# Christmas Roses

NEW YORK TIMES BESTSELLING AUTHORS

# SUSAN KING
# MARY JO PUTNEY
# PATRICIA RICE

*Christmas Roses*

This is a work of fiction. Any references to historical
events, real people, or real locales are used fictitiously.
Other names, characters, places, and incidents are the
product of the author's imagination, and any resemblance
to actual events or locales or persons, living or dead, is
entirely coincidental.

ISBN ebook 978-0-9964641-3-0
ISBN print 978-0-9964641-4-7

Published by Story Cauldron Publishing,
Baltimore, Maryland

Story ● Cauldron

Cover Design and Interior Format

*To our friends and families with whom
we share our own Christmas joys.*

# The Snow Rose

## SUSAN KING

# THE SNOW ROSE

## SUSAN KING

WRITING THIS LITTLE story is one of my happiest creative experiences, and I'm delighted to be able to share it with readers again. "The Snow Rose" was my first novella, a spinoff of my second novel, *The Raven's Wish*. Both stories are set amid the ongoing feud between the Frasers and the MacDonalds in 16th century Scotland. I love clan legends, and I'm part Fraser, so now and again I write something about the historical Frasers to see what sort of fictional mischief I can stir for them.

"The Snow Rose" is the story of Kenneth Fraser, one of the many cousins of Elspeth Fraser in *The Raven's Wish* (among eighty Fraser cousins all born within the same year, Elspeth is the only girl—it's based on a legend of Clan Fraser). I loved Kenneth, with his dry wit, his long, braided dark hair and his sexy Highlander look, and I wanted him to have a special romance of his own. His soulmate turned out to be Catriona MacDonald, who desperately needs help one snowy New Year's Eve—or Hogmanay, as this is Scotland.

Kenneth is the "first foot" arriving at Catriona's snowbound cottage one New Year's Eve—that is, first to set foot on the threshold after midnight. A dark-haired handsome man is a good omen, and these two bring luck to each other in the midst of a clan feud—but their New Year's beginning is a bit calamitous. A collapsed roof, a cow and a horse inside the cottage, a cat named Dog, a lost and valuable brooch, and, of course, the MacBaddies after our hero and heroine, who are getting to know each other even while the snow falls through a hole in the roof and a cow tumbles head over heels for the hero.

# CHAPTER ONE

*Christmas Day, 1573*
*Scotland, The Highlands*

"I AM CATRIONA MACDONALD of Kiler-nan, and I need your help." Her soft Gaelic echoed in the silence. Catriona held her breath, and waited for a response from several men gathered near the hearth in the great hall at Glenran Castle. She lifted her chin slightly, determined to show no fear, though these were Frasers, and enemies of her clan.

No one spoke. Although she stood in the center of a hall filled with men, women and children, amid the Yuletide scents of pine and juniper, of spices and cakes and roasted meats, she felt utterly alone in that instant. Still, she could not blame the Frasers for staring at her so warily. She had broken the peace of their Christmas by coming to their castle.

As the silence continued, Catriona lifted trembling fingers to the red plaid she wore draped over her frayed green gown, and unfastened the silver brooch that she had owned since infancy. She held it out toward Callum Fraser, the laird of Glenran.

"This brooch marks an honorable pledge, made on Christmas Eve twenty years past, by your father," she said. "I have treasured the snow rose all my life."

"Snow rose?" Callum asked as he accepted the brooch.

She nodded. "I called it that when I was a child, because of the silver setting, and the rose quartz stone."

He examined the piece thoughtfully. "I remember seeing it when I was a child."

"Lachlann Fraser gave it to me on Christmas Eve, when I was but a few days old. He pinned it to my swaddling and told my mother that it marked his pledge of protection for me. He said that if I ever was in need, my mother or I should come to him."

"And you are in need now?" Callum asked.

"I am," she said quietly. "Though I am a Mac-Donald, and you are Frasers, and our clans have feuded for generations, I must call upon this pledge. I know that Lachlann of Glenran died several years ago, but I hope that his son will honor his promise, in the spirit of the Yuletide season."

Callum watched her somberly, then leaned over to murmur to the man seated beside him; that man had dark hair and brilliantly blue eyes, and seemed older than the others. Callum listened to him carefully.

The other Frasers murmured among themselves, most of them standing with their backs to
the yellow light that spilled from the stone fireplace. While Catriona could not see their faces
clearly, she saw that they were tall and well-made,
blond, dark and red-headed, wearing plaids of
deep green and midnight blue, colors favored by
the Glenran Frasers.

Another dark-haired man watched her intently
from where he stood in a shadowed corner near
the hearth. He leaned against the wall and folded
his arms over his wrapped plaid, crossing his long,
muscular legs, cased in deerhide boots. His gaze
never wavered from her face.

Although her heart thumped, Catriona looked
at him boldly. He inclined his head in acknowledgment; Catriona soon lowered her eyes, her
cheeks heated.

She waited, ignoring the sting of her chilled
fingers and toes as they warmed after hours of
riding in the cold. She ignored, too, the rum-
bling of her empty stomach, roused by the scents
of the Frasers' Christmas feast. She stood straight
and held her head high, feeling the weight of her
black hair as it spilled down her back, and curling
her toes inside her worn leather boots. Her knees
shook, her heart pounded, but on the outside, she
remained quiet and still.

Finally the laird leaned forward, his strong,
handsome face lined with a frown. "My father
told us the story of a Christmas Eve when the
widow of Iain MacDonald of Kilernan saved his
life."

Catriona nodded. "My mother took Lachlann Fraser in during a blizzard. He had been hunting and stopped at Kilernan, unable to make it back to Glenran because of the storm. My mother was still in childbed, and could have directed her men not to admit him," she continued. "He was a Fraser, and she had been recently widowed by the hand of a Fraser. But she honored the custom of Highland hospitality, which is offered to any visitor, friend or foe. Lachlann gave me the brooch and the pledge in return."

"My father was deeply touched by your mother's generosity," Callum said. "I recall that he mentioned a babe, whom he promised to protect. But the MacDonald widow never contacted him again." He glanced at the other men. "My father would expect his kinsmen to honor this vow." A few of them nodded agreement. Callum turned to her. "What is it you need?"

Catriona sighed in relief, and gathered boldness in her next breath. "My uncle, Hugh MacDonald, holds Kilernan Castle. I am the Maid of Kilernan, my father's only heir. My uncle will not acknowledge my claim unless I wed the man he has chose for me." She paused. "I want you to take the castle from Hugh MacDonald."

Callum stared at her. His kinsmen stared at her too. From across the room, she sensed the gazes of the women as well.

The laird cleared his throat. "Take it?"

"Take it," she said, "and give it into my keeping. I have loyal kinsmen living at Kilernan who will help me hold it."

"Then let them take it for you," a red-haired Fraser said.

"My kinsmen are afraid to go against my uncle, although they disapprove of his actions."

"Hugh MacDonald is a drunken fool," the red-headed Fraser said. "Surely when he sobers, he will honor your claim."

"He refuses to do that unless I wed Parlan Mac-Donald, my third cousin." She drew a breath. "The Glenran Frasers are well known for fear-lessness and clever raiding. You can take the castle and give it into my keeping."

"We will not take Kilernan by force," Callum said. "Surely you are aware of our signed pledge to end the feud with Clan Donald." He handed the brooch back to her. Catriona pinned it to her plaid. "Let us help you some other way," Callum said.

"Lachlann Fraser promised whatever I needed," she said.

"Lachlann did not promise to kill MacDonalds for you," someone said in a precise, deep tone; the dark-haired man standing in the shadows spoke. His frowning gaze pierced hers.

"Kenneth is right." The man beside Callum leaned forward. "The Frasers signed a bond years ago that forbids them to fight MacDonalds. Your clansmen signed the same pledge, though they have not kept it. The Frasers honor it."

"Are you not a Glenran Fraser?" she asked the man.

"I am Duncan Macrae of Dulsie, kin by mar-riage to the Frasers. And I am a lawyer for the

Privy Council. What is the dispute with your
uncle? There may be another way to solve it."

She shook her head. "My uncle took over Kilernan when I was a babe. My mother never wed
again, and died a few years ago. Now my uncle
insists that I marry Parlan. I fear that I will lose
Kilernan."

"He is within his rights as your guardian to
choose a husband for you," Macrae said. "But I
will look into your legal position when I go to
Edinburgh in the spring, if you like."

"By then, I will be wed, unless you help me,"
she said.

"This is no affair for Frasers," Callum said. "Go
home, girl, and listen to your uncle."

"I cannot. I fled Kilernan a few months past,
to stay in a shieling hut in the hills above Loch
Garry. Parlan and my uncle want me to return to
Kilernan, but I have refused, until the castle has
been promised to my keeping."

"Take your troubles to your clan chief," Kenneth Fraser said. "We cannot solve this for you."
Catriona glanced toward the shadows again. His
deep voice had a soothing quality, despite his
harsh words.

"I sent word to the MacDonald," she said. "He
refused to take Kilernan from Hugh, and promised to send a silver spoon to my first born."

"Then you have his blessing to marry Parlan,"
Kenneth said. "Do that, and you will have Kilernan. You have no choice."

"I do," she pointed out. "I came to you."

His dark eyes gleamed in the firelight. "Stubborn girl," he said softly. "Let us add to your sheepfold, or give you oats and barley to see you through the winter. We cannot attack a MacDonald castle for you."

"Then take the castle without bloodshed," she said impulsively. "The Glenran Frasers are said to be very clever."

"Without bloodshed? That," Kenneth said, "is impossible."

"We will gladly help you some other way," Callum said.

Hopelessness wrenched through her. "I must have Kilernan," she whispered. She had not told them the whole truth. Now that they had rejected her plea, her throat tightened over the words. She doubted they would care that she wanted to provide a home for eight children, her cousins. Hugh had not cared, either; he had said she was a fool to take on the responsibility. The Frasers might agree.

She saw the dark-haired Fraser frown, watching her. His eyes seemed kind, and his gaze warmed her like a hearthfire. But he offered her no aid. None of them did.

"Catriona," Callum said. "You are welcome to stay and share our feast."

Food would not solve her dilemma, though her stomach clenched in hunger; she had eaten little that day. Catriona glanced at the tables loaded with dishes, greenery, and blazing candlelight, and then looked away. Her pride told her to accept nothing from the Frasers now.

But eight hungry children awaited her. She

could not deny them a chance for a Christmas feast.

"I cannot stay," she finally said. "But I will accept a gift of food for my cousins, who have little to eat this day."

Callum nodded. "And for yourself?"

"I want nothing from you," she replied, head high. "Farewell, and blessings of the season to you." She turned away.

A woman stepped away from the tables and came toward her, carrying a sturdy toddler in her arms. The mother was delicately beautiful, with copper gold hair and wide gray eyes. A boy with dark hair stood behind her, and two young children clung to her skirts, a boy and a girl who shared their mother's striking gray eyes. The children watched her curiously, and the babe sucked a finger and babbled, grinning. Catriona smiled at him.

"I am Elspeth Fraser, wife to Macrae of Dulsie, the lawyer," the woman said. "The Frasers here are my cousins. We were all fostered by Lachlann of Glenran. We do not mean to dishonor his vow to you, but please understand our position. I will urge my husband and my kin to look into the matter for you."

Catriona nodded. "Thank you. Farewell—"

"You look cold and tired," Elspeth said. "Warm yourself by our fire. Eat with us, and share songs and dances with us. It is Christmas, Catriona MacDonald. Be of good cheer this day." Catriona hesitated, urged by her empty stomach, her cold feet, her lonely heart. She looked into Elspeth's silver eyes, and smiled at her beautiful children. She glanced at the tantalizing burden of cakes, meats, and cheeses on the table, and inhaled the scents of beeswax candles and fragrant greenery.

She glanced at the other women and children who watched her. They were all handsome, keen-eyed, looking at her with interest, and without suspicion. No one seemed anxious for her to be gone.

She sensed the warmth and love among these Frasers, as tangible as the aromas of ginger cakes and evergreens. Suddenly Catriona wanted to share in what they had. The desire and the need nearly buckled her knees. She starved for more than food.

But she could not endure pity or charity in place of the real help she desperately needed. When Christmas was done, the Frasers would still be enemies of the MacDonalds.

"I must go," she murmured. "Others wait for me."

Elspeth touched her arm gently. "Take this, then," she said. The older boy held a cloth bundle toward her.

"Cheese, cakes, and roasted meat," Elspeth explained. "The cheese has holes in it. Look through a slice, and you will see what will come to you in the new year. And there are candles to bring the blessing of light in the coming year. I added a flask of *uisge beatha* too. May it warm you well."

Catriona took the bundle, blinking away the tears that pooled in her eyes. "Thank you," she whispered. "A happy Christmas and luck in the new year to all of you." She moved toward the door. Behind her, she heard a strong tread as a man strode the length of the hall.

"Catriona MacDonald." The voice of the dark Fraser, deep and mellow, sounded. She turned to see Kenneth Fraser walking toward her. "Stay. We will escort you home later."

She gazed up into his strong, lean face, into heavily lashed eyes of brilliant, warm brown, like firelight shot through polished, dark cairngorm. Somehow all the tempting, wondrous comforts of this place seemed to gather in those deep, rich eyes.

She shook her head. "I must go. A good new year to you."

"*Bliadhna Sona,*" he said. "A lucky new year to you."

"Luck," she said softly, "is what I need." She went toward the door, aware that he watched her.

Though they had refused to help her in the way that she needed, the Frasers' kindness made her ache inside, down deep where she had felt empty for so long. Their charity reminded her keenly that she lacked what existed in such abundance here. Loving kin, comfort, safety, and companionship were commonplace to them—and as rare as gold to her.

She shoved open the door and ran down the stone steps. During Yuletide, charity always flowed like wine, she told herself. They would gladly share with her now. Later, after the new year, the Frasers would once again be her enemies. Fraser pledges would prove false after all, just as her uncle had often said whenever he saw the snow rose brooch pinned to her plaid.

She ran through the yard, fighting back a sob. Then she tore the silver brooch from her plaid and tossed it into the ice-crusted mud.

Kenneth Fraser walked through the yard as the girl cantered away on her garron pony. He watched her until she was a dark speck moving over the snow-coated hills. He sighed and turned.

Something sparkled in the mud beside his boot, and he bent down to pick up the silver brooch. The snow rose, she had called it. Silver tracery, curved like flower petals, circled a pink stone. He imagined Catriona as a little girl, naming the brooch, cherishing the pledge it represented. But the Frasers had disappointed her.

Gripping the brooch, he walked toward the tower entrance, and looked up to see Duncan Macrae standing in the doorway.

"You want to help the girl," Duncan observed calmly.

Kenneth shrugged. "Someone should help her."

"If blood is spilled in feud between Frasers and MacDonalds, the crown will send fire and sword upon your heads. The Regent will not hesitate this time."

"I know." Kenneth frowned as he studied the sparkling brooch. He thought of the MacDonald girl, shining like a Christmas angel come to earth: gentle, graceful, and yet filled with a marvelous strength.

She stood proudly, but he had noticed the worn hem of her green woolen gown, and the peeled edges of her leather boots. He had seen the haunted look in her brilliant blue eyes, and the quick touch of her tongue to her lips when she had looked at the food heaped upon the tables. The girl had many needs, yet asked for only one favor, nearly impossible to meet.

"Lachlann pledged protection to her," Kenneth said. "We owe her something for that."

Duncan nodded. "But we all signed that bond, Kenneth. We cannot do what she wants of us."

"True." Kenneth frowned. "Perhaps I should ride out to her shieling hut in a few days, just to be certain she is well. I do not like to think of her alone during the Yuletide season. She reminds me—" he stopped.

Duncan watched him evenly. "The girl does have a little of the look of Anna."

Kenneth nodded curtly. Anna, his betrothed, had died of an illness three years ago on New Year's Day. Since then, the Yuletide season had proved hard for him to endure.

Like Anna, Catriona MacDonald was slim and black-haired, graceful and strong. But Anna had always glimmered with humor and joy, her rosy cheeks dimpling often. Catriona MacDonald was somber and sad, her skin as pale and delicate as the rose quartz stone in her brooch.

She was not Anna; no one could be like Anna, ever. But he did not like the thought of Catriona suffering and alone on Christmas, or on New

Year's, the day that Anna had died.

"You could ride out in a few days," Duncan agreed. "Make certain that the girl is well, and bring her provisions. We can at least see that she is safe through the winter. By spring, she will likely marry this Parlan MacDonald."

Kenneth smoothed his thumb over the cold surface of the brooch. "And I will return this to her," he said. "She should know that it does have some meaning, after all."

# CHAPTER TWO

JUNIPER SMOKE BILLOWED up from the central firepit in a gray, stinging cloud. The tears that wet her lashes were the first she had allowed herself to shed in a long while. Catriona blinked hard, wiped her eyes, and grasped an iron poker to prod the high pile of evergreen branches that smoldered over glowing peat bricks.

Coughing, she waved her hands to spread the smoke to every corner of the little shieling hut to cleanse and purify and protect, just as her mother had done on every *Oidhche Challuinn,* New Year's Eve, when she had been a child. Such memories, bringing back her mother's kindness and loving companionship, had sustained her during these months of living alone here, without hope for her future.

The hut was hardly a fine fortress, but it was her home. Castle Kilernan was lost to her now. The memory of Christmas Day, and the Frasers' refusal to help her stung as harshly as the smoke in her eyes. New Year's Eve was a time to gather blessings and attract luck to the household, and she would honor her little home with the proper traditions, and hopefully turn her luck for the better.

She waved at the billowing juniper smoke. When she could scarcely breathe—her mother had taught her that the smoke must be thick enough to drive everyone from the room—she went to the door and pulled it open. Cold air and swirling snowflakes rushed inside.

She coughed and pulled her plaid snugly over her frayed gown as she watched the storm. Bitter chill snapped at her cheeks, and she ducked deeper into the plaid, keeping the door open while the smoke dispersed.

A small, solid body stropped against her leg. She glanced down at the black cat who blinked up at her with pale green eyes.

"Pardon the smoke, Cù," Catriona said. "But you and I will have some wonderful luck after the juniper is burned," she said with forced brightness. She reached down and scooped up the cat, and watched the snow pile wild and thick over the hills. The darkness had a soft blue tint, and the air felt gentle somehow, filled with promise and hope.

But she knew the dangerous reality of such a storm. Behind her, the dim hut offered shelter and warmth. Tonight, she would not set foot beyond the wedge of light that spilled into the flurrying snow.

No one else would venture outside tonight, either, although it was New Year's Eve, and likely near midnight by now. No one would come up to her hut for a traditional visit after midnight, bringing small gifts of food or drink or coin as tokens of good luck. The storm and the distance would keep visitors away. She was disappointed, but relieved to know that Parlan MacDonald would not ride out to see her.

"Little Mairead MacGhille told me a wonderful surprise would come to me this New Year's, Cù," she whispered to the cat. "She spoke of it when I visited the children earlier today. Perhaps she felt the approaching storm, though. All that snow is wondrous and peaceful. Ah, Cù—I hope the children are not alarmed by the storm. The snow had not begun when I left them."

Cù mewled and poured out of her arms. Thumping down to the rushed-coated earthen floor, he stretched beside the warm stones that encircled the fire. Catriona began to close the door, but a faint, steady sound caught her attention. She peered out, seeing little beyond the fluttering, lacy whiteness.

But she could hear the drums of the *gillean Callaig,* the lads of New Year's Eve, as they marched around the *clachan,* a cluster of a few farms and kale-yards. Even a blizzard would not stop them, although she doubted they would walk far with their torches and drums and songs. The young lads, with a few young men among them, would pound intense, driving rhythms on hide-stretched drums, and chant loudly; from this distance, only the strong beat penetrated the drifting curtains of snow.

She smiled, imagining their antics. They would be disguised in robes and animal hides, some wearing horns and acting like oxen, while others chased them, carrying blazing torches. Chanting and beating drums, they would circle each house to frighten away evil spirits, sending out the old year to make room for the new. They were given wine, *uisge beatha*, and sweet bannock cakes in return for bringing luck for the new year.

"Just as well no one will come up here in this weather," Catriona told the cat. "I have little food or drink to offer. Another poor omen for the new year." She sighed. "Who will set first foot in my home after midnight, to bless it for the year?"

When she had been young, the adults at Kilernan had laughed and celebrated with midnight visitors, singing and drinking fine drams until the small hours. Whoever set foot first in the hall after midnight would determine good or ill fortune for that year. Tall, dark-haired men with pleasant natures, bearing small gifts, were the luckiest New Year's visitors of all. Blond men were quite unfavorable, and women, according to hair color and disposition, might be lucky or not.

But Catriona would have no midnight visitors at all, surely an unfavorable omen. She sighed, and watched the cat stretch on the floor. "You may not be tall, Cù, but you are a dark-haired male. You will have to set first-foot in the door. We have to make our own luck this year." The cat only looked at her with disinterest.

Closing the door, she went to the table and picked up a flaming beeswax candle, part of the

Frasers' Christmas bundle, and placed it on the
narrow windowsill. The glow would attract lucky
spirits toward her home and help to bless the
coming year.

She had given the other candles and most of
the food to the MacGhille children, keeping a little cheese and oatmeal for herself along with the
flask of *uisge beatha,* which the children should
not have.

Remembering the Frasers' gifts, she went to
the cupboard and sliced off a bit of cheese, which
was pierced with round holes. As she passed the
circle of hearth stones, the fire blazed brightly for
an instant. Catriona frowned, aware that a sudden burst of flame could foretell the coming of a
stranger. A chill slid through her.

She opened the door, then held the cheese
slice up to one eye. Elspeth Fraser had told her
that looking through a hole in the cheese would
show her what would come in the new year. She
peered through the hole, partly dreading whatever omen she might see, convinced that good
fortune had forgotten her existence.

Seeing only fluttering snow and darkness, she
wondered dismally if the view portended a cold,
lonely year for her.

Then she gasped. Through the small hole,
something moved out in the falling snow. She
narrowed her eyes, and saw a man and a horse
coming slowly along the ridge of the hill. Lowering the cheese, staring in disbelief, she watched
the horse advance with high, labored steps
through the deep drifts. The man was enveloped

in a thick plaid, unrecognizable through the darkness, though he was a tall, large man.

*Parlan*. Surely Parlan rode toward her house for a New Year's visit. Catriona stepped backward to slam the door shut, and leaned against it.

Regardless of his thick blond hair, Parlan MacDonald was a poor omen indeed. She would not let him into her house.

He was thoroughly lost, and his head ached fiercely. Not an auspicious end to the old year, nor a lucky start to the next, Kenneth thought in irritation. Icy, slanting snow stung his face and hands, and he shivered in the bitter cold. He drew his plaid higher over his head and peered through swirling veils of white.

Snow smothered the hillsides and filled the air. He had little sense of his location now. A few hours ago, when the snowfall had been a mild, pretty flutter, he had approached Loch Garry and turned toward the hills that edged its northern side, certain that the MacDonald girl's shieling hut would be there.

Riding upward, he had met three MacDonalds, who had ridden toward him with suspicious glances, no doubt recognizing the Fraser badge, a sprig of fresh yew stuck in his woolen bonnet, and the Glenran pattern of his plaid. And he knew the distinctive red and green design that they wore: Kilernan MacDonalds. Kenneth nodded politely as he passed.

"Fraser! A Fraser!" The MacDonalds turned to

chase him. Leaning forward, he urged his garron to a canter, but his mount slipped on the
icy slope. The MacDonalds caught up to him,
shouting threats. One swiped an unstrung bow
at him, another swung a sword, and the third
kicked at him. Struggling to dodge their blows,
wary of fighting them, Kenneth noticed that they
wavered and laughed drunkenly; they had already
begun to celebrate the New Year, and saw him as
some sport.

His garron stumbled and went down, pitching
Kenneth from the saddle. He rolled to avoid the
MacDonalds, who landed on him in a brawling,
hooting cluster. The force of their attack drove
his head against a rock. As he faded from awareness, he heard them swearing and running back
to their horses.

When he awoke, the snow gathered silently
around him in the darkness. Groggy and shivering, grateful that two thick plaids had saved him
from freezing, he struggled to his feet, found his
garron, and managed to ride onward.

Now he touched his fingers to the painful
lump on the back of his head and felt the swelling there, then felt his bruised and cut lip. The
horse walked ahead slowly, impeded by heavy
snow and dim light. Kenneth did his utmost to
stay warm, and to stay upright in the saddle as
dizziness swamped him.

"What a pair we are," Kenneth muttered.
"Ambushed and wounded, and now caught in
a blizzard. Luck is not following us into the new
year." He glanced around, certain that the hour

must be close to midnight. The MacDonald girl's shieling hut was somewhere in these hills, but he would not find it this night.

He would take shelter wherever he could, in a stranger's home, an empty shieling, even a cave. Tomorrow would be time enough to find the girl and deliver the pack of food and household items that was tied to the saddle behind him.

He shivered with cold, despite the protection of two plaids, a leather doublet, woolen trews and deer hide boots. He patted the horse's neck with a note of encouragement he did not feel; riding through MacDonald territory was dangerous enough for a Fraser, but exposure and death were a far more real threat now.

He remembered the tale Lachlann Fraser had told of traveling one Christmas Eve through a fierce snowstorm. No wonder Lachlann had promised protection to the newborn child of the woman who gave him hospitality. Just now, Kenneth would give anything he had for the barest sort of welcome.

He peered through the snowy veil that obscured his surroundings. A moment later, he saw a faint sparkle of golden light ahead. He narrowed his eyes, wondering if the light was a trick of the blow to his head, but the glow flickered and held.

Riding forward, he saw a small house, a single candle glowing in the window. Grateful for his good fortune, Kenneth dismounted stiffly. When his dizziness abated, he untied the bundle from the saddle, wanting to offer something in return for hospitality. He waded through the deep snow to knock at the door. Silence followed. He knocked again.

"Be gone from here!" a woman's voice called out.

"I am in need of shelter for the night," he called.

"Go away, Parlan MacDonald!" she returned.

Hearing that name, and the woman's soft voice, he realized that he had found the MacDonald girl's shieling after all, through sheer luck. "Catriona MacDonald," he called, knocking again. "I am a Glenran Fraser. Let me in." A long silence followed his statement. He pounded on the door. "I am in need of shelter for myself and my horse."

She opened the door a crack and peered at him. "A Glenran Fraser! What are you doing here on such a night?"

"Let me in, if you will, and I will tell you," he said. The firelight that haloed her form darkened oddly as he looked at her. He leaned against the doorframe. "Let me in, girl," he said wearily. "I have come far."

"Which Fraser are you? Are you the blond man? If so, then I must let black Cù go out and come in again before you enter."

Confused, he realized that it must be after midnight. If only for the color of his hair, he would be welcome. He lowered the plaid that covered his head.

"I am the dark-haired one," he answered. "Kenneth Fraser. May I come in?" His legs felt strangely weak. He willed the sensation to pass. It did not.

The girl opened the door, and Kenneth stepped

across the threshold. He heard her speak faintly, as if from a distance. Then darkness gathered around him like a thundercloud.

# CHAPTER THREE

**H**E WENT DOWN at her feet like a felled oak. Catriona dropped to her knees and slipped her hand under his head. His tall, muscular body took up much of the space in her tiny home: his feet were on the threshold, his head lay near the hearth. The cat, who had leaped upward when the man fell, now sniffed gingerly at him.

"Kenneth Fraser!" Catriona said anxiously. "Kenneth!" After a few moments, he groaned and moved slowly, then raised himself to his knees. Catriona helped him to stand, but he leaned so heavily against her that his weight and height threatened to topple her to the floor.

She half-dragged him the few feet toward the bed, a narrow mattress boxed in the wall by wooden panels and a heavy curtain. Shoving the curtain aside, she let the man drop to the bed. He sank, face downward.

"You may have dark hair," she said, as she lifted one of his legs, then the other, to the mattress, "but a drunken, staggering first-foot must be a poor omen, and I do not thank you for it."

"I am not drunk," he said. His voice was slurred.
"I came to bring you blessings of the new year.
Am I your first foot?" He put a hand to his head
and rolled to his back, groaning.

"You are," she said, "and an unlucky one, I am
sure." She scowled down at him. She had thought
him a handsome man when she had seen him
at Glenran, but now he was bedraggled, bruised,
and near frozen; his lip was cut and swollen, and
his expression was stupefied. She had seen men
in this condition at Kilernan, men who drank
and brawled on New Year's Eve, and indeed celebrated heavily from Christmas through Twelfth
Night. Her uncle was the worst of the lot.

"*Tcha,*" she muttered. "This sort of blessing I
do not need. You are drunk, wet, and frozen."

"I am not drunk," he said, sitting up. "*Ach,* my
horse is outside. I must—" he stood, swayed, and
grabbed the frame of the box-bed for support.

Catriona slipped beneath his arm to keep him
from falling over. He laid an arm over her shoulders, and walked, unsteady and stumbling, toward
the door.

"Lie down," Catriona said, turning with him. "I
will see to your horse." She led him back to the
bed, and pulled the fur covers over him.

She threw her spare plaid over her shoulders,
and went to the door, nearly tripping over the
cat, who pawed tentatively at the snow piled on
the doorstep, then slid back into the house.

"*Cù!*" Catriona pushed the cat aside. "Stay in
here. Both of you," she ordered, glancing at the

man on the bed, who mumbled indistinctly.

Catriona trudged through icy winds and hazy snowfall, took the garron by the bridle, and led him to the small byre, where her own horse and a cow, lent her by a neighbor, were stabled. She murmured reassuringly to the animals, filled their manger with oats, and hurried back to the hut.

Kenneth had removed his damp plaid and sat on the bed in trews and a shirt, the fur covers pulled around his shoulders. His face seemed grayish, and he sagged against the bedframe. Catriona stamped her feet and shook the snow from her skirt, then undid her plaid. "However did you find my house, as drunk as you are?" she asked.

"I am not drunk, girl," he growled. "And it was pure luck that I found you."

"Luck? I have little of that, and your arrival like this, on New Year's, is certain proof." She hammocked their plaids between the table and the bed, then edged her way past Kenneth as she approached the central hearth. "Are you hungry? I can offer you oats and hot *uisge beatha* to warm you—but perhaps you have had enough of that."

He glowered at her. "Porridge would be kind," he said curtly. "I nearly forgot—that sack by the door is for you, with blessings of the New Year from the Frasers."

Catriona looked at him in surprise, and retrieved the bundle that he had dropped inside the door when he fell at her feet. She took it to the table and opened it. Inside, she found an abundance of goods: wrapped cheeses and roasted meat, more candles, milled oats and barley in cloth sacks, a flask of claret, a sack of currants, parchment papers holding spices, and even a sack of white sugar. Catriona dipped a finger in the sugar to taste its sweetness, then glanced at Kenneth.

His dark eyes gleamed warm in the amber light. "Luck in the New Year to you, Catriona Mac-Donald," he said softly.

"Thank you," she whispered, her throat tightening. This man, a Fraser, had ridden a long way in foul weather to bring her a New Year's blessing. No one had ever done such a thing for her. She glanced away from his steady gaze uncertainly. "I will make the food. It will cleanse the drink from your head."

He sighed, a half laugh. "Well, I am hungry," he said. Catriona cooked oats and water in a kettle over the fire, stirred in some of the roasted beef he had brought, and ladled the food into a wooden bowl, handing it to him with a wooden spoon.

"Will you not eat too?" he asked. When she shook her head, he frowned. "When was the last time you ate a meal?" he asked. She shrugged; she wanted to bring his gift of food to the children when the weather cleared.

Kenneth scooped up a spoonful of porridge and offered it to her. She shook her head again. "*Ach,* girl, you cannot refuse my New Year's gift. You will offend me and bring ill luck to us both. Here, eat."

She leaned forward and Kenneth touched the spoon to her lips, slipping the warm, salty oats inside. She swallowed, knowing he watched her, and felt a hot blush seep into her cheeks, and an intimate swirl ripple through her body. He offered her more. She shook her head, but he insisted, until she took the spoon from him and ate some. Kenneth finished the rest. "There," he said. "That should bring us both some luck."

"I hope so," she said softly. "I need some luck."

"Believe me, girl, after being lost in that snowstorm, I am glad to bring some to you."  He smiled a little.

She smiled too, and felt oddly safe and peaceful then, as if he was not a stranger, or an enemy of her clan. She liked his smile, liked the quiet lilt in his voice, his gentle, teasing manner, and the bronze lights in his hair and his eyes. She liked the comforting weight of Fraser beef in her stomach. Most of all, she was glad to have her loneliness eased on the first night of the year.

Kenneth looked toward the shuttered window, which trembled as the wind shoved it. "I cannot leave until the weather clears. May I sleep by your fire?"

"You are too weak to go anywhere. You may stay as long as you need. Cù sleeps by the fire, but he will make room for you."

"*Cù*? A dog? Where is it?" He glanced around the room.

She laughed. "Cù is my cat. A very little girl once saw him as a kitten, and called him a black puppy, so `Dog' is his name. Mairead, the child, is nearly blind," she added softly.

"Ah. So, a cat named Dog," he murmured. "I

am sure he protects you well." He smiled, and the boyish quirk of his lips charmed a quick, shy smile from her.

He stood slowly, his weakness evident, and picked up his plaid, wavering unsteadily as Cù shot between his feet to snatch at the cloth. Kenneth spun to avoid stepping on the cat, and sat heavily on the bed.

Catriona picked up Cù. "The house is small, I know," she told Kenneth. "It is just a shieling, meant for use by the men who bring their herds into the hills to graze in the springtime. It lacks the comforts of a true home."

"Some of the comforts are here," he said, watching her steadily. "It only has to house two of us—and your cat named Dog—for one night. I will leave in the morning." He cradled the back of his head and grimaced as he took his hand away.

She frowned, seeing blood on his fingers. "You are hurt! What happened? Were you in a drunken New Year's brawl?"

"My horse and I went down on the ice. I am fine," he said shortly, when she leaned forward to part his hair.

Catriona winced in sympathy as she looked at the wound. The swollen, bloody lump looked painful. "Fine? Hardly. And these bruises on your jaw and your lip—" Leaning close to look, she did not smell strong drink on his breath. "You are not drunk," she said. "My pardon for thinking you were. What happened? Were you attacked as you came here? *Ach*, it was MacDonalds!"

"I went down on the ice," he repeated sharply.

She narrowed her eyes. "And just who took you down?" He was silent. Catriona shook her head. Here was trouble indeed, if her kin had attacked a Fraser and tracked him here. She went to a shelf, fetched a folded cloth and a bowl of water, and went back to the bed. "Now let me tend to your head," she ordered.

He turned obediently. She cleansed his wounds carefully, then gently raked her fingers through his dark hair to ease his headache. His tangled hair felt like heavy silk. He groaned softly as she worked.

"I did not mean to hurt you," she said, lifting her hands.

"Such gentle hands could never deal out hurt," he murmured. "My thanks. I know you are not fond of Frasers." He opened his doublet, took it off and set it aside, then unpinned a small brooch from his linen shirt. He held it out. "This is yours." The snow rose brooch winked in the low light. She began to reach out, then closed her hand tightly. "I—I do not want it."

"Take it, Catriona," he said. "Let it continue to serve as a token of the Frasers' good will. We wish you no harm."

She glanced at him. "Have you come here to take Kilernan from Hugh MacDonald?"

"You know I have not."

"Then the snow rose means nothing to me." She stood. "You keep it. Good night." She snatched up her plaid and spread it on the floor like a pallet.

"What are you doing?" he asked.

"I will sleep here," she said, as she sat on the plaid and began to remove her boots. "You are injured, and need the bed."

"I will not take your bed, girl." He stood. In the dim light of the peat fire, she saw his face go suddenly pale.

"Lie down. Will you refuse my hospitality and bring us both ill luck?" She echoed his own words. "The hearthfire cannot be allowed to go out on this night of the year, as anyone knows. I need to watch over it. Go to sleep, now." She stretched out and pulled the plaid over her.

After a moment, she thought she heard him swear a low oath. Soon, she heard his boots thud to the floor, and heard the bed creak as he lay down.

The peat fire crackled, the wind howled cold and bleak outside, and the man sighed in her bed. Catriona tossed on the flat, hard pallet, and wondered just what this odd evening portended for the new year.

Kenneth opened his eyes again. Restless for a while now, he had laid in the bed listening as the girl shifted and sighed, huddled in the plaid on the cold floor. He peered toward her. The light from the glowing embers revealed that she curled tightly, shivering.

"Catriona," he said softly.

"Kenneth? What is it? Are you ill?" She sat up.

He flung back the plaid and the furs. "Get in

the bed."

"I will not!" She turned away abruptly.

He sighed in exasperation. "I will sleep by the hearth. Get in and get warm," he ordered, sitting up. "Your knocking teeth have kept me awake all the night."

She sighed, then got up and came toward him. "It is freezing on the floor. We can share the bed. But if you touch me, I will use the poker." She lay down and deliberately stuffed part of the fur robe between them.

"You can always call out your Dog on me," he muttered, and shifted to his side, his back to the cold wall. The box-bed was narrow, and they were jammed together as if in a snug nest. Kenneth felt the tension in her shoulders as she lay stiffly against him. "Relax," he said, adjusting his position. "I must rest my arm somewhere. If I lay it just here, will you attack me with your poker?" He balanced his forearm gently on her hip.

"I might," she said. He smiled at her wry tone. He settled, inhaling the sweet smell of her hair and enjoying the feel of her, close and warm on a cold night. Their bodies fit comfortably together—far too comfortably, he thought, and stirred slightly away from her.

He thought of Anna, for it was New Year's and the third anniversary of her death. But he was deeply exhausted, and her image seemed distant. He sighed, feeling strangely content, almost peaceful. Listening to Catriona's even breathing, he slipped into a heavy, dreamless sleep.

Catriona opened her eyes once again, wanting to be certain that the banked fire still burned. She lay half-awake and heard the wind shove at the outer walls, and heard Kenneth snore. Snuggling against his solid warmth, she felt safe and comfortable, although he was a Fraser, and largely unknown to her. In the morning, daylight would bring a new year, and cold reality. But now, while darkness spun a bridge from the old year to the new, she felt a brief respite from loneliness.

Turning, she felt his arm, heavy with sleep, fall across her abdomen. His breath stirred her hair. Lured by his warmth and strength, hungry for the reassurance of simple touch, she rested her head against his chest. He sighed in his sleep and wrapped his arms around her.

Drawn into that shelter, Catriona suddenly felt tears sting her eyes. Kenneth did not awaken, but pulled her closer, as if he sensed her need for solace even in his sleep.

Curled into the curve of his body, listening to the deep, even beat of his heart, she sniffled and wiped her eyes. Finally growing drowsy, she knew that she would sleep peacefully and without fear.

# CHAPTER FOUR

KENNETH AWOKE TO silence, but for the low crackle in the hearth, and sat up to see that Catriona was gone. Shoving his fingers through his hair, he felt a throbbing reminder of his injury, and still felt the grogginess of total exhaustion. Judging by the light, he must have slept late into the morning. He crossed the room and pull open the window shutter, then blinked at the brightness.

Snow blanketed the hills and piled high in drifts of down. After a few moments, he saw Catriona wading through the yard. She entered the house on a draft of bitter wind, shaking the snow from her clothing and setting down a small bucket of fresh milk. Her cheeks were a high, clear pink as she unwound her plaid.

"Blessings of the New Year to you, Kenneth Fraser," she said. "I have been out to see to the animals. The snow is quite deep. I could hardly walk from the hut to the byre." She sat on the bench to remove her boots.

"Luck of the New Year," he returned. "You

should have asked me to see to the animals."

"You were asleep," she said. "And why should I ask you?"

"Because I owe you for sheltering me."

"You are injured and fatigued, and you brought gifts to me. I will repay you with hospitality," she said. "After that, we owe each other nothing. Our clans are at feud, after all."

"Catriona." He glanced at her somberly. "We are not at feud, you and I. I know a promise was made to you when you were born. I came here to honor Lachlann's pledge as best I could."

She sent him a swift glance. "With food and candles, or with men at your back and a sword in your hand?"

"I came here to see that you were well," he said firmly. "I came here to protect you, if you need that."

She looked away. "I need nothing from a Fraser."

He sighed, watching her profile, delicate but precisely made, as if stubbornness began in her core, in her bones. "I know you want us to reconsider, but we cannot. We signed a bond given us by the Privy Council," he explained. "If we fight with MacDonalds, the man who serves as pledge for our bond can be imprisoned and even executed. That man is Duncan Macrae, my cousin Elspeth's husband."

"The lawyer?" she asked.

He nodded. "I owe Duncan my life. He once saved me from a beheading." She glanced at him, her eyes wide. "We all owe him," he continued,

"and we will not endanger him. The MacDonalds do not honor this bond as cautiously as we
do, but no Glenran Fraser will willingly shed
MacDonald blood ever again."

"I understand," she said, and sighed. "But my
uncle has done me a great wrong, and I need help
to right it. I may never be able to go back to my
home again." She bit at her lower lip.

He undid the silver brooch, which he had
repinned to his shirt, and held it out to her. "Take
the snow rose, Catriona," he said. "Take it, and let
me help you some other way."

She did not touch the brooch. "Oats and candles are kind gifts, and brooches are pretty. But
none of those help me."

"Kilernan cannot be taken without starting a
blood feud."

"Then take it without bloodshed," she said
simply.

He shook his head. "That cannot be done."

"I need only that. All else I can do for myself."

He bowed his head in exasperation. He wanted
to help her, but she would accept only what he
could not give her.

"Do it without blood, Kenneth," she said. "If
you want to help me, find some way to take Kilernan. Please." He heard the pleading in her soft
voice, and heard a tremble of fear there.

He frowned, and grabbed up the brooch. Standing, he went to the door and yanked it open. He
stared out over the hills, white and vast and end-
lessly pure. Behind him, Catriona knelt by the
hearth. He heard a wooden spoon stir inside an

iron kettle, heard the splash of liquid as she began to prepare a meal.

"You will have to stay another night, because of the snow," she said as she worked. "And with that head wound, you need rest before you can travel. When you return to Glenran, please thank your kin for the New Year's gifts."

He said nothing. The pin of the snow rose pierced his skin as he grasped it. He looked down, and saw a bright drop of blood on his fingertip.

They ate a hot meal of barley and beef, and oatcakes made with a hole in the center, traditionally shaped New Year's bannocks, although Kenneth noticed that Catriona did not add the sugar and currants he had brought, as would have been customary. She made a spiced, watered wine with the claret, but sipped only a little herself.

After the meal, Kenneth slept heavily, as if he had not rested for days, and awoke to find that his headache had lessened a good deal. He looked around. Near the door, Catriona wound her thick plaid around her head and shoulders, over her gown and another plaid. Her hands were covered in heavy stockings. She picked up the cloth bundle that he had brought, opened the door quietly, and stepped outside.

Frowning, he sat up and dressed, wrapping and belting his own plaid over his leather doublet and long trews. Yanking on his deerhide boots, he followed her outside.

She rode her garron away from the yard, through

deep drifts. Kenneth ran to the byre and saddled his own horse to follow Catriona. He rode after her steadily, his breath frosting in small clouds, his eyes narrowed against the glare of sun on snow.

"Catriona! Go back!" Kenneth called as he neared her. "These drifts are too deep."

She turned. "You go back! You need to rest. I am not going far."

He rode alongside of her, determined to watch over her. If her garron became stranded, at least she would not be alone. She rode ahead of him while their ponies struggled through the drifts. They crossed a long ridge and waded down a hill.

"It is but a short way now," she said after a while. She urged her garron over a moor. Kenneth followed, his garron, like hers, plowing through deep snow. Cold nipped through his boots and plaid. Finally he saw a small stone house set in the lee of a hill. Gray smoke twisted up from the roofhole. In the yard, a snow fortress, piled high with snowballs, was flanked by crudely shaped snowmen, wearing flat Highland bonnets.

Catriona dismounted and led her horse into a small, crowded byre, which already contained a goat, four sheep, two cows and two dark garrons. She motioned for Kenneth to stable his horse as well. Then she handed him the bundle she had brought, and knocked on a small door in the wall.

"You must enter as the first-foot," she told Kenneth. "A dark-haired man, holding gifts, will bring them good luck. And besides, they will adore you for it."

Kenneth gave her a puzzled look and stepped

through. He stared in amazement as a swarm of children rushed past him, shouting and laughing, to throw themselves at Catriona. She hugged them, each in turn, from a tall, dark-haired boy to a tiny blond boy—and every size in between, Kenneth thought, stunned. Finally she embraced a little red-haired girl, kissed her soundly, and turned to Kenneth.

"These," she said, "are my children."

He blinked at her, while the children laughed loudly, and Catriona smiled. He looked around, hardly able to take in the din, the laughter, the jostling and giggling of six, seven, eight children in all, seven boys and one girl.

"Your children?" he asked uncertainly.

She laughed sweetly, like a small bell. "Well," she said. "I wish they were mine. But they are my cousins, and...orphaned. This is Kenneth Fraser," she told the children. Kenneth nodded, and received sober stares in return.

"This is Patrick MacGhille," she said, touching the tallest boy's arm. Kenneth saw Patrick frown, his beard-wisped cheeks flushed, as if he disapproved of a Fraser in his home. Those of the name MacGhille, Kenneth knew, were loyal to Clan MacDonald.

"And here are Angus, Malcolm, David"—she touched each lower head as she spoke, like going down a stair—"and Donald, Edan, and Tomas. And their sister, Mairead." Kenneth nodded hesitantly to each; the little girl, he observed, was only a bit older than the two youngest boys, Edan and Tomas.

"Triona, Triona!" Edan tugged at her hand and pointed to Kenneth. "What does he have in that sack?"

"Wonderful things, but you must be patient," she said.

"*Bliadhna Sona*, Triona," the little girl piped.

"And a lucky New Year to you, my Mairead," Catriona said, smoothing her hair. Kenneth saw then that the child's left eye was milky-blue and wandered to the side. This, then, must be the little half-blind girl who had named the cat `Dog'.

"Tell me, how did you fare in the storm?" Catriona asked them. The children began to chatter of their adventures as she crossed the dim, smoky room and sat on a bench beside the table, lifting Tomas to her lap. The boys sat too, on the bench, on stools, on the earthen floor. Kenneth stood while Catriona and the children spoke about the storm.

As he listened, he realized that Patrick and his brother Angus, who seemed to be proud, capable lads, had taken responsibility for their younger siblings. The children clearly loved Catriona, and Kenneth saw that they depended on her for support and friendship.

He glanced around the house. Snug and well-made of stone, earth, and thatch, the crofter's hut had one room with a central hearth; the furnishings were simple and few, and he saw two box-beds in the wall. Overhead was a dark, narrow loft, likely with more beds. Behind him, he heard—and smelled—the animals in the byre, separated from the house by a wattle and daub wall.

He looked at Catriona, who gathered the children close to tell them about her New Year's adventure. They gasped as she told them about her first-foot, and turned to stare at Kenneth.

"But he is a Fraser!" one boy said. "He is not lucky!"

"He has dark hair," Mairead said, in his defense.

"Why would a Fraser come to see you?" Patrick asked.

"I came as Catriona's friend," Kenneth answered.

"He brought gifts," Catriona said. "I will show you."

"He is the one," Mairead said, nodding. "The lucky one."

The smaller boys tugged at Catriona's skirt. She smiled at them and looked at Kenneth. He handed the bundle he still held to an older boy, Angus, who untied it on the floor.

The younger children exclaimed over the packets of food and spices and goods. Mairead sat on the floor to examine the contents eagerly, while Patrick and Angus watched, frowning, as if too old to be excited by simple things.

Mairead, Edan, and Tomas, the blond toddler, dug their fingers into the sugar sack until Catriona whisked it away. Malcolm, David, and Donald began swordplay with the candles, which Patrick grabbed from them with a fatherly growl.

Kenneth watched, thoughtful as he recognized the items as the Frasers' gifts to her. So the children were the reason that Catriona had not used the sugar and spices at home. They were the reason that she used one candle frugally when she had been given several. She gave what she could to them.

"The Fraser brought these things?" Malcolm asked Catriona.

"I did," Kenneth affirmed. "My kin and I are friends to Catriona." The children looked at him in amazement.

"Kenneth and his kin know all about my children," Catriona said. "They wanted to share their wealth and good fortune with you on New Year's Day." She slid a keen glance toward Kenneth.

"That we did." He nodded. "Your good luck is ours."

"This Fraser is a good omen," Mairead said. "He is Triona's New Year's surprise."

"Triona's what?" Kenneth asked her.

Mairead licked sugar from her fingers and nodded. Her left, milk-blue eye appeared totally blind, while her right was vivid blue; she gazed at him in an oddly wise manner. "I told Triona that New Year's Eve would bring her something wonderful. You are her New Year's gift. We can have the other things," she added brightly.

Kenneth raised a brow in astonishment. Catriona blushed and gave him a faltering smile. "Mairead did say that New Year's would bring me a lucky omen. She has the Sight."

"My cousin Elspeth has the Sight," he told Mairead. "She sees visions that come true. You must meet her one day."

"Is she a Fraser too?" Mairead asked.

"She is," Catriona said, "and a very nice woman, too. Come here to the hearth, Mairead, Patrick, Angus—I will show you how to make New Year's bannocks with oats, sugar, and spices. But you must promise not to let Tomas eat sugar from the sack. Store it up high, where he cannot get to it."

They gathered around Catriona as she knelt by the hearth and made several sweet cakes, which she cooked on a flat griddle over the fire. Then she made a thick soup with onions and beef, and prepared a hot, watered, spicy wine. When the meal was ready, the children helped Catriona serve the food in wooden bowls.

Kenneth shared their New Year's meal, eating as lightly as Catriona did. He answered the boys' curious questions about the feud between Frasers and MacDonalds, and about hunting, herding, and winter care of livestock. The older boys soaked in whatever Kenneth told them, nodding and asking more, as if thirsty for the knowledge and guidance he offered.

Later, while they gathered near the peat fire, David, Donald, and Malcolm began to sing Gaelic songs traditional to the New Year. Their voices were high and pure, and filled the room with peace and serenity. Kenneth watched their faces shining in the warm light, and thought of his own childhood.

Lachlann Fraser had fostered fifteen Fraser children after their fathers had died in a battle between Frasers and MacDonalds. Although Kenneth had been an orphan, he had never felt isolated or unwanted under Lachlann's generous care.

He looked at Catriona, who held Mairead and Tomas in her lap. She glanced around the room at each child while the boys sang, her blue eyes full of kindness, pride, love. Kenneth was fascinated by the depth of spirit that he saw in her.

When she dipped her head to kiss Tomas's sleepy head, he felt some lost, forlorn part of his soul stir. In that moment, he felt the strength of her love for these children, and felt as if she included him, too, in the warm circle created by her gaze.

But he knew that wine and firelight and good cheer created that sense. In truth, she regarded him as a Fraser who did not keep promises. The rare privilege of Catriona MacDonald's love was not meant for him. The thought made him infinitely sad.

He shook his head to clear it, and listened to the song.

Later, he watched as Catriona said farewell to each child with a soft word and an embrace. Kenneth bid them good fortune and peace in the new year, and he and Catriona led their rested garrons outside to ride back to her shieling hut.

"How long have the MacGhille children been alone?" he asked, as they waded through snowdrifts.

"Their mother died when Tomas was born three years ago," Catriona said. "She was my second cousin. Their father was a farmer. He died a few months past, when he went out on a cattle raid with my uncle Hugh."

"And you alone are helping them?"

"I am their only kin here, except for Uncle Hugh. But when I asked him to see to their welfare, he refused—he said that they would be far too much trouble, and someone else should do it." She sighed, shook her head. "Patrick is fifteen, and he and Angus think themselves old enough to watch over the younger ones. They have hunted and fished and protected them, and they have done well so far, but—" she shrugged.

"But the winter will be hard for them," Kenneth said.

She nodded. "Patrick and Angus are quite proud. I have offered to take the youngest ones to live with me, but none of them want to be separated."

"Your little house is not much bigger than theirs."

"Nor do I have the means to care for eight children." She looked directly at him, her eyes snapping blue. "I want to bring them to Kilernan to live. Hugh will not allow it."

"Ah. So that is why you want Kilernan so desperately." He gazed at her thoughtfully; she considered the children's welfare more important than her own.

"It is my rightful home, after all." They rode in silence until the shieling hut appeared on the next hill.

In the yard, they dismounted, and Catriona looked up at him. "Thank you for coming with me," she said. "Perhaps your first-foot into the children's house will bring them good luck."

He moved closer to her, his breath misting the air between them. "And will it bring luck for you?" he asked. "You said Mairead predicted a good omen for you this New Year's Eve."

She looked up at him, holding her horse's bridle. "That I do not know," she said. "Tell me, Fraser, was it good fortune that you set first-foot in my house, hurt and bleeding and in need of shelter? Or will the whole year be shadowed by that moment?" She turned away.

Kenneth stepped after her, ready to reply. But Catriona stopped so quickly that he nearly knocked into her, laying a hand on her shoulder.

"The poor luck may have already begun for the year," she said grimly. "Look." She pointed toward the front door.

Kenneth saw the flattened, trampled snow near the doorway, saw the troughs made by large feet and deep hoofprints. "We did not make those marks," he said slowly.

"Parlan MacDonald has been here, I think." She sent him a worried glance. "He may come back."

Kenneth shrugged. "If he does, I am here with you."

"If he finds a Fraser here, there will be trouble. You are forbidden to fight with MacDonalds."

"We are forbidden to *begin* a fight with MacDonalds," he explained. "But if they start a dispute, we certainly can defend ourselves."

She reached up, her fingers muffled in a thick stocking, and brushed his tender lower lip. "Who took you down on the ice?"

He could not hold back the truth when he looked into her deep blue eyes; her gaze was too serious, too perceptive. "Three men," he said. "MacDonalds. One of them was a huge blond man."

"That," she said, pulling on her horse's bridle, "was Parlan. Your fight with MacDonalds has already begun, Fraser."

# CHAPTER FIVE

CATRIONA PEERED OUT the window often, and listened for the thud of hoofbeats, but heard only the whip of the rising wind. She tried to ignore her apprehension by attending to simple tasks: sweeping the floor, repairing frayed woolen stockings, and stirring a thick soup in a kettle suspended over the hearthfire.

She spoke with Kenneth, softly and leisurely, of snow and the Highland hills, discovering that like her he loved them in any season or weather; they spoke of food, and hunting, and the best weave for a good plaid; they went on to share events from their childhoods. Neither mentioned feuding clans, or the disputes and pledges that lay unresolved between them.

Kenneth told her some amusing adventures he had experienced with his cousins, while she shared comments about her childhood, spent with her mother as her closest friend, isolated in Kilernan Castle from Hugh MacDonald's world of raids, drink and hunting.

Finally, seeing Kenneth yawn, his beard-shadowed cheeks pale, she told him to rest for a while. When the last of the daylight faded to blue dusk, she lit the beeswax candle.

"New Year's Day is not yet over," she said, when he sat up from his rest and looked at her. "Candlelight attracts good spirits to a house."

"Ah," he said. "That must be why I came here last night."

She turned to scowl at him, but he grinned at her, boyish and charming, and she laughed. Setting the candle on the windowsill, she turned back and caught his somber gaze.

His brown eyes gleamed deep, dark and rich. She remembered the warmth and comfort of his arms last night when they had shared the narrow bed. Blushing at the thought, she reminded herself sharply that he was a Fraser. He and his kin had denied her what she most needed. Any comfort she sensed in him was surely false.

A week ago, even a day ago, she would have believed that easily. Now, she found it harder to hold on to the hurt and anger that the Frasers' refusal had roused in her. He was more than a Fraser to her; she considered him a friend.

After supper, Kenneth sat on the floor with Cù, dangling a woolen stocking for the cat to snatch, and rubbing the cat's head and stomach. Catriona laughed when Kenneth dropped to his hands and knees and faced the cat, making growling sounds.

Kenneth glanced at her. "If he is determined to carry a proud name like `Dog'," he drawled, "he should learn to behave like one." The cat batted at him gently, and tangled his claws in Kenneth's long hair. When Kenneth's playful growl turned to a howl of genuine pain, Catriona sank to her knees to rescue him, chuckling softly as she freed the glossy strands.

"Ah, but some dogs have claws, I think," she said.

Kenneth slid her a look of chagrin. The cat leaped away as Catriona sat close to Kenneth, her fingers wound in his warm, soft hair. She sensed the heat of his body, and could smell an intriguing blend of smoke and leather and maleness about him. Looking up, she met his brown eyes directly.

"Triona—" he murmured. Her gaze dropped to the dusky curve of his mouth, to his chin, sanded with black whiskers. She was keenly aware of small, fascinating details—the sooty thickness of his lashes, the spicy scent of wine on his breath, his strong, warm fingers resting beside hers on the floor.

"What?" she asked him. Inside, her heart pounded like a drum. She lowered her fingers from his hair.

"Triona." He sat up and leaned close. "Come to Glenran." She shook her head. "I cannot do that."

"You can hardly stay here for the winter."

"It is comfortable enough here," she said defensively.

"You need food, fuel—"

"I will manage. Patrick and Angus will help me to hunt and fish and find fuel."

"We can support you at Glenran," he said. She

shook her head again and looked away. "It is dangerous for you to stay here. Even if you had enough supplies, you are alone."

*Alone.* But she was discovering how much she wanted his solace, his companionship—and more. She rose briskly to her feet and turned toward the window. "I will be fine here."

"Catriona." He stood and touched her shoulder. His soft voice and the heat of his hand made her want to turn toward him. She stayed still. "Come with me," he said.

"I need to be here," she said. "The children need me."

Behind her, he heaved an exasperated breath. "I am sure your cousins can come as well. Callum will not turn them away. His father took in many orphans for fostering, all cousins, by the way. I was one of them," he added.

She tilted her head. "You were orphaned?"

He nodded. "By MacDonalds."

She turned then. His somber gaze and the muscle that thumped in his cheek told her that he knew the pain of growing up without a natural father, as she had done, as the MacGhille children would have to do.

She sighed. "I had heard that Lachlann fostered several fatherless babes. You were one of those, then."

"Fortunately, I was. He was a good man."

"He was generous to me, too, when I was born." She paused. "A Fraser killed my father, a MacDonald killed yours. And Lachlann of Glenran helped us both."

"Then let his kindness be our bond," he murmured. "Lachlann would not want us to continue the bitter feud between our kin. Come to Glenran with me."

She shook her head. "That will not gain back Kilernan."

"It will not," he agreed. "But you will be protected."

"I do not need protection. I need my home. The children are the only kin I have, other than my uncle. Help me gain a home for them." She looked up at him, and felt the rising sting of tears. She blinked them back.

He tilted her chin with his fingers. "I wish I could tell you what you want to hear. I cannot."

"There must be a way," she said. His hand on her chin, his warm, steady gaze, held her pinioned as she stared up at him. When his thumb brushed over her lower lip, she felt a flood of need rush through her. He lowered his head.

"Stubborn girl," he whispered. His gaze moved down to her mouth, traced up again. His fingers were warm and firm as they slid to cup her cheek, and his breath was soft on her skin. "Let me help you. Let me protect you."

Her heart quickened. Frasers and MacDonalds, Kilernan and promises, seemed far distant suddenly. She watched his lips, his eyes, and moved closer to him by a breath, tilting her head in silent answer. Her body, her heart, surged toward him, seeking.

His mouth covered hers then, gently, poignantly. Joy curled sudden and deep within her, and rose like a wave of the sea. She let out a little moan as he pulled her into the circle of his arms and slanted his lips over hers, drinking there, his hands warm and strong on her back.

Beside her, Cù leaped to the windowsill, nearly upsetting the candle. Startled, Catriona broke away from Kenneth, her cheeks hot, heart slamming. The cat mewled and jumped down, striding to the front door and meowing there.

"Cù wants to go out, I think," she breathed.

Kenneth leaned past her, his hand at her waist, and peered through the crack in the shutter. "That cat is more of a watch dog than I thought," he said grimly. "Look."

Catriona did, and saw three horsemen riding into the yard. "Parlan, and his kin!" she gasped, and pushed at Kenneth's chest. "Hide, quickly— get into the box-bed!"

"Hide? I owe them a beating, and I have the right to deliver it."

"I will not have bloodshed and fighting in my home on New Year's Day! You might be hurt! And it is hardly a good omen!"

He sighed. "Talk to Parlan through the door, then, and do not let him in. That should keep your house free of poor omens." She slid him a sharp look, bit back a remark about wounded first-footers, and went to the door.

Kenneth folded his arms over his chest and waited, watching Catriona. She pressed her hands against the door and sent him a nervous glance.

When the first knock sounded, she jumped.

"Who's there?" she called quickly.

"Parlan MacDonald." His voice, through the door, was thick and deep. Kenneth peered stealthily through the shutter crack; he saw a blond, huge young man, wrapped in a red plaid that added more bulk to his heavy build. Surely Parlan was the same man who had attacked him on New Year's Eve; the other MacDonalds looked familiar too. Kenneth scowled, feeling a gut-centered urge to go outside and settle a debt. But he had promised Catriona that no violence would mar her New Year's Day.

"What do you want, Parlan?" Catriona asked. "It is after dark. You should be at home on such a cold night."

"I came to wish you well for the New Year," Parlan answered. "I came earlier with my cousins, but you were not here, and your horse was gone. So we came back."

"I went to see the MacGhille children," she said. "Thank you for thinking of me. Good night."

"Catriona," Parlan said, knocking again. "Let me come in."

"I will not," she said. "It is late."

"Hugh told me to come here and see that you were well. Let me in, Catriona. Let me in, girl." His voice sounded slurred.

Kenneth moved toward Catriona and leaned a shoulder firmly against the door. He glanced down at her pale face.

"He's drunk," she whispered. "He is usually so."

Parlan knocked again. "The wind is strong, and

the air is cold. Will you not offer me a dram?"

"You have had your share of drams tonight," she said primly. "And you must not be my first foot of the New Year. You are blond-headed."

"Then let my cousin Niall in first. He is dark-haired."

"He is a gloomy man, and is surely unlucky too," she said.

"No one lets me inside first on New Year's," Parlan grumbled. "Hugh would not let me in the hall this morning until someone else set foot in there before me."

"Go back to Kilernan," she said firmly. "I am tired, and I want no visitors just now. Good night."

"Catriona, your uncle sends a message," Parlan said. "He wants you to stop this nonsense and come home."

"Nonsense!" she exclaimed.

"We both think this hiding in the hills is silliness. Come home, and wed me. Hugh expects you to be the queen at his Twelfth Night feast in three days."

"Tell him I have no mood for revelry," she said.

"If you are not at Kilernan by Twelfth Night Eve, Hugh says he will ride here himself and carry you back."

Catriona sighed wearily. "I will think about his invitation. Go home, now."

"Catriona—we saw a Fraser in these hills yesterday. We knocked him from his horse. Have you seen any strangers?"

She glanced swiftly at Kenneth. "None at all. But I will be careful."

"If you are anxious, I could stay with you," Parlan said.

"I will be fine. Good night, Parlan."

"Catriona, I do not like to leave you alone here."

"Good night!" She faced Kenneth, waiting silently with him. When hoof beats thudded out of the yard, Catriona sighed and looked up. "He will come back tomorrow. If he finds you here—"

"I will be gone by then. Come with me." Kenneth brushed back a lock of her hair. When he touched her, the memory of the kiss they had shared rushed through him like lightning.

She turned away abruptly. "Every man I know wants me to do what pleases him," she said. "None of you cares what pleases me." Grabbing a folded plaid, she shook it out vigorously and laid it on the floor near the hearthstones.

"You do not have to sleep on the floor," he said.

"I know," she said. "This pallet is for you. I want my own bed tonight." She knelt by the hearth to stir the soup that simmered in the kettle.

Kenneth accepted the bowl she handed him with quiet thanks. They ate in silence, and afterward Catriona stacked the bowls and spoons. "I will clean them tomorrow," she said. "It is poor luck to clean dishes on New Year's Day."

"You are careful of such things," Kenneth said.

"I need to be, to improve my luck," she said.

"Good fortune will come to you this year, Catriona," he said. "I promise." He reached out and took her hand, pulling her down to sit beside him on the bench.

She slid him a wary look. "I do not trust Fraser promises." He smoothed his thumb over the back of her hand. "Trust this one," he said. "Good luck will be yours this year."

Her look was still doubtful. "You sound like a soothsayer."

"My cousin is one. And she would tell you that you need a strong good luck charm to cleanse away the old year and seal the luck of the new."

"The best omen I have had so far this year was a beaten and bleeding first-foot." She scowled at him, but he smiled in return. "It would take a strong omen to balance that out."

"True. Did you know," he murmured, "that the most powerful charm of all for New Year's Day... is a kiss?"

A blush colored her cheek. "We did that."

"We could bless the year again. If you like," he added.

She watched him, her eyes deep blue wells, filled with of uncertainty, and a hint of yearning. Slowly, she closed her eyes and lifted her face. He leaned toward her.

She tasted salty, like the broth, and sweet, like warm honey. Kenneth sank his fingers in her hair, cupping the back of her head as he kissed her deeply, gently, touching his lips to hers, lifting, touching again. She sighed out and raised a trembling hand to his cheek. Sliding her fingers through his hair, she tilted her mouth beneath his, her lips opening tentatively.

His body surged. He had not touched a woman in a long while; but the need that made him quaver now, that stirred through him like flame after darkness, was far deeper than physical. He wanted her profoundly, in his heart, his blood.

He remembered, distantly, vaguely, as if it had happened decades ago, that he had felt a shadow of this for Anna. But what swept through him now was more powerful, soul-deep. He could not explain it, but knew its strength was great.

Wanting her fiercely, he held back, sensing that her willful nature had a fragile side, too. He kissed her gently, pressing a hand against the sweet curve in her lower back, but no more than that. She sighed and broke the kiss, tipping her brow against his shoulder.

"Enough blessing," she said breathlessly.

He smiled, his cheek against her hair. "That should bring us both some luck." He drew a breath and waited for the thudding in his heart to calm.

Catriona laughed, a breathy gulp, and sat up, her cheeks were flushed and velvety. She stood and picked up her plaid, throwing it around her shoulders.

He stood too. "I will see to the animals," he said, guessing what she intended to do. "You stay here, by the fire. Stay warm. That wind sounds wickedly strong." He fetched his spare plaid and wrapped it over his head and shoulders. Catriona opened the door for him, and he stepped into a rough, icy wind.

By the time he returned, Catriona had gone to bed. The bed curtains were closed. Kenneth took off his plaid and moved toward the window, where the candle still burned.

"Do not blow it out," she said from behind the curtain.

"The light will attract good spirits. And please watch the fire, to see that it does not go out on the first day of the year."

"I will. Good night, then." He stretched out by the hearth. The cat jumped up on him, and Kenneth made room for both of them. He watched the glowing fire and listened to the wind howl and push past the little house; he thought about luck, and promises, and the unknown year.

Catriona had enjoyed too little luck, he knew. He wished he knew a charm to grant whatever she wanted, safety for her and the children, home, happiness. He thought of Anna, who had never known lack or struggle until her brief illness. Kenneth had been her betrothed, her lover; but she had not truly needed him until the last days of her life. Her death had left him lacking.

Catriona needed him. He knew that, even if she did not. He would leave tomorrow, but he would return to bring her food and goods, and to watch over her. Lachlann would have wanted someone at Glenran to fulfill his promise. And he had made his own pledge to her to improve her luck. He felt an odd sense of obligation; the Frasers owed her something—and he had been her first-foot of the year.

As he drifted to sleep, he wondered if Kilernan could be taken without attack; then he sighed, for it was impossible. And he realized that, once he left here, Catriona might not accept further visits or gifts from him. He was a Fraser, after all. She was not fond of Frasers.

He wished, suddenly, that she was.

# CHAPTER SIX

SLEET HURTLED DOWNWARD on shriek-ing winds, rattling against the walls and the roof. Catriona slid out of bed in a murky gray light, and wondered if it was morning yet. She pulled her plaid over her linen chemise and went to the door, cracking it open.

Icicles hung crystalline from the doorway, the byre, and the trees. Frozen rain poured down in fine sheets from a dark sky. Catriona shivered as the wind cut past her, and stepped back, bumping into Kenneth, who now stood just behind her.

He peered out. "Poor weather," he commented dryly. "I had better go see to the horses and the cow. They could freeze to death in this." He shut the door and turned. "Even with a hearthfire, it will be hard to stay warm inside today."

"You cannot ride to Glenran in this," she said.

"I cannot. Will you mind if I stay a bit longer?" He smiled and shoved a hand through his tan-gled hair. She noticed the sleepy creases around his brown eyes, and the heavier beard shadowing his firm jaw. He looked tousled and comfortable, standing beside her in his rumpled shirt and trews. Suddenly she did not want him to leave, regardless of the weather.

"Please stay," she said. "I would like the company."

He nodded and turned to gather his plaid and boots, pulling them on to go outside. When he was gone, Catriona dressed quickly and warmly, built up the smoldering fire with peat, and made a thick, salty porridge in a kettle over the hearth.

Her thoughts turned to the children. Although she trusted Patrick and Angus to watch over the younger ones, she was deeply concerned for them in such a dangerous storm. She would go there as soon as travel was possible.

After a while, Kenneth returned, his face red with cold. He blew on his hands to warm them, and ate quickly. "Thick ice has formed on this roof, and the byre," he told her. "I have to clear it off, or the thatch could collapse."

"I will help you," she said. He protested, but she grabbed her spare plaid and soon followed him outside.

The wind shoved at her, and the raw, bitter chill stung her hands and toes while she and Kenneth used broken tree limbs to prod at the ice on the low thatched roof of the shieling. When they turned toward the byre, they saw that the sloped, low-slung roof sagged under a burden of ice.

Fighting the keening wind, Kenneth opened the door of the byre, and held her back with his arm. "Stay here," he told her. "The roof could fall.

We will have to move the animals to safety. There is no choice but to bring them inside the hut."

"I know," she said. "We will make room for them somehow." He led the two garrons and the cow out of the byre, and she helped him guide the animals through the doorway of the hut.

Cù hid under a bench when they came inside, although Catriona got down on her knees to speak reassuringly to him. She turned to the agitated horses, patting their broad necks while Kenneth tipped the table, bench, and stools to build a makeshift stable area. Going back outside, he returned with oats for feed, and straw to spread on the floor.

Catriona perched on the bed, the only remaining seat, and watched while Kenneth soothed the horses with gentle hands. He spoke calmly to the cow, a small, shaggy, black creature who stared at him with limpid eyes. Then he stepped over the barrier and skirted the hearth to come toward her.

"The animals will be warm and safe," he said, "though it will be crowded in here."

"We will manage," she said brightly.

He unwound his damp plaid and hung it over the table to dry, then sat beside her to unlace his boots. "When the weather improves, I will repair the byre roof. I suppose"—he looked at her—" you would not consider coming to Glenran."

"With my cow and my horse, and eight children?" she asked.

He shrugged. "Lachlann and his wife raised fifteen fosterlings and their own son at Glenran.

There is room." He stripped down to his shirt, trews, and bare feet as he spoke, and began to rub his pale, blotched toes with a blanket from the bed.

"Your feet look frostbitten!" Kneeling, she took his foot in her hands and rubbed gently for a while, then warmed some water and sluiced it over his feet.

She felt the power and grace in his long bones and lean muscles. Even when his feet looked improved, she continued to stroke his ankles and knotted calf muscles. The rhythm and warmth was as soothing to her as she hoped it was to him.

"Thank you," he murmured.

She nodded, and turned away to fetch the flask of *uisge beatha* that the Fraser women had given her. Heating some of the liquid in an iron pot, she added cream, ground oats, and pinches of spices and sugar from Kenneth's New Year's gift. She poured it into a bowl and handed it to him.

"Drink this brose. It will warm you inside and out."

He sipped. "Ah. This is good. Thank you. I thought you gave the sugar and spices to the MacGhille children."

"I kept some for you," she admitted shyly.

He raised an eyebrow. "Girl dear, you are generous with your guest, but not with yourself. Come here." He patted the mattress. She sat beside him, and he held the bowl to her lips. "Drink," he said. "I am not the only one who is cold."

She sipped, feeling the hot, sweet burn of the brose slide down her throat. They shared more between them, and then Kenneth reached out to remove the outer plaid that she still wore.

The cow lowed morosely as Kenneth draped her damp plaid beside his to dry. He patted the animal's head affectionately and murmured to her. She nuzzled after him for a moment when he left her side to return to the bed, kneeling beside it.

"Let me warm your feet, now," he told Catriona. She allowed him to unlace her damp leather boots and pull them off; then he reached under her skirt to peel off her knee stockings as if she were a child. He kneaded her bare feet between his strong hands, then bathed them in the water that remained in the bowl.

His touch sent subtle shivers of pleasure throughout her body. She sighed, and watched his dark head and wide shoulders as he gently stroked her feet, coaxing warmth into her toes. No one, since her mother's death, had taken care of her like this man did now. No one had shown concern about her comfort.

And no one, other than the children, had touched her with gentleness or affection. She blinked back tears and closed her eyes, relaxing under his languid touch. Her feet and ankles seemed to glow with luscious warmth. When he set her foot down, she curled her toes and made a playful little moan, as if begging for more.

He smiled. "Enough, I think. Who knows what kind of an omen this might be."

"What do you mean?" she asked, frowning.

He raised a brow. "Do you not know about the

ritual of foot washing for a bride and groom, the night before they marry?"

A hot blush flooded her face. "I forgot about that," she said hastily, and drew her feet up to pull on thick, dry woolen stockings, folding her legs beneath her.

He sat on the bed again, his weight shifting her against him slightly. He sipped brose and offered her more. "The MacGhille children," he said, as they listened to the steady torrent of sleet. "How will they fare in this storm?"

"I have been thinking about them too," she said. "Patrick and Angus are clever lads, and they will do their best to keep the others safe. But if ice collects on their roof, as it did here, or if one of them gets hurt or sick—" she sighed. "I wish we could go there."

"I will ride there as soon as the weather allows. Patrick will take care of them. He's a smart lad, and nearly a man."

She nodded and sipped the brose. The thick, sweet stuff slipped down her throat like fire and honey, warming her despite the pervasive chill in the hut. The wind shrieked past the house, but the blazing hearth and the presence of the man beside her were vastly comforting.

Kenneth stood to toss a few sticks of kindling over the peat chunks, and used the iron poker to coax a bright, leaping fire.

"Do you see those little blue flames?" she asked. "Those are the spirits of the hearth."

"Good omens, I hope," he said, as he sat beside her again.

"Very good. That square bit of peat, there, fore-tells wealth coming into a house. And that long, round shape means a stranger will come into the house."

"Ah," he said. "I told you I was lucky for you."

She rolled her eyes. "That remains to be seen."

He smiled. "You will be surrounded with luck, Catriona MacDonald. A dark-haired man fell across your doorstep, loaded down with good fortune and goodwill." She laughed softly at his gentle teasing. "Ah, look," he said. "More square chunks in the fire. They predict much wealth for you this year. What does that fat little chunk of peat mean?"

"That?" She frowned. "A birth within the year, I think."

"Ah. Well," he said, "perhaps your cow will calf."

"Perhaps." She wrinkled her nose. "It is begin-ning to smell like a stable in here."

He chuckled. "I will have to shovel out the straw sooner than I thought, if we are to share this place with them."

"This will help." Catriona grabbed a slen-der juniper branch from the kindling pile, and tossed it on the fire. Soon the smoky evergreen fragrance of the juniper began to counter some of the animals' pungency. She climbed back into the warm nest of the bed and sat beside Kenneth; they both welcomed Cù there when he slid out from his hiding place to curl between them.

Kenneth smoothed his hand over the cat's sleek-ness, as did Catriona, and their fingers touched.

His hand moved past hers slowly. She shivered, but knew it was not from the chill, and remained silent, as he did, both of them stroking the cat.

She listened to the thrust and whine of the storm, and the purring cat, watched the fire and sensed the peacefulness of Kenneth's silence. Delicious currents of heat and contentment poured through her, and she sighed. She felt truly sheltered, while bitterness raged outside.

"The storm is fierce. The cold and the ice could last for days," Kenneth murmured.

"It could," she agreed. Then this heaven of peace would continue, she thought dreamily.

"I should leave soon," he said.

"But you planned to stay," she said, looking up at him.

"Tomorrow my horse should be able to manage the hills, and I will ride out to see the children. Then I must return to Glenran. My cousins will be wondering what happened to me." He smiled at her. "But I am not leaving just yet."

"I am glad," she whispered.

"Are you?" His gaze was steady and deep.

She nodded. "And I am glad you set first foot in my house. You have brought me good fortune after all. You saved the animals from the cold, and cleared the ice on the roof. It was good luck that brought you here in that storm. I might have been alone here, to deal with the ice."

His fingers covered hers over the cat's back. "Perhaps I shall be your first-foot next year," he murmured, "if you like."

"I would like that," she whispered. He leaned

closer, and she tilted her head toward him, hoping suddenly.

The first touch of his lips was soft and tentative,
but the next kiss, deep and full, swept her breath
away. She circled her arms around his neck, pulling him closer. Kenneth pushed the cat gently
out of the way and wrapped her in his arms.

His mouth delved over hers with such strength
and heat that she seemed to melt, like butter in
hot brose. She felt the light caress of his tongue
across the seam of her lips, and she sighed out,
loving the strange intimacy of it.

She leaned back and let him take her down
to pile of pillows and furs on the narrow bed.
His lean, hard body fit against her curves, even
through layered wool, and his lips moved over
hers in a breathless rhythm. What rushed through
her was more heady, more dizzying than the
strong drink that still coursed, hot and languid,
through her blood.

He drifted his fingers over her cheek, along her
neck and shoulder, touching her as if she were
fragile. His fingers grazed over her breast and
moved downward, pulling her hips toward his.
She gasped and tightened her arms around his
neck, pressing the length of her body to his. Her
heart beat in a fierce cadence, and she sensed the
heavy pounding of his heart, too, when her fingers skimmed over his chest.

He traced his lips over her cheek, her ear, along
her jaw. Shivers cascaded through her, and she
moaned softly, turning to find his lips with her
own. She moved against him, craving more of his

grazing touches and deep, luscious kisses. She had not known this kind of tenderness existed. All she wanted was to float in its luxury, in its slow, effortless current; no matter where it took her, she knew she would be safe.

Once, Parlan had kissed her in a dark corridor at Kilernan, swift, sour wine kisses followed by the heavy thrust of his tongue. She had arched away from him, and slapped him when his large hands rounded boldly over her behind, pulling her hips against the hard swelling beneath his plaid. He had claimed drunkenness; but she had known that, drunk or not, Parlan would never be a tender husband.

But this Fraser, a stranger who had no reason to care about her, touched her as if she were made of silk and roses. His kisses were kind and yet strong, surging through her like bursts of flame. No threat, no sense of wrongness spun awry in her gut, as she had felt with Parlan. She felt herself relax and sink into the warm ocean of comfort Kenneth provided with his lips, his hands, his breath.

His hand soothed over her breasts, rousing a shiver of need that spooled deep within her. She felt as if she had found the heart of a fire, and never wanted to leave its comfort.

When he hesitated, as if offering her a chance to stop what grew between them, she let her silence, and the kiss she returned, answer his unspoken question. When he drew the lacings of her bodice loose, when his fingers found her breast, she pulled in a breath. Slipping her hands over his wide, tightly muscled shoulders and chest, she sighed out.

His touch, his kisses, roused a sudden swell of joy in her, and she smiled to herself, loving this—loving him. The thought stunned her, and she paused, wrapped in his arms, knowing, in a strange, complete, wordless way, that she was where she belonged. She sank into a cocoon of warmth and comfort he provided, and wanted more, anything, all, from him. He glided his lips to her breast, and a deep, thunderous tremor rippled through her, as if strong enough to shake the bed, shake the room—

Kenneth sat up quickly, bolting from the bed with a muttered oath. "The roof! It's close to collapsing!" he yelled. He leaped past the hearth toward the animals.

Bewildered, Catriona scrambled out of the bed. The walls trembled, and noise and chaos flooded the room. She swept the cat into her arms and watched as the ceiling over the stable area sagged and groaned. The horses and the cow shifted, bumped, and kicked out at the furniture and the walls.

The cow stumbled against the upturned table, which crashed to the ground. Kenneth struggled to pull and push and cajole the three animals to safety across the room. Then the thatched roof above the abandoned corner emitted an unearthly groan, and shivered down in a heap of ice, snow, and straw.

# CHAPTER SEVEN

"ARGH," KENNETH SAID, leaning back into the recess of the box-bed, "she seems to like me." He held up an arm to protect his face and turned his head, trying to avoid the cow's hot breath as she snuffled sloppily at his hair. Beside him, Catriona laughed with delight. He shot her a wry look.

"She adores you," Catriona agreed, and shoved helpfully at the cow's massive shoulder. The animal turned and swatted her tail at Catriona as she moved away, only to bump into one of the horses. Sidestepping, the cow knocked over a stool.

"She'll step in the hearth fire! Here, move!" Catriona said. "You'll burn yourself—*ach*, silly cow, go that way!"

"What's her name?" Kenneth asked, as he reached out and guided the cow's hindquarters away from the hearth.

"I do not know," she said. "A neighbor stabled her here so that I could have milk over the winter. What shall we call her?"

"Well, the cat is called Dog"—he frowned in

a pretense of concentration—" how about Pig?"

Catriona laughed in that bell-like sound that made him smile to himself. Ever since the roof had caved in, their shared laughter over the mishap had made the work of cleaning and repairing the damage easier. Now she bounced off the bed and danced quickly around the hearth, intent on keeping a horse from knocking over the remains of the ruined table, which Kenneth had set up as a crude fire screen.

"You are giddy as a lark in spring," Kenneth said, watching her. She moved lightly, with a kind of joy he had not seen in her before. "Your little house is in shambles, and yet you are happy as a child."

She chuckled sweetly as she patted one of the garrons. Kenneth smiled, and glanced past her toward the dark corner of the house where the roof had fallen. He stretched his shoulders, weary from a day spent clearing the wreckage and repairing the roof. He and Catriona had worked together to drag out chunks of ice, shovel dirty snow and straw, and haul timber and straw from the collapsed byre to shore up the ceiling of the hut. The repairs had sealed out the sleet and the wind for now, but he was not sure how long the roof would hold, particularly if the ice storm continued.

Another onslaught of wind and sleet battered the outer walls, but soup steamed, fragrant and savory, in the hanging kettle, and the crackling flames in the hearth warmed the snug, overcrowded hut. Kenneth felt oddly content;

Catriona's smile, directed toward him, told him she felt the same.

"What makes you so happy now, Catriona MacDonald?" he asked softly. "Surely a fallen roof is a poor omen, and yet you smile."

She sat beside him on the bed. "I do not know," she said. "I feel good, safe, somehow, in here, with the storm outside." She grinned, quick and charming. "And you made me laugh all through the day, just watching you try to repair the damage, with the cow licking your face and the horses bumping into you." Kenneth chuckled. "But a fallen roof must be a very unfavorable sign, as you say," she added somberly.

"It would be favorable enough, if it forced you to find a better place to live," he said. "You cannot stay here now. Come to Glenran with me."

She shook her head. "You know I will not do that."

"I am concerned for your welfare," he said. "Come with me. Please. Will you make me get down on my knees and beg?"

"I might," she said saucily. "Would you do it?"

"*Tcha.*" He smothered a grin. "I will more likely toss you in my plaid and carry you off. No Fraser will beg for a favor."

"Abducting the Maid of Kilernan is probably grounds for a feud," she said. "My uncle would be after you then."

Kenneth watched her sparkling blue eyes, and his heart swelled within him. He realized, with a sudden, powerful clarity, that he had begun to love her. He drew a long breath, relishing the feeling, and an idea burst into his mind, stunning him with its strength, and its undeniable truth.

"Catriona," he said, "what if the Maid of Kilernan wed a Fraser?" He spoke slowly, wondering, his heart pounding.

She stared at him, her cheeks flushing high pink. "That—that would surely start a feud between Kilernan and Glenran."

The bold step he was about to take felt wholly right. "A marriage can sometimes end a feud," he said.

She lowered her head, her cheeks gone pale, as if all the joy drained out of her. "Go back to your kin in safety, Kenneth Fraser," she said. He barely heard her.

"I will not go back without you," he said.

"My uncle and Parlan might kill you if we—if we wed."

"I have faced death before," he said. "A sure death, with the executioner's mask already about my eyes, and his ax a swing away from my neck. Yet I am here beside you now." She glanced at him, frowning in concern. "That happened years ago, when I was wrongly accused of breaking the signed bond with the MacDonalds," he explained. "My kin stood by me then. I will stand by you now, Catriona. Your uncle might approve of a marriage between us. Surely he knows that any attempt to heal this feud will please the Council."

She twisted her hands in her lap. "He would not like it."

"Shall we find out?" He watched her steadily.

She began to speak, then shook her head.

Kenneth leaned toward her. "Am I such a poor omen?"

"You are not a poor omen," she said. Her voice quavered. "But Parlan and my uncle would seek you out, bond or none."

"*Ach*, my girl," he said, touching her shoulder. "Who would you rather take to husband—me or Parlan?"

"You," she breathed out, without hesitation. "But I will not do it." She turned away, curling up to lay on the bed, her back to him. He heard her sniffle, as if she fought tears.

He sighed and shoved a hand through his hair, regretting that his impulsive words had upset her. But he knew his mind, and his heart; the past few years, with Anna and then without her, had taught him much about himself, and about what he needed.

In the space of a few days, Catriona had blessed his lonely existence fully, kindly, like candlelight dispels shadow. Still, he had spoken his thoughts far too fast—not for him, but for her. Stretching out beside her, he circled his arms around her.

"All I ask is that you consider it," he murmured.

"It would never work," she answered. "Go back to Glenran, and remember your bond. Keep your distance from the MacDonalds."

"Remember the brooch, Catriona," he said softly. "The Frasers have a pledge to fulfill to you."

She shook her head, curled away. "I fear that misfortune would befall both of us this way. Forget the brooch." She drew a shaky breath. "I should never have come to Glenran asking for payment of Lachlann's pledge. I always hoped that the snow rose would bring me luck. Marriage between us would"—she paused—" would only invite danger for the Frasers, and the MacDonalds."

"The snow rose will bring you luck, if you let it," he said. "If not for the brooch, I would never have set foot across your threshold. I will be your luck, Catriona," he whispered. "I *am* your luck. Depend on it."

She caught back a sob and grasped his hand tightly. He held her, but she did not turn, did not speak. He felt her cry silently, and knew she kept her fears and her thoughts within. After a while, her breaths grew more even, and she slept, exhausted, in his arms.

He kissed her damp cheek, then sighed and sat up, aware that he must keep watch over the animals, so that none of them stepped into the open hearth, or knocked something into the fire.

He leaned against the bedframe. The cow wandered toward the bed and nuzzled at his chest. Kenneth patted her huge head gently, distracted by his thoughts: he meant to find a way to fulfill a promise made twenty years ago.

The ruined shieling sat on the hill like a pile of broken dreams. Catriona sighed, looking at it as she stood outside in the yard. The thatched roof sagged sadly at one end, its hole filled with straw and timber scraps; the small byre beside the house resembled a large pile of kindling.

She turned away to watch the cow and horses, who wandered close to the house, where the snow was packed flat. She had brought them outside to milk the cow and let the garrons walk a bit; she would guide them inside soon, for the air was still frigid, although the sleet had stopped. Cù had stepped out briefly, and had gone inside, making his preference clear.

Ice slicked the hills to milky smoothness, and turned the trees to bare, delicate sculptures. Catriona walked carefully over the slippery, crusted snow, her boots sinking with each step, and glanced back at the house.

Kenneth still slept, although it was well into the day. She knew that he had been awake much of the night. Just after dawn, when Catriona had awoken and got out of bed, he had been sitting beside her. They had said little to each other beyond a somber morning greeting, and he had laid down and drifted to sleep quickly. She was not sure what she would tell him when he awoke.

She sighed and began to crush the snow around her with her boot, making idle patterns while she thought. She had to convince Kenneth to go back to Glenran. If he stayed with her, if he wed her, the risks to him, and to the Glenran Frasers and Kilernan MacDonalds, frightened her. If she wed him, she feared that she would be widowed too soon, as her mother had been.

But the thought of being wed to him spun through her like a whirlwind, stealing her breath. To have him near her always, strong and calm, kind and comforting—but that was a dream, a wish. No matter how much she desired it, it could not happen.

Gazing at the broken, sad little house, she sighed. She had no choice now but to return to Kilernan. Twelfth Night Eve, when her uncle expected her, was two days away; by then the weather would allow travel. Kenneth would leave, and so would she.

She pressed her foot down again and again, turning in a slow circle as she thought. Before Christmas, all she had wanted was a rescue from her dilemma, and better luck in the future. But since Kenneth had fallen through her door at midnight on New Year's Eve, as if fate had guided him there, all had changed.

Somehow, fate had swept through her life like snow and ice, covering all that she thought existed, leaving a new, pure vista, filled with possibility and risk. But she would not risk Kenneth's life to grasp at joy.

*I am your luck*, he had said. She wished it could be true. His words had been filled with devotion and love; they were a pledge in themselves. Tears stung her eyes, and she wiped them away. She rarely allowed herself to cry, but last night she had been flooded by bitter joy. Desperate to turn into his arms, knowing he wanted her, too, she had not; she feared what would happen if she let herself love him as she wanted to do.

Kenneth was more than her luck. He was her life, the soul of what she needed and desired. The heart-wrenching choice she faced was no choice at all: she wanted him to live, wanted peace for him and their clans. If she had to return to Kilernan to ensure that—if she had to marry Parlan—then she would.

She stepped back, and looked down at the design she had made. Spreading around her like an opened flower, her footprints formed a rose in the snow.

# CHAPTER EIGHT

KENNETH LOOKED UP from lacing his boots to see Catriona open the door and guide the cow into the house ahead of her. She shut the door against a blast of frigid air, and turned toward him. Her pink cheeks grew even brighter.

"You are awake," she said. "Have you eaten?" She took off her outer plaid and folded it as she spoke.

"Not yet." He stood. "How is the weather?"

She knelt by the low fire and poured water from a bucket into a kettle, swinging it over the fire to heat while she scooped ground oats from a sack. "Bitterly cold, but the sleet has stopped. Walking is difficult, and riding might be nearly impossible on some of the hills. You may have to stay another day or so." She seemed to be avoiding his gaze.

He watched her add the oats. "Catriona, I—" he stopped, having much to say, and unsure where to begin.

"I will not wed you, Kenneth," she said quietly,

stirring the porridge. "But thank you for wanting to help me."

He walked over to stand beside her. She did not look up. "I did not suggest it as a way to help you," he said, "although I think it would solve your situation. I suggested it because I want to wed you, Catriona MacDonald. Just that."

She stirred silently. The cow lowed and shoved gently at him, and the cat slid over his feet to sit by the warm hearth stones and lick his paws. Kenneth did not move. He studied the dark sheen of Catriona's braided hair, and noted the proud, tense set of her slender neck and shoulders.

"I will not wed you," she repeated, adding salt.

He sighed in exasperation, annoyed with himself for bumbling through this matter impulsively and foolishly, and distressing her. He would have to begin again.

Catriona knew little about him beyond what he had mentioned of his childhood and his cousins. He wanted to tell her about the last few lost years of his life. Perhaps then she would understand him better; perhaps then she would believe that he knew what he wanted in his life.

He sighed, rubbed at his jaw, wondered where to begin. "I was betrothed just over three years ago," he said finally.

She frowned, tilted her head. "I did not know," she said.

"I loved Anna very much," he said quietly. "She was a sweet, happy girl, and easy for anyone to love. But she died three years ago of a quick, fierce illness, on New Year's Day."

Catriona glanced up at him, her blue eyes wide and sympathetic. "New Year's? Dear God."

He tensed his jaw, looked away. As much as he trusted Catriona, he found it difficult to reveal the hidden corners of his heart to anyone. "Since her death, I have dreaded the Yuletide season, every day of it, from Christmas to Twelfth Night," he said. "I thought only about what I had lost. I did not want to be happy if she was not there."

She lowered her lashes, bit her lip, and said nothing as she circled the spoon in the thick porridge.

"I had set my mind to loneliness," he said. "I was content, in a bitter way, to be discontent. Then you walked into Castle Glenran on Christmas Day." She glanced quickly at him. "At first, I thought how much you resembled Anna," he told her.

"Oh." She looked away. "Now I see—"

"You do not see," he said firmly. "Listen to me well. I know that you are different from Anna," he said. "Black-haired, blue-eyed, kind-hearted, that much is true of both of you. But now, though I fell through your doorway only days ago, I feel as if I know you well, as if I have known you for years."

She sucked in a little breath. "I—I feel the same," she said. "But we have spent much time together, shut in here." She sighed as she stirred the porridge. "I am sorry about Anna, Kenneth. It must be hard to lose the one you love."

"It is," he murmured. "Do not make me endure it again." He met her gaze evenly, though his heart thumped like a wild thing.

"You do not know me well enough to...love me," she whispered, looking down.

"Do I not?" He knelt beside her. "I know that you are strong and determined," he murmured, watching her. "You are keen-witted, and beautiful, and hopelessly willful."

She frowned, but her cheeks blushed brightly. He smiled. "You laugh like a child, and make me want to laugh too. And you have the heart of an angel where others are concerned," he continued. "I think you might do anything for those you love." His fingers curled over hers while she continued to stir the porridge. "And I know that you are scared just now," he added.

"I am not," she said stiffly, knocking the spoon against the side of the kettle, and lifting the pot away from the fire.

"Are you not? Well, I am," he said. He tugged at the spoon, but she would not give it up. She stirred resolutely, though her cheeks bloomed with color and her breath quickened. "Catriona," he said patiently. "Let go of the damned spoon."

"Why?" she asked. "Are you hungry?"

"I am that," he growled, and flung the spoon away, turning her in his arms. He pulled her close, kneeling with her beside the hearth stones, and kissed her profoundly.

For a moment, she hesitated. Then she sighed out and her lips softened beneath his, as if she struggled within herself, and found the strength to surrender.

She circled her arms around his neck and tilted

her head beneath his, framing his jaw with her slender hands, kissing him with a trembling joy- fulness that made him want to weep suddenly, not for what he had lost, but for what he had found.

He slanted his mouth over hers and kissed her deep and certain, and let his hands skim the curv- ing contours of her body. A wealth of thick wool separated them, but he felt her graceful, willing undulations against him. That silent eloquence poured through him like fire, and the hardening strength in his body urged him onward.

She slid her fingers through his hair, returning his kiss with a fervency that took his breath. He circled his hands around her waist, beneath the drape of her plaid, and moved upward to find the slope of her breasts. He caught her little glad cry between his lips, and knew that she shared his need.

He hoped, ardently, desperately, that she also shared the love he felt. Like sunlight bursting through clouds, the feelings that burgeoned inside of him streamed through his blood and being, adding fire to his touch as he held her.

If he let go of her, then and there—if he walked out into the cold and let the lust that flamed in his body cool to ice—he would still feel this fiery yearning that fueled his desire. She charmed him, nurtured him, filled the emptiness within him like light poured over shadow. Kin and feuds and promises aside, he loved her, simply, deeply. He could not do without her now.

Kneeling with her as they kissed, he wanted

more of her, more of this. He touched the
incredible softness of her breast, warm and hidden beneath wool and linen, felt his own breath
and blood pulse through him like wind-driven
waves. He stood, lifting her as if she were made
of no more than silk and a soul.

Setting her down on the fur-covered, rumpled
bed, he looked into her eyes, questioning, waiting. Silently, she reached past him and drew the
curtain shut. Her fingers closed around his arm,
pulling him toward her in the darkness. He knelt,
leaning over her, hands to either side of her, and
kissed her gently.

"Catriona," he whispered, "listen to me, now. I
love you." He kissed her again, letting his mouth,
his breath, linger and blend with hers. "Whether
we have been together for days or years is not
important. What has begun will only grow stronger."

She closed her eyes, sighed, lifted her mouth
to his. He caressed her lips, then lifted his head
to gaze at her through the shadows. "I may be a
Fraser, but I will be your luck, the whole soul of
it," he murmured, "if you want me."

She made a small sound, half sob, half laugh, and
drew him down to lie beside her. He wrapped his
arms around her, his heart pounding against the
rhythm of hers.

"I do want you," she answered. "Good omen or
poor, you fell at my feet on New Year's Eve, and I
want you for my own, so much," she whispered.
"But you must not ask me to wed you."

He opened his mouth to speak, to protest, but

she laid a silencing finger against his lips. He felt a poignant tug of deep emotion in his chest, and sank his fingers into the silk of her hair as he kissed her gently. The hunger of her returned kiss surprised him, fired his craving for more. Meeting her lips again, he thought he tasted the salt of tears. But she smiled when he looked at her.

He savored the small, moist cave of her mouth, and his hands traced over the graceful shape of her, impeded by wool and linen. She caressed his arms, his waist, and tugged at his plaid; he shifted, letting her divest him, while he pulled at her laces, slid wool gently away from her, until they lay bare together. The curves of her body were luscious in shadow, touched by tiny stars of daylight that fell through the curtain weave.

He was aware that they hurtled fast toward a brink that would carry them forward, and change them both forever. Heart pounding, he kissed her mouth and slowed, giving her time to think, to stop him. She sighed and traced her fingers down his arm, a welcoming, loving gesture.

He kissed her throat, the soft, globed sides of her breasts, her velvet-firm nipples at last, until desire rendered him breathless. When he traced his hand over her flat abdomen, she gasped and shifted closer, settling her hips to his so sweetly, so intently, that he groaned and tilted himself away from her.

"Hold," he whispered. "Hold, love. You must be certain."

"I am," she said. "Did you not say yourself that I am quick to decide, and hopelessly willful?"

"Hopelessly," he murmured, and kissed her again. He slid his fingers gently along her waist, over her abdomen and down; he found the small, soft seam and parted it delicately. She sighed, and swayed against his caressing fingertips, showing him the cadence with her breath and motion. Her seeking, tender fingers explored the hard map of his torso until he gasped and groaned low and rolled to his back, pulling her over him.

His heart thundered, his blood and breath pulsed heavily, and he could hardly hold back. She moved over him with gentle, inexorable power, like a wave of the sea, sweeping him into her current. He held her, kissed her, shifted toward her; she opened over him in a graceful arching motion, and he was lost.

He sucked in a long, full breath and slipped inside the warm haven of her body, rocking beneath her with a lingering, aching, heartfelt rhythm. Her body thrilled him, nurtured him, gave him solace. He felt her love then, genuine and deep, flowing over his heart like warm, restoring rain. And he knew, as if these exquisite moments worked subtle magic, that now he was forever blended to her, body and soul.

He held her in his arms while the shared rhythm of their breathing slowed, while their bodies parted reluctantly. She curled beside him under the warm fur covers, while wind whistled against the outer walls. After a long while, she looked up.

"I love you well, Kenneth Fraser," she murmured. "I want you to know that." Her voice was soft and sad. "But I will not wed you. I will not risk that for you."

"*Ach*, stubborn girl," he said gruffly. "It is my risk, and I will take it."

"I will not have you die at the hands of the MacDonalds for loving me." She sat up, grabbing her clothing, pulling her shift and her gown over her head. He reached for her, but she slipped out of the enclosed bed. He snatched up his shirt and trews and yanked them on, then moved toward her, where she stood by the window.

He touched her shoulder. "Surely you have changed your mind now," he murmured, tracing a finger over her cheek.

She shook her head, sadly, firmly, and looked through a crack in the shutter. "The sleet has stopped," she said. Her voice sounded faraway, as if she had withdrawn to some place where he could not follow. "You will be able to ride out soon.

I hope you will go to the children. I am concerned about them."

"Did I not promise that already? Come with me."

"The cow would trample this house to bits if I left her alone," she answered. "If the children are fine, I want you to go on to Glenran from there."

He sucked in a breath, his heart pounding, aching. "What of the pledge the Frasers owe you?" he asked.

She stared out the window. "You have honored that," she said. "You helped me when I was...in need." He heard the tremor in her voice. "Now you are free. Go back."

"Not without you." He reached out for her.

She stepped away to gather oatcakes and cheese and wrap them in a cloth. She took up his plaid and handed it to him.

"You must go," she said. "Parlan and Hugh will come here, for it is the eve of Twelfth Night. You must leave, Kenneth."

"Catriona," he said softly. "What if a child comes of this between us?"

She lowered her head. "Then I would be glad," she said.

He stepped toward her, but she turned away. He sighed, sensing that she would not waver in this, not now. He knew her well enough to know that she needed time alone to think; he hoped that she would realize that her love was stronger than her fear.

"I will ride to see the MacGhille children," he said. "And then I will be back." She began to protest, and he held up a hand. "This is not over between us. I owe you a pledge, and I will fulfill it."

"I think Lachlann's pledge has been met."

"Perhaps." He watched her slender back, her proud head. "The snow rose brooch is but silver and stone, and its promise is easily met," he said. "But my pledge to you is priceless, endless. Do not make it worthless." He snatched up his plaid and led his horse toward the door.

# CHAPTER NINE

CRISP SMACKING SOUNDS and the high trill of children laughing soared through the air. Kenneth guided his garron carefully along the ridge of an icy hill, and looked down.

Below, on a small, frozen pond amid leafless trees, the eight MacGhille children slid and laughed and yelled. They brandished long sticks in their mittened hands, and batted a rock back and forth across the pond surface, then ran, skidded, and slipped in pursuit of the missile.

Kenneth smiled, recognizing the game as one he and his cousins played often in the winter. He urged his horse down the slope. As he approached, one of the younger boys saw him and yelled to the others, pointing. The children dropped their sticks and ran toward him.

"Kenneth Fraser!" Angus called as he ran at the head of the pack. "Where is Triona?"

"At the shieling," he said as he dismounted. "She sent me to see how you fared in the storm." Soon all eight of them, from Patrick to little

Tomas, gathered near his horse.

"We did well enough," Angus said. "Patrick and I watched after everyone. Edan and Donald were scared, but—"

"We were not!" Donald protested, pouting.

"I'm proud of all of you," Kenneth said, smiling. "Catriona will be, too."

Edan pulled at his sleeve. "Did you bring gifts?"

"Cheese, and some oatcakes." Kenneth patted the bundle that hung on his saddle.

"We could not open the door of our house yesterday," Mairead said. She smiled up at him, her milky, glazed left eye drifted to the side. "Patrick and Angus had to push and push. It was frozen shut, but we were warm inside. And Tomas got a burn."

Kenneth frowned, and bent toward Tomas, who stood with his hand in Mairead's. "Let me see, lad," he said.

Tomas held up a blistered finger. "Fire hurts," he said.

"It does that," Kenneth said, sighing as he thought of the dangers these children faced without an adult to watch over them. He patted the child's head and stood. "How is the game of *sinteag* going?"

"We have no wooden ball to play the shinty properly," Angus said. "But we found a round rock. Patrick's team is winning, because my team is smaller, and we have Tomas."

"I can do it," Tomas insisted.

"I will be on your team, if I may," Kenneth said. With enthusiastic hoots, Angus and Malcolm ran off and returned with a broken tree limb. "Ah, this will do for a *caman*," Kenneth said, hefting the stick as he walked with the children toward the pond.

The game was lively and fast-paced. They slid over the ice in their boots, laughing and falling, and sweeping the smooth stone back and forth across the ice between their goals. Kenneth helped Tomas to skim the rock over the ice several times, raising cheers from everyone, none louder than Tomas. Kenneth made certain that each of the little ones managed to slide the stone past the opposite team's goal; he had rarely laughed so hard, or enjoyed a game so much, in his life.

When their cheeks were red with cold and their toes were numb, they left the pond and walked carefully over an icy hill. Kenneth perched Mairead, Tomas and Edan on the horse, and led the pack, walking beside Patrick.

He smiled, hearing their chatter, and thought of his own childhood. He and his cousins, most of them orphans, had been as close as siblings, playing, teasing, laughing and competing, though always fiercely loyal to each other. But Lachlann had always been there to guide the young Glenran Frasers. Beyond Catriona's loving concern for them, the MacGhille children were guiding themselves through life for now.

He sighed, glancing at the children, and realized that they had stolen into his heart, easily and completely, just as if they had always been there— and just as their beautiful cousin had done. With a strangely certain sense of rightness, he felt as if he had acquired a family of his own. He could not leave these children to fend for themselves, just as he could not return to Glenran and leave Catriona alone.

As they approached the house, Kenneth laughed aloud. A garden of snowmen filled the yard, tall and short, fat and fallen over, decked with bonnets and plaids. Beyond them, the snow fortress was partly collapsed and clearly well-used. "You have all been busy," he remarked to Patrick.

The boy grinned. "We built most of them after you and Catriona left the other day," he said. "But after the ice storm, I would not let the younger ones outside until this afternoon."

"You take good care of them, lad," Kenneth observed.

Patrick raised his head proudly. "I promised my parents that I would. A Highlandman never breaks a pledge."

Kenneth nodded silently, thinking of the pledges he owed to Catriona. If he could have taken Kilernan Castle from Hugh MacDonald alone, without bloodshed, he would have already done it. He wanted Catriona to be content, but he could not perform the impossible. He sighed heavily, wondering if he could ever convince her and the children to come to Glenran with him.

Later, while the children sat by the fire and ate cheese and oatcakes, Kenneth looked up to see Mairead, Malcolm and David take long white robes from a chest; they pulled them over their heads and pranced around the room while their siblings chuckled.

"We are practicing for our Twelfth Night feast tomorrow," Mairead announced. She tripped, her poor vision further obscured by a large white hood, and Kenneth righted her. "Will you and Catriona come? We shall have singing and dancing, and we shall all be guisers," she said. She spread her arms wide, long sleeves hanging limp. "My mother made these guising robes for my father and my older brothers to use at Yuletide. There are more things in a chest in the loft. They used to go about the hills with the other lads and men. Have you ever been a guiser?"

"I have been out with my cousins," he said, "on New Year's Eve and on Twelfth Night, wearing robes and animal hides and horns. We marched around singing, and beating drums and making merry while we frightened away the bad spirits." He grinned.

"Will you come to our feast?" Mairead asked. "Though we shall have only porridge and not a roasted beef. But Patrick said we could make a large oatcake to hide the bean, so that we could have a King of the Revels. Or a queen," she added. She reached past Kenneth and picked up a slice of cheese full of holes, and held it to her right eye. "I wonder if this will show me who will get the bean this year." She squinted playfully through a hole in the cheese and looked toward the fire.

Kenneth smiled. "I'm sure your brothers will let you be the queen of the feast," he said. "And I will ride back to the shieling and fetch Catriona for your Twelfth Night revels."

Mairead frowned as she peered at the fire. "*Ach,*

Kenneth Fraser," she murmured. "Triona will not come. She does not want you to ride back for her. She wants you to ride home."

A chill ran along his neck and arms. He remembered that the child had the Sight; he respected the natural ability of seers like his cousin Elspeth, whose visions often proved true. "Mairead," he said quietly. "What do you see?"

"Triona cannot come to our feast, because she is not at home," she answered. Behind them, her brothers turned to listen. "She has gone to Kilernan." She turned, her eyes wide, her cheeks pale. "I saw Parlan MacDonald and Catriona in the fire just now, through the hole in the cheese. They were holding hands, as if they were about to be married." Mairead leaned toward Kenneth. "But she would rather wed you," she whispered. "Even though you are a Fraser."

He drew in a long breath, and looked around at the other children, who watched him somberly. "I will ride back to the shieling." He stood. "And I will be back—with Catriona."

"You will have to go to Kilernan to get her, then," Mairead said easily, and fed the cheese to Tomas.


She was gone when he arrived. The hut was empty but for the cow, and the hearth was cold. He frowned over that; Catriona had been careful never to let the fire go out, fearing bad luck.

The cow lowed, a mournful, lonely sound, and stepped across the disheveled room, knocking over a stool as she went, bending her head to nibble some oats left in a sack. The other garron was gone; even Cù was gone.

Kenneth patted the cow's shoulder and fetched a bucket of water for her, frowning as he worked. He looked at the neatly made bed, then glanced away; haunting memories of the love they had made there hurt him keenly.

Catriona had clearly gone back to Kilernan. Had she decided to marry Parlan after all, finding a MacDonald more to her liking than a Fraser? He sucked in an angry, wounded breath and stomped out of the house, shutting the door firmly behind him.

Hoofprints marred the snow all around him as he trudged toward his garron. Several horses had been in the yard since he had left earlier. The MacDonalds had come for her, then; Parlan and his cousins, or even Hugh MacDonald, who had sent word through Parlan that he would fetch his niece for Twelfth Night.

Kenneth scowled as he swung up into the saddle. Had she gone willingly, or had she gone with regrets? Had she decided to wed Parlan after all, to gain a MacDonald home for her eight cousins? He squeezed his eyes shut in grief at the thought.

He spun the garron and began to ride out of the yard, but something in the snow caught his gaze. Reining in, he looked down at an image of a flower in the snow, made by the repeated impressions of a slender, graceful foot.

A snow rose, he realized with a sense of shock. Nearby, glinting on the crusted snow, he noticed the discarded silver brooch, its rose quartz stone pale and perfect. Dismounting, he picked up the jewelry piece and stared at the design in the snow.

The brooch, he was sure, had been flung down in haste. The flower design had been made earlier, for its edges were blurred. He wondered if his anger and sense of rejection were misplaced. Perhaps Catriona had not left here voluntarily.

Perhaps she had dropped the brooch as a message, as a plea for help. He could not ignore the possibility.

He would ride to Kilernan and face Hugh and Parlan—and Catriona as well. Only then would he know for certain how she felt about him. Only then could he prove to her that the MacDonalds were no threat to him.

An idea occurred to him then, wild in its newness, bringing with it fresh hope. Perhaps, if he acted on it, he could honor all the pledges: Lachlann's, the legal bond, and, most importantly, his own to Catriona. He thrust the crosspin of the brooch into his plaid, and rode out.

"And so, Catriona needs our assistance," Kenneth finished. He looked at the steady, caring gazes that watched him somberly. "It is a risk, I know, but we must ride to Kilernan and free her if she needs it. I cannot do it alone. I need your help."

Patrick nodded first, and looked at his brothers and sister. Each one in turn nodded, including Tomas and Edan. "We would do anything to help Triona," Patrick said. "But what can we do against Hugh MacDonald?" He inclined his head toward the younger ones. "They are children, and you are a Fraser. The MacDonalds will not even let you into Kilernan Castle."

"They will not let a Fraser inside, true," Kenneth said. "But they will let you in, I think. Listen, now. We have much work to do before the feast tomorrow evening."

# CHAPTER TEN

A RAUCOUS MIXTURE OF laughter, rough voices, and the strong thrum of a wire harp filled the vaulted hall of Kilernan Castle. High stone walls soared into shadow deepened by the rising smoke of wall torches. Benches creaked under the weight of fifty MacDonalds seated at tables, eating a variety of roasted meats, savory vegetable dishes, and sweet cakes, and drinking wines and *uisge beatha* from flasks and cups handed back and forth.

Catriona sat beside her uncle at a table near the blazing hearth, and flicked at a small, dry pea, spinning it idly on the table; she had found it in her cake earlier, and had been named the Twelfth Night Queen. Parlan had put it there, forcing this night of revelry upon her, just as he and her uncle had taken her away from the shieling the day before. But she had quiesced and gone with them. She knew that she must leave before Kenneth returned for her, or she would have to surrender to the strength of her love for him.

Sighing, she glanced at him, and at her uncle,

who sat to either side of her. They ate with lusty appetites and swallowed drink strong enough to take most men to their knees. She had eaten little, and had sipped less.

"The Queen is not merry tonight," Hugh Mac-Donald remarked. "Eat up, girl, and drink. And smile. Soon you will be wed, and Kilernan will be yours. I will announce your marriage soon."

She looked at him, noting the florid stain in his cheeks and his constant grin, which meant that he was quite drunk. She was familiar with that flushed, hearty look, having seen it on her uncle's face frequently throughout her life.

"I wish to go to bed," she said, beginning to stand.

Hugh MacDonald grabbed her arm. "Stay," he barked. "You are the Queen of the Revels tonight. You cannot go until the celebration is over. We are waiting for you to choose your king." He grinned and waved his hand toward Parlan.

Parlan leaned toward her, grinning, his breath soured by wine and meat, and held a bit of cake near her mouth. The spicy, sweet fragrance nearly made her ill. Catriona shook her head in refusal. "Eat it," Parlan said. "The cook made it for this feast, from English flour, and sugar and raisins and ginger. You will not taste a finer Twelfth Night cake in all the Highlands."

She shook her head again, and Parlan crammed the piece into his own mouth. "You will do as I say when we marry."

"I did not agree to wed you," she said, between her teeth.

Hugh leaned over. "You came back to Kilernan, girl, and that means you agree to many things," he said, and belched.

"You both must promise to bring the Mac-Ghille children to live here," she said. "Then I will consider wedding Parlan."

"Hah! You have a will like an ox," her uncle said. "My nephew will do well to wed such a strong woman." He grinned.

"Parlan! Did you find that Fraser who was about last week?"

Parlan shook his head. "He went back home, I'm sure."

"The rascal," Hugh said. He lifted a brow at Catriona. "Where is that silver brooch you always wear?"

"I—I lost it," she said.

He scowled. "You did not send it to a Fraser and ask them to honor that foolish promise, did you? They would take the silver, and leave you, girl. You know that. I've told you their pledges are worthless. MacDonalds keep pledges, not Frasers."

"I believe that the Frasers are men of their word, Uncle," she said quietly.

He growled in disagreement and swallowed more drink. "Ah!" he called suddenly. "Good! Now the revelry begins at last! The guisers are here from the *clachan!*" He gestured toward the door.

Catriona barely looked up as the troupe of guisers entered the hall. The men cheered and laughed as the lads danced and sang, wending their way through the large chamber. One of them beat a skin-covered drum and another played notes on a wooden pipe; all but one wore loose, hooded robes of pale wool, their faces painted in frightening or comical masks. The oldest lad, taller and larger than the rest, wore an animal hide.

The old bard played a tune on his wire-strung harp to keep time with the spirited rhythms of the drum and pipe. Clapping and singing began among the MacDonalds who watched, howling with glee as the guisers pranced and chanted, tumbled and cavorted.

Catriona watched, her attention captured by the music and antics. The group of guisers included children, but that was not unusual. The smallest child, robed like the rest, was lifted and passed among the older lads; guisers traditionally celebrated the youngest among them as a symbol of luck.

Any household on New Year's Eve and on Twelfth Night would welcome a group of guisers, both as light-hearted entertainment and as a means of clearing away lingering evil spirits. Catriona sighed, watching the performers, and thought of Kenneth, who had come to her house on New Year's Eve, and had vowed to bring her good luck. But she would not let him attempt it, fearing what her uncle and Parlan might do to a Fraser in their midst.

Now the guisers began a mock battle, initiated by one of the smaller lads, who kept tripping on the hem of his voluminous robe, raising hearty laughs from the men watching. He fought a "bull" in the form of the tallest lad, who wore an animal hide that covered his head and torso, with deer antlers fixed to his head. Beneath the hide, Catriona saw a red-and-green MacDonald plaid, and long, muscled legs cased in deerhide boots.

The comical battle continued between the roaring "bull" and the robed little hunter, who bravely climbed on his quarry's back and rode him around the hall. Then Catriona sat up abruptly.

She had seen those deerhide boots before; just yesterday she had watched a pair of strong, agile hands lace them, hands that later had loved her into ecstasy. Chills cascaded down her spine. She narrowed her eyes and watched more carefully.

Her uncle chuckled beside her, enjoying the simple, amusing battle. "Look at that brave little one! Punching the bull with his tiny fist—and the bull goes down! And again! Hah hah!"

Catriona did not laugh. Parlan guffawed beside her, and choked on his drink, coughing until he was red-faced. Catriona stared at the bull, and at each guiser in turn. She recognized every one of them, from Kenneth down to little Tomas, carried by his older brothers. And the hunter, quite clearly, was Mairead.

She frowned, wondering why Kenneth had come to Kilernan Castle, and why he had brought the MacGhille children. She twisted her hands in her lap anxiously and watched the antics.

The little hunter won the battle, but the fallen bull sprang to life again. He chased the guisers from the hall—and perhaps to safety if trouble began, Catriona thought—but for one older lad;

Patrick, she guessed. The bull ran, roaring, around the hall, with this guiser in pursuit, banging on the drum.

They came to the table where Catriona sat with her uncle and Parlan. The white-robed guiser, his face painted green and black, bowed low. "Queen of Twelfth Night," he said, "your wish is ours to fulfill. Whatever you want shall be yours. Who shall be your king? Who shall rule your hall?"

Catriona glanced at him and at her kinsmen, and at the bull, whose face and torso were covered in the shapeless animal hide. She straightened.

"What better king for a Twelfth Night queen than a bull who cannot be defeated, even in death?" she said. "Surely he is an enchanted king from some magical land." She held out her hand to the bull. Beside her, Parlan sputtered a protest, and Hugh chortled with laughter, guzzling his drink.

Kenneth bowed low in acceptance, snorting and pawing the ground. He came closer and shifted until he stood between her and Hugh MacDonald. She could smell the animal hide, and saw his hand, long-fingered and strong, at his belt. He wore a red plaid, borrowed, she guessed, from the children; his own blue-and-green tartan would be recognized here as a Fraser weave.

"And who shall rule your hall?" the guiser, Patrick, asked.

She paused, and saw Kenneth's hand tighten in the shadows beneath the hide. She saw Parlan scowl, and saw her uncle slit his eyes toward her, waiting.

"I rule this hall," she announced. "And I shall send the bull out to graze." She gestured imperiously, earnestly. "Go, now. Please. Go!"

Laughter rose around the hall. Parlan chuckled heartily, and her uncle slapped his knee and pointed, imitating her.

The bull moved like lightning then, tearing off his disguise. Shoving Hugh face down on the table, Kenneth twisted the man's arm and pressed a knee hard into his back. Then he touched the point of his dirk to Hugh's neck. Patrick dove at the same time, wrenching Parlan's arm behind him, and holding a dirk to his neck as well.

Catriona gasped and jumped to her feet, backing away. Throughout the hall, men rose to their feet, shouting as they came toward the main table.

"Hold!" Kenneth roared. "Hold! If any man comes near, your laird will die at the point of a Fraser blade! And his nephew will follow, cut by one of your own pups! Hold, now!"

Breathing hard beneath Kenneth's restraining hand and knee, glancing wild-eyed at the dirk near his head, Hugh managed to nod. "Listen to him!" he bellowed. He swiveled his eyes. "I know you! You are a Glenran Fraser! By God! Catriona, you sent that damned brooch to them! And look what treachery!"

"Catriona did not invite me here," Kenneth said. "I am Kenneth Fraser of Glenran, come of my own will, with something to say to you, Hugh MacDonald, and to all the MacDonalds of Kilernan. First, though, I ask your pardon for the blade at your throat; we do not trust one another

well just now. And I thank you for your hospitality." He smiled easily.

"Hospitality?" Hugh choked out. "What do
you want here?"

"Peace," Kenneth said clearly. "And promises. I wish to remind you of a paper pledge you
signed long ago, when you agreed to end the
feud between our clans. Let it be newly agreed
in words between you and I, and witnessed by all
men here."

"*Ach,*" Hugh grunted. "You know I must agree
to that, on pain of death from the crown. I have
no choice, whether or not you hold a blade to
my throat."

"I will not draw your blood," Kenneth said,
sliding a meaningful glance toward Catriona, "if
you will listen well, and give your solemn promise before all men here."

"Promise what?" Hugh growled.

Watching, Catriona fisted her hands at her
sides, wondering what Kenneth meant to do. She
glanced from Kenneth to Hugh, then from Patrick to Parlan, who looked ill. Kenneth looked at
her once, his dark eyes full of storm and determination. His presence, his intensity, swept through
her like the pull of a lodestone.

"Tell me, Hugh," he said. "Who owns Kilernan? Who holds it by right of the Regent of
Scotland?"

Hugh was silent, his face florid, his breath coming in gasps. "Catriona," he growled at last. "It is
hers by right."

"And you have kept the property well for her,

for which she surely thanks you. But now, I think, she is ready to rule it with her own hand and her own judgement. Tell her."

"A bargain," Hugh managed. "If Catriona promises to wed the man I choose for her, I will make this pledge. Kilernan must remain a stronghold for Clan MacDonald."

Catriona sucked in a breath and stared at Kenneth. His mouth tightened. "Catriona?" he asked, without looking at her.

She had no choice. For the sake of Kenneth's life after this moment, for the children, for Kilernan, she had no choice. "I—I promise," she murmured.

"Then I bestow Kilernan back into your keeping, now that you are old enough," Hugh said. "Before all men here, I pledge this," he added, when Kenneth pressed the dirk point to his neck. Kenneth looked at the silent, frowning Highlanders gathered nearby. "Catriona MacDonald is the owner of this castle. Your loyalty is owed to her now. She is her father's daughter, brave and strong and fair-minded."

Catriona watched him, tears glinting in her eyes. Kenneth Fraser had fulfilled the promise of the snow rose, but the price was high: she must lose the man she loved.

He barely glanced at her as he looked down at Hugh. "Now, MacDonald," Kenneth continued. "The Twelfth Night after Christmas is the Epiphany, when three wise kings offered gifts and homage to a child in a manger. Will you honor that by offering gifts and protection to a few children in need?"

"The MacGhille children," Hugh muttered. "Catriona holds Kilernan, and she has the right to bring the waifs inside its walls." He groaned. "Let me up, Fraser. I will not come after you, nor send my men."

"Then I will trust you." Kenneth let go and stepped back, though he held the blade steady. Beside him, Patrick slowly released Parlan. Hugh muttered to him, and laid a hand on his arm. Catriona sensed no threat there, though; Parlan looked as if he might faint or be sick, either from strong drink, or the shock of being bested so easily.

Kenneth glanced at Catriona. "You wanted Kilernan taken without bloodshed," he said softly. "It is done. You wanted a home for your young cousins. That, too, is done. Hugh MacDonald will not go back on his word to you. Every man here will hold him to his promise."

"Uncle?" Catriona asked. "Will you forget this pledge later, when it suits you?"

Hugh wiped sweat from his brow. "I gave you my word before a host of men, on a holy day," he muttered. "I will not break that. I have pride and a heart, girl, though you do not think so. Kilernan is yours, as it always was. I only kept it until you found a strong husband. Parlan will do well by you."

Catriona hesitated, dreading what she must do next. "Thank you, Kenneth Fraser. Thank you—" Her voice trembled uncertainly. "Go, now," she urged him. "Please."

Hugh watched them. "You know this Fraser!"

"I know him well," she said softly. "Let him return to his home in peace, Uncle."  Hugh scratched his head, muttering.

"If I must go," Kenneth said, looking at her evenly, "let me first ask a favor of the Twelfth Night Queen. She may grant requests on the last night of the Yule season."

Catriona inclined her head, determined to answer whatever he asked her with calm and pride, though her breathing grew quick. She knew that Kenneth must leave here; yet she longed for him to stay, however foolish the thought.

"What is your request?" she asked.

"All I want," he said, "is to know the queen's dearest wish."  He stepped toward her. "Then I will leave."

Her heart surged. She watched him, and sensed the hush all around her. She drew a quivering breath. "All I truly want," she murmured in a soft voice, "is for you to be my luck, and my own. Forever."  She looked up at him through a glaze of tears, then glanced away. "But that is just a wish."

"Wishes are often blessings." He stepped closer. "Catriona MacDonald, listen to me well."  He tipped her chin up with a finger. "I am your luck, and I am yours."

"Holy saints," Hugh mumbled.

"And if I leave here," Kenneth continued, in a whisper so low only she could hear it, "I will never give up. I will be back for you."

A hot tear slid down her cheek. She took his

hand and turned to her uncle, who watched her with a stunned expression.

"I choose my king for this night," she said.

"You would choose him for your husband," Hugh murmured.

"I would," she said softly. "But I made you a promise."

Hugh sighed. "I may be drunk, but I am no fool. I know a brave, good man, a man to respect, when I meet one—though he be a Fraser." He rubbed his whiskery jaw. Then he looked at Kenneth. "Will you hold Kilernan for MacDonalds, or Frasers?"

"Kilernan will be a fortress of truce between our clans," Kenneth answered. "The pledge will always hold here."

Hugh nodded brusquely. "Catriona, wed this man." He grinned. "And do it soon."

She smiled. "I will, Uncle."

Parlan sputtered. "Hugh—"

"Hush up," Hugh snapped. "I have other nieces."

Catriona looked at Kenneth through joyful tears. He drew her into his arms and kissed her, his lips gentle, his breath full of life. "I told you I would bring you luck," he said.

"Ah, and you did," she answered, smiling.

"The star!" A murmur rose among the men gathered in the hall. "The Epiphany star!" The crowd parted to admit one of the guisers, who walked toward the main table, carrying a candle.

Kenneth put his arm around Catriona as they watched the final ceremony of Twelfth Night.

Catriona rested her head on his shoulder and let the tears glide freely down her cheeks.

Mairead came toward them, her white robe trailing, her small hands clasped around a thick, flaming candle. The light pierced the shadows in the dimly lit hall as she held the flame high. She lifted her face to the golden light, and her eyes, blind and seeing, glittered like pale jewels.

"Twelfth Night is the last night of the Yule season," Catriona murmured. "It is the day of hope, the day when we truly see all the blessings of the year to come."

"There will be many years full of blessings for us, love."

"Is it so?" she asked, her tone light.

"I pledge that it will be so," Kenneth whispered. "Here. This belongs to you." He lifted his hand and pinned the snow rose brooch to the shoulder of her plaid. Then he kissed her, while the child circled the light of promise and hope around them.

HERE'S A LOVELY wee recipe for a whiskey brose that's straight from the story, and just right for your own Hogmanay or New Year's Eve. Best wishes of the New Year to you!

# OATMEAL BROSE
## (also known as Atholl Brose)

Measure out about ½ cup of oatmeal and twice that in boiling water; soak the oats in the water until you can extract the liquid, or the brose (oat broth). In the hot brose, dissolve 1 tablespoon honey (preferably heather honey!), and add 4 tablespoons heavy cream and 6 tablespoons or so of your favorite Scottish whiskey. Blend together, chill, pour into glasses, sprinkle with some cinnamon and nutmeg, and enjoy!

# About the Author

Susan King is a bestselling, award-winning author of 27 historical novels and novellas (so far). From historical romances written as Susan King and Sarah Gabriel to mainstream historical novels as Susan Fraser King, including *Lady Macbeth: A Novel* and *Queen Hereafter: A Novel of Margaret of Scotland,* her work is consistently praised for historical accuracy, storytelling, and lyricism. In the nonfiction world of education, she is the author of one book and many magazine articles.

Her fiction has earned awards and nominations, including RT Book Reviews Reviewer's Choice awards for Best Scottish Historical, Best Medieval Historical, Best British Isles Historical, and Career Achievement, along with an RWA RITA nomination. She has earned several starred reviews from Publishers Weekly, Library Journal, and Book List, and her books frequently appear in #1 spots on several Amazon lists.

A former college lecturer in art history and a founding member of the author blog WordWenches. com, Susan holds a bachelor's degree in studio art and literature, and a graduate degree in medieval art history. She lives in Maryland with her family, and is currently working on new books.

Learn more at *http://www.susankingbooks.com/* and *http://www.wordwenches.com/*.

# The Black Beast of Belleterre

## MARY JO PUTNEY

# THE BLACK BEAST
# OF BELLETERRE

## MARY JO PUTNEY

"THE BLACK BEAST of Belleterre" was my miracle novella. In an excess of enthusiasm for Christmas stories, which I love, I committed to writing them for two different holiday anthologies the same year.

As always, things take longer than they take, and all of sudden I was up against a drop dead delivery date: my editor needed the story delivered in less that two weeks. In nine days I was booked for a conference in Savannah, and I hadn't started the story. So I did the only thing I could: sat down at my computer and started to work.

Then came the miracle. Each day for the next eight days, I wrote ten pages. At the end, I had eighty pages and the story was done. I have *never* written with that kind of speed and regular pacing!

And the miracle didn't end there. "The Black Beast of Belleterre" is one of my very favorite novellas. Well, it's a beauty and the beast story, and that's a surefire winner. Plus, it was a Victorian setting, which gave me fun elements to play with that wouldn't fit into my usual Regency tales.

But most of all, Ariel and Falconer were a gift. I loved writing about them, and when I reread this story for inclusion in this anthology, I loved them still. I hope you do also.

Happy reading,
*Mary Jo Putney*

*To Binnie Braunstein, who has more
Beauties and Beasties than anyone I know!*

# PROLOGUE

H E WAS UGLY, very ugly. He hadn't known that when he was young and had a mother who loved him in spite of his face. When people looked at him oddly, he had assumed it was because he was the son of a lord. Since there were a few children who were willing to be friends with him, he thought no more about it.

It was only later, when his mother had died and accident had augmented his natural ugliness, that James Markland realized how different he was. People stared, or if they were polite, quickly looked away.

His own father would not look directly at him on the rare occasions when they met. The sixth Baron Falconer had been a very handsome man; James didn't blame him for despising a son who was so clearly unworthy of the ancient, noble name they both bore.

Nonetheless James was the heir, so Lord Falconer had handled the distasteful matter with consummate, aristocratic grace. He installed the boy at a small, remote estate, seen that competent tutors were hired, and thought no more about him.

The chief tutor, Mr. Grice, was a harsh and pious man, generous both with beatings and lectures on the inescapable evil of human nature. On his more jovial days, Mr. Grice would tell his student how fortunate the boy was to be beastly in a way that all the world could see. Most men carried their ugliness in their souls, where they could too easily forget their basic wickedness. James should feel grateful that he had been granted such a signal opportunity to be humble.

James was not grateful, but he was resigned. His life could have been worse. The servants were paid enough to tolerate the boy they served, and one of the grooms was even friendly. So James had a friend, a library, and a horse. He was content, most of the time.

When the sixth lord died—in a gentlemanly fashion, while playing whist—James had become the seventh Baron Falconer. In the twenty-one years of his life, he had spent a total of perhaps ten nights under the same roof as his late father.

He had felt very little at his father's death. Not grief, not triumph, not guilt. Perhaps there had been regret, but only a little. It was hard to regret not being better acquainted with a man who had chosen to be a stranger to his only son.

As soon as his father died, James had taken two trusted servants and flown into a wider world, like the soaring bird of the family crest. Egypt, Africa, India, Australia; he visited them all during his years of travel. The life of an eccentric English lord suited him and he developed habits that enabled him to keep the world at a safe distance. Seeing the monks in a monastery in Cyprus had given him the idea of wearing a heavily cowled robe that would conceal him from casual curiosity. Ever after, he wore a similar robe or hood when he had to go among strangers.

Because he was young and unable to repress his shameful lusts, he had also taken advantage of his wealth and distance from home to educate himself about the sins of the flesh. For the right price, it was easy to engage deft, experienced women who would not only lie with him, but would even pretend they didn't care how he looked.

One or two, the best actresses of the lot, had been almost convincing when they claimed to enjoy his company, and his touch. He did not resent their lies; the world was a hard place, and if lying might earn a girl more money, one couldn't expect her to tell the truth. Nonetheless, his pleasure was tainted by the bitter awareness that only his wealth made him acceptable.

He returned to England at the age of twenty-six, stronger for having seen the world beyond the borders of his homeland. Strong enough to accept the limits of his life. He would never have a wife, for no gently bred girl would marry him if she had a choice, and hence he would never have a child.

Nor would he have a mistress, no matter how much his body yearned for the brief, joyous forgetting that only a woman could provide. Though he was philosophical by nature and had decided very early that he would not allow self-pity, there were limits to philosophy. The only reasons why a woman would submit to his embraces were for money or from pity. Neither reason was endurable. Though he could bear his ugliness and isolation, he could not have borne the knowledge that he was pathetic.

Rather than dwell in bitterness, he was grateful for the wealth that buffered him from the world. Unlike ugly men who were poor, Falconer was in a position to create his own world, and he did.

What made his life worth living was the fact that when he returned to England, he had fallen in love. Not with a person, of course, but with a place. Belleterre, in the lush southeastern county of Kent, was the principal Markland family estate. As a boy James had never gone there, for his father had not wished to see him. Instead, James had been raised at a small family property in the industrial Midlands. He had not minded, for it was the only home he had ever known and not without its own austere charm.

Yet when he returned from his tour of the world after his father's death and first saw Belleterre, for a brief moment he had hated his father for keeping him away from his heritage. *Belleterre* meant "beautiful land" and never was a name more appropriate. The rich fields and woods, the ancient, castle-like stone manor house, were a worthy object for the love he yearned to express. It became his life's work to see that Belleterre was cared for as tenderly as a child.

Ten years had passed since he had come to Belleterre, and he had the satisfaction of seeing the land and people prosper under his stewardship. If he was lonely, it was no more than he expected. Books had been invented to salve human loneliness, and they were friends without peer, friends who never sneered or flinched or laughed behind a man's back. Books revealed their treasures to all who took the effort to seek.

Belleterre, books, and his animals. He needed nothing more.

# SPRING

SOMETIMES, REGRETTABLY, IT was necessary for Falconer to leave Belleterre, and today was such a day. The air was warm and full of the scents and songs of spring. He enjoyed the ten-mile ride, though he was not looking forward to the interview that would take place when he reached his destination.

He frowned when he reined in his horse at the main gate of Gardsley Manor, for the ironwork was rusty and the mortar crumbling between the bricks of the pillars that bracketed the entrance. When he rang the bell to summon the gatekeeper, five minutes passed before a sullen, badly dressed man appeared.

Crisply he said, "I'm Falconer. Sir Edwin is expecting me."

The gatekeeper stiffened and quickly opened the gate, keeping his gaze away from the cloaked figure that rode past. Falconer was unsurprised by the man's reaction. Doubtless the country folk told many stories about the mysterious hooded lord of Belleterre. What kind of stories, Falconer neither knew nor cared.

Before meeting Sir Edwin, Falconer knew that he must ascertain the condition of the property. That was his reason for visiting Gardsley in person rather than summoning the baronet to Belleterre. Once he was out of sight of the gatekeeper, he turned from the main road onto a track that swung west, roughly paralleling the edge of the estate.

On the side of a beech-crowned hill, he tethered his mount and pulled a pair of field glasses from his saddlebag, then climbed to the summit. Since there was no one in sight, he pushed his hood back, enjoying the feel of the balmy spring breeze against his face and head.

As he had hoped, the hill gave a clear view of the rolling Kentish countryside. In the distance he could even see steam from a Dover-bound train. But what lay closer did not please him. The field glasses showed Gardsley in regrettable detail, from crumbling fences to overgrown fields to poor quality stock. The more he saw, the more his mouth tightened, for the property had clearly been neglected for years.

Five years earlier, Sir Edwin Hawthorne had come to Falconer and asked for a loan to help him improve his estate. Though Falconer had not much liked the baronet, he had been impressed and amused by the man's sheer audacity in asking a complete stranger for money.

Probably Hawthorne had been inspired by stories of Falconer's generosity to charity and decided that he had nothing to lose by requesting a loan. Sir Edwin had been very eloquent, speaking emotionally of his wife's expensive illness and recent death, of his only daughter, and how the property that had been in his family for generations desperately needed investment to become prosperous again.

Though Falconer knew he was being foolish, he had given in to impulse and lent the baronet the ten thousand pounds requested. It was a sizable fortune, but Falconer could well afford it, and if Hawthorne really cared so much for his estate, he deserved an opportunity to save it.

But wherever the ten thousand pounds had gone, it hadn't been into Gardsley. The loan had come due a year earlier, and Falconer had granted a twelve-month extension. Now that grace period was over, the money had not been repaid, and Falconer must decide what to do.

If there had been any sign that the baronet cared for his land, Falconer would have been willing to extend the loan indefinitely. But this ... ! Hawthorne deserved to be flogged and turned out on the road as a beggar for his neglect of his responsibilities.

Falconer was about to descend to his horse when he caught a flash of blue on the opposite side of the hill. Thinking it might be a kingfisher, he raised his field glasses again and scanned the lower slope until he found the color he was seeking.

He caught his breath when he saw that it was not a kingfisher but a girl. She sat cross-legged beneath a flowering apple tree and sketched with charcoal on a tablet laid across her lap. As he watched, she made a face and ripped away her current drawing. Then she crumpled the paper and dropped it on a pile of similarly rejected work.

His first impression was that she was a child, for she was small and her silver-gilt tresses spilled loosely over her shoulders rather than being pinned up. But when he adjusted the focus of the field glasses, the increased clarity showed that her figure and face were those of a woman, albeit a young one. She was eighteen, perhaps twenty at the outside, and graceful even when seated on the ground.

She must be Hawthorne's daughter, for she was no farm girl despite the simplicity of her blue dress. But she did not resemble her florid father. Instead, she had a quality of bright, sweetness that riveted Falconer's attention. His view was from the side and her pure profile reminded him of the image of a goddess on a Greek coin. If his old tutor, Mr. Grice, could have seen this girl under the apple tree, even that old curmudgeon might have wondered if all humans were inherently sinful.

She was so lovely that Falconer's heart hurt. He did not know if his pain was derived from sadness that he would never know her, or joy that such beauty could exist in the world. Both emotions, perhaps.

Unconsciously he raised one hand and pulled the dark hood over his head, so that if by chance she looked his way, she would be unable to see him. He would rather die than cause that sweet face to show fear or disgust.

When he had made his plea for money five years earlier, Sir Edwin had mentioned his daughter's name. It was something fanciful that had made Falconer think her mother must have loved Shakespeare. Titania, the fairy queen? No, not that. Ophelia or Desdemona? No, neither of those.

*Ariel.* Her name was Ariel. Now that Falconer saw the girl, he realized that her name was perfect, for she seemed not quite mortal, a creature of air and sunshine.

Though he knew it was wrong to spy on her, he could not bring himself to look away. Her glance went up and down as she sketched the old oak tree in front of her. She had the deft quickness of hand of a true artist who races time to capture a private vision of the world. He was sure that she saw more deeply than mere bark and spring leaves.

A puff of breeze blew across the hillside, lifting strands of her bright hair, driving one of her crumpled drawings across the grass and loosening blossoms from the tree. Pink, sun struck petals showered over the girl as if even nature felt compelled to celebrate her beauty. As the scent of apples drifted up the hill, Falconer knew he would never forget the image that she made, gilded by sunshine and haunted by flowers.

He was about to turn away when the girl stood and brushed the petals from her gown. After gathering her discarded drawings, she turned and walked down the opposite side of the hill away from him. Her strides were as graceful as he had known they would be and her hair was a shimmering, silver-gilt mantle.

But she had overlooked the drawing that had blown away. After the girl was gone from view, Falconer went down and retrieved the crumpled sheet from the tuft of cow parsley where it had lodged. Then he flattened the paper, careful not to smudge the charcoal.

As he had guessed, the girl's drawing of the gnarled oak went far beyond mere illustration. In a handful of strong, spare lines, she implied harsh winters and fertile, acorn-rich summers; sun and rain and drought; the long history of a tree that had first sprouted generations before the girl was born and should survive for centuries more. That slight, golden child was a true artist.

Since she had not wanted the drawing, surely there was no harm in keeping it. Knowing himself for a sentimental fool, he also plucked a few strands of the grass that had been crushed beneath her when she worked.

He watched for the girl as he completed his ride to the manor house, but without success. If not for the evidence of the drawing in his saddlebag, he might have wondered if he had imagined her.

Sir Edwin Hawthorne greeted his guest nervously, gushing welcomes and excuses. He had been a handsome man, but lines of dissolution marred his face and sweat shone on his brow.

As Falconer expected, the baronet was unable

to repay the loan. "The last two years have been difficult, my lord," he said, his eyes darting around the room, anything to avoid looking at the cowled figure who sat motionless in his study. "Lazy tenants, disease among the sheep. You know how hard it is to make a profit on farming."

Falconer knew no such thing. His own estate was amazingly profitable, for it flourished under loving hands. Not just the hands of its master, but those of his tenants and employees, for he would have no one at Belleterre who did not love the land. "I've already given you a year beyond the term of the original loan. Can you make partial payment?"

"Not today, my lord, but very soon," Sir Edwin said. "Within the next month or two, I should be in a position to repay at least half the sum."

Under his concealing hood, Falconer's mouth twisted. "Are you a gamester, Sir Edwin? The turn of a card or the speed of a horse is unlikely to save you from ruin."

The baronet twitched at his guest's comment, but it was the shock of guilt, not surprise. "All gentlemen gamble a bit, of course, but I'm no gamester. I assure you, if you will give me just a little more time ..."

Falconer remembered the neglected fields, the shabby laborers' cottages, and almost refused. Then he thought of the girl. What would become of Ariel if her father's property was sold to pay his debts? She should be in London now, fluttering through the Season with the rest of the bright, wellborn butterflies. She should have a husband who would cherish her and give her children.

But a London debut was expensive, and likely any money her father managed to beg or borrow went on his own vices. In spite of the isolation of his life, Falconer was not naive about his fellow man. He was surely not Hawthorne's only creditor. The man had probably borrowed money in every direction and had debts that could not be repaid even if Gardsley was sold.

Falconer felt a surge of anger. A man who would neglect his land would also neglect his family, and a girl who should have been garbed in silks and adored by the noblest men in the land was wearing cotton and sitting alone in a field. Not that she had looked unhappy; he guessed that she had the gift of being happy anywhere. But she deserved so much more.

If Falconer insisted on payment now, her father would be ruined, and the girl would probably end up a poor relation in someone else's house. Unable to bear the thought, Falconer found himself saying, "I'll give you three more months. If you can repay half of the principal by then, I'll renegotiate the balance. But if you can't pay ... " It was unnecessary to complete the sentence.

Babbling with relief, Sir Edwin said, "Splendid, splendid! I assure you I'll have your five thousand pounds three months from now. Likely I'll be able to repay the whole amount then."

Falconer looked at the baronet and despised him. He was a weak, shallow man, unable to see beyond the fact that he had been spared the consequences of his actions for a little longer. "I'll be back three months from today."

But as he rode home to Belleterre, he was haunted by one thought. What would happen to the girl?

Ariel returned to the house for lunch, pleased that she had done several sketches worth keeping. Her satisfaction died when she found that her father had taken the train down from London that morning. As soon as the butler told her, Ariel put one hand to her untidy hair, then darted up the back stairs to her room.

As she brushed the snarls from her hair, she wondered how long Sir Edwin would stay at Gardsley this time. Life was always pleasanter when he was away, which was most of the time. But while he was here, she must tread warily and keep out of his sight. Alas, she could not escape her daughterly duty to dine with him every night. He would criticize her unladylike appearance; he always did. He would also be quite specific about the many ways in which she was a disappoint- ment to him.

Once or twice Ariel had considered pointing out that he didn't allow her enough money to be fashionably dressed even if she had been so inclined, but caution always curbed her tongue. Though not a truly vicious man, Sir Edwin was capable of lashing out when he had been drink- ing, or when he was particularly frustrated with his circumstances.

Still brushing her hair, she wandered to her

window and looked out. She loved this particular view. The clouds were dramatic this afternoon. Perhaps she could go up on the roof and try to capture the sunset in watercolors. But no, that wouldn't be possible tonight, since she would have to dine with her father.

She was regretfully turning away from the window when a strange figure came down the front steps. A tall man wearing a swirling black robe with a deep, cowled hood that totally obscured his face. Since Gardsley was said to have a ghost or two, Ariel wondered if one of them was making an appearance.

But the man who moved so lithely down the steps seemed quite real. Certainly the horse and the Gardsley footman who brought it were not phantoms.

Abruptly she realized that the figure could only be the mysterious, reclusive Lord Falconer, sometimes called the Black Beast of Belleterre. He was a legend in Kent, and the maids often talked about him in hushed, deliciously scandalized whispers.

Ariel had heard him described as both saint and devil, sometimes in the same breath. It was said that he gave much to charity and had endowed a hospital for paupers in nearby Maidstone. It was also said that he held wild, midnight orgies on his estate. Though Ariel had looked up the word orgy, the definition had been so vague that she hadn't been able to puzzle out what was involved. But it had sounded alarming.

Stripped of rumors and titillated guesses, the

gossip about him boiled down to three facts: he had grown up in the Midlands, he was so hideously deformed that his own father had been unable to bear the sight of him, and he now concealed himself from the gazes of all but a handful of trusted servants, none of whom would say a word about him. Whether their silence was a product of fear or devotion was a source of much speculation.

As Ariel watched him swing effortlessly onto his horse, she decided that his deformity could not be of the body, for he was tall and broad-shouldered and he moved like an athlete. She wondered what made him so unwilling to show his face to the world.

Even more, she wondered why Lord Falconer was at Gardsley. He must have had business with her father. That would explain why Sir Edwin had unexpectedly returned from London.

Ariel had just reached that conclusion when Lord Falconer glanced up at the facade of the house. His gaze seemed to go right to her, though it was hard to be sure since his face was shadowed. Instinctively she stepped back, not wanting to be caught in the act of staring. Although, she thought with a hint of acerbity, a man who dressed like a medieval monk had to expect to attract attention.

Dropping his gaze, he turned his horse and cantered away. He rode beautifully, so much in tune with his mount that it seemed to move without the use of reins or knees. Stepping forward again, Ariel watched him disappear from sight.

The Black Beast of Belleterre. There was a larger-than-life quality about the man that was as romantic as it was tragic. She began considering different ways to portray him. Not watercolor, that wasn't strong enough. It would have to be either the starkness of pen and ink or the voluptuous richness of oils.

She stood by the window for quite some time, lost in contemplation, until her attention was caught by another figure coming down the steps. This time it was her father, followed by his valet. As she watched, the carriage came around from the stables. After the two men had climbed in, she heard her father order the driver to take him to the station. So he was going back to London without even asking to see her.

Silly of her to feel hurt when their meetings were so uncomfortable for both of them. Besides, now she would be free to go up on the roof and paint the sunset. But Ariel found that unexpectedly thin comfort. A sunset no longer seemed as interesting, not when she had just seen the enigmatic Lord Falconer.

Yes, pen and ink would be best for him.

# SUMMER

FALCONER RETURNED TO Gardsley exactly
three months after his first visit. The day was
another fine one, so, despising himself for his weakness, he took the same detour across the estate that he
had taken before. The land was in no better shape and
the hay would be ruined if it wasn't cut immediately,
but he did not care for that. His real purpose was a
wistful hope that he might catch a glimpse of the girl.

But she was not sketching on the hill today. The
blossoms were long gone from the tree and now
small, hard green apples hung from the branches.
Regretfully he turned his horse and rode to the
house.

He'd had his solicitor make inquiries about Sir
Edwin Hawthorne and the results had confirmed
all of Falconer's suspicions. The baronet was a
gambler and a notorious seducer of other men's
wives. He was away from Gardsley for months
on end, and had been hovering on the brink of
financial disaster for years.

The solicitor's report had gone on to say that

Sir Edwin's only daughter, Ariel, was twenty years old. She'd had a governess until she was eighteen. Since then, she had apparently lived alone at Gardsley with only servants for company. On the rare occasions when she was invited into county society, she was much admired for her beauty and modesty, but her father's reputation and her own lack of dowry must have barred her from receiving any eligible marriage offers.

Falconer had trouble believing that part of the report. Surely the men of Kent could not be so blind, so greedy, as to overlook such a jewel simply because she had no fortune.

The butler admitted Falconer and left him in a drawing room at the front of the house, saying that Sir Edwin would be with his guest in a moment. Falconer smiled mirthlessly. If the baronet had the money, he would have been waiting with a bank draft in hand. Now he was probably in his study trying desperately to think of a way to save his profligate hide.

Falconer was pacing the drawing room when he heard the sound of raised voices, the baronet's nervous tenor clashing with the lighter tones of a woman. The drawing room had double doors that led to another reception room behind, so Falconer went through. The voices were much louder now, and he saw that another set of double doors led into Sir Edwin's study, where the quarrel was taking place. The baronet was saying, "You'll marry him because I say so! It's the only way to save us from ruin!"

Though Falconer had never heard Ariel's voice,

he knew instantly that the sweet, light tones belonged to her. "You mean it will save *you* from ruin, at the cost of ruining me! Even I have heard of Bratchett! The man is notorious. I will not marry him!"

Falconer felt as if he had been struck in the stomach. Bratchett was indeed notorious, a pox-ridden lecher who had driven three young wives to their graves. Not only did he have an evil reputation, but he must be over forty years older than Ariel. Surely Sir Edwin could not be so vile as to offer his only daughter to such a man! Yet Bratchett was wealthy and Ariel's father needed money.

In a feeble attempt to sound reassuring, Sir Edwin said, "You shouldn't listen to backstairs gossip. Lord Bratchett is a wealthy, distinguished man. As his wife, you'll have a position in London's most amusing society."

"I don't want to be part of London society!" his daughter retorted. "All I want is to be left alone here at Gardsley. Is that so much to ask?"

"Yes, dammit, it is!" the baronet barked. "A girl with your beauty could be a great asset to me. Instead, you hide here and play with pencils and paints. In spite of your lack of cooperation, I've managed to arrange a splendid marriage for you, and by God, you'll behave as a proper daughter and obey me!"

Voice quavering but defiant, Ariel said, "I won't! I'll be twenty-one soon. You can't make me!"

She was stronger than she looked, that delicate, golden girl. But even as the admiring thought passed through Falconer's mind, he heard the flat, sharp sound of flesh slapping flesh and Ariel cried out.

*Sir Edwin had struck his daughter.* Nearly blinded by rage, Falconer put his hand on the knob to the study. He was about to fling the door open when he heard Ariel speak again. "You won't change my mind this way, Papa."

Though he could hear tears in her voice, she did not speak as if she had been seriously injured, so Falconer paused, his hand still on the door-knob. What happened between Sir Edwin and his daughter was none of his business. If he inter-vened, the baronet would surely punish the girl for it later when her champion was not around.

"I'll find a way that will change your mind," Sir Edwin snarled. "If you don't marry Bratchett, you won't have a roof over your head, for Gard-sley will have to be sold. Then what will you do, missy? Go to your room and think about that while I talk with that ugly brute in the drawing room! If I can't persuade him to give me another extension of my loan, I'll be a pauper, and so will you."

Falconer turned and retreated noiselessly to the drawing room at the front of the house. He was standing there, looking out the window, hands linked behind his back, when the baronet entered the room.

"Good day, my lord," Sir Edwin said in a voice of forced amiability. "You've come just in time to hear good news. My daughter is about to con-tract an advantageous alliance, and I will be able to repay you out of the settlement money. You need only wait a few weeks longer, for the bridegroom is anxious for an early wedding."

Falconer turned and stared at his host. As the silence stretched, Sir Edwin became increasingly nervous. Falconer knew that his stillness disturbed people. Once, behind his back, someone had said that it was like being watched by the angel of death.

When he could bear the silence no longer, the baronet said, "Are you unwell, my lord?"

After another ominous pause, Falconer said, "I've already extended the loan twice. Since Gardsley is your collateral, I can have you evicted from here tomorrow if I choose."

Sir Edwin paled. "But you can't ruin me now, not when a solution is so close at hand! I swear that within a month…"

Falconer cut the other off with a sharp motion of his hand. "I can indeed ruin you, and by God, perhaps I will, for you deserve to be ruined!"

Almost weeping, the baronet said, "Is there nothing I can do to persuade you to reconsider? Surely it is the duty of a Christian to show mercy." He paused, groping for other arguments. "And my daughter … will you destroy her life as well? This is the only home she has ever known."

His daughter, whom the villain proposed to sell to Bratchett. Falconer's hands curled into fists when he thought of that golden child defiled by such a loathsome creature. He could not allow the girl to marry Bratchett. *He could not.* But how could he prevent it?

A shocking idea occurred to him. To even consider it was wrong, blasphemous. Yet by committing a wrong, he could prevent a greater wrong. When he was sure his voice would be even, Falconer said, "There's one thing that would change my mind."

Eagerly Sir Edwin said, "What is it? I swear I'll do anything you wish!"

"The girl." Falconer's voice broke. "I'll take the girl."

Half an hour after Ariel was sent to her bedroom, her father came up after her. She steeled herself when he entered, praying that she would be strong enough to resist his threats and blandishments. She was still shaken by what he had revealed earlier. Though Sir Edwin had never spent money on his estate or her, she had always assumed that he had a decent private income or he could not have afforded to live in London. But today he had informed her that his entire fortune was gone and she must marry the despicable Lord Bratchett.

Yet she couldn't possibly marry Bratchett. A fortnight earlier her father had brought the man to Kent for the weekend. In retrospect it was obvious that the real purpose of the visit had been for the old satyr to look Ariel over.

Once he had caught her alone and pounced on her like a dog discovering a meaty bone. His foul breath and pawing hands were disgusting. After escaping his embrace, she had spent the days in distant fields and had barred her door at night until he left.

Without preamble her father said, "You didn't want to marry Bratchett, and now you don't have to. Another candidate for your hand has appeared. Sight unseen, Lord Falconer wants you."

"Lord Falconer?" Ariel gasped, her mind going to the dark, enigmatic figure she had so briefly seen. "How can he want to marry a female he has never even met?"

"Ask him yourself," Sir Edwin replied. "He's in the drawing room and wants to speak with you." Mockingly he stepped back and gestured her to go ahead of him. "It appears that you'll be the salvation of me in spite of yourself. You can't say I haven't done well by you, missy. You have your choice of two wealthy, titled husbands! Most girls would cut off their right arms to be in your position."

Ariel doubted that many girls would sacrifice a limb for the privilege of being forced to choose between a revolting old lecher and a faceless man known as the Black Beast, but she kept her chin high when she walked past her father.

She gave a fleeting thought to her loose hair, but there was no time to tidy herself. In this her father was right. If she'd behaved like a young lady, sipping tea instead of roaming the fields, she would be prepared for such a momentous interview. Surely if she were dressed properly, she would be less afraid.

She entered the drawing room with her father's heavy hand on her arm. The Black Beast of Belleterre stood in front of the unlit fireplace, tall and dark and so still that the folds of his robe might have been carved from stone. Trying to conceal the trembling of her hands, Ariel linked them together behind her.

"Here's the girl," Sir Edwin boomed. "So excited by the prospect of receiving your addresses that she rushed right down! Ariel, make a curtsy to his lordship."

As she obediently dipped down, the hooded man said, "Leave us, Sir Edwin."

"That wouldn't be proper." Though the baronet's tone was virtuous, his hard glance at his daughter showed that he didn't trust her to say the right thing without him there.

Sharply Falconer repeated, "Leave us! I will speak with Miss Hawthorne privately."

Ariel surreptitiously wiped her damp palms on her skirt as her father reluctantly left the room. In spite of what he had said and done earlier, she watched him go with regret, for he was a known quantity, unlike the frightening man by the fireplace. Even without the hood, he would have been hard to see clearly for he had chosen to stand in the darkest part of the room.

Falconer turned to her. "Your father told you why I wish to speak with you?"

Not trusting her voice, she nodded.

His voice was the deepest she'd ever heard, but the commanding tone he had used to address her father was gone. In fact he sounded almost shy when he said, "Don't be afraid of me, Ariel. I asked your father to leave so we could speak freely. I know you're in a difficult position and I want to help. Unfortunately the only way I can do so is by marrying you."

Startled, she said, "You know about Bratchett?"

"While I was waiting to speak to your father, I overheard the discussion between you."

Unconsciously Ariel raised one hand to her cheek where a bruise was forming. When she did, the folds of Falconer's robe quivered slightly and the atmosphere changed, as if a thundercloud had entered the room.

Her face colored and she dropped her hand, embarrassed that this stranger had heard what had passed between her and her father. Apparently the Black Beast of Belleterre was enough of a gentleman that he had been upset by her father's bullying.

But that didn't answer a more basic question. Thinking of those ill-defined orgies, she asked, "Why are you offering marriage to someone you've never met?"

"No young lady should be forced to wed Bratchett. I had not intended ever to marry, so offering you the protection of my name will not deprive me of anything." His tone became intense. "And that is exactly what I am offering a home and the protection of my name. I will not require ... marital intimacy of you."

Her blush returned, this time burningly hot. The maids always lowered their voices when they spoke of the marriage bed, or of the non-marital haystack. Ariel guessed that the subject might be related to orgies, but that told her nothing worthwhile. Haltingly she said, "Do you mean that it will be a ... a marriage in name only?"

He grasped at the phrase with relief. "Exactly! You told your father that you wished to be left alone at Gardsley. I can't give you that, for it's only a matter of time until he loses the estate, but if you like the country, you'll be happy at Belleterre. You'll be free to draw or paint or do anything else you desire. I promise not to interfere with you in any way."

Her eyes widened. How could he know about her art and how important it was to her? Vainly she tried to see Falconer's face within the shadows of the cowl, but without success. There was something uncanny about the man; no wonder he had such an alarming reputation. "Your offer is very generous, but what benefit will you derive from such a marriage?"

"The warm glow that comes from knowledge of a deed well done," he said with unmistakable irony. Seeing her expression, he said more quietly, "It will please me if you are happy."

She began twisting a lock of hair that fell over her shoulder. He seemed kind, but what did she know of him? She wasn't sure she trusted disinterested generosity. If she became his wife, she would be his property, to do with as he wished.

Guessing her thoughts, he said, ''Are you wondering if you can trust the Black Beast of Belleterre to keep his word?"

So he knew his nickname. This time when she blushed, it was for her fellow man for inventing such a cruel title. "I'm confused," she said honestly. "An hour ago, I scarcely knew you existed. Now I'm considering an offer of marriage from you. There's something very medieval about it."

He gave an unexpected rumble of laughter. "If we were in the Middle Ages, you would have no choice at all, and the man offering for you wouldn't be wearing a monk's robe."

So he had a sense of humor. For some reason that surprised her, for he was such a dark, melo-dramatic figure. She sank down into a chair and linked her hands in her lap while she considered her choices. Marrying Bratchett she dismissed instantly; she'd become a beggar first.

Perhaps she could stay at Gardsley for a while longer, but sadly she accepted that her days at the only home she had ever known were numbered. Even if her father received some unexpected financial windfall, he would soon squander it. He cared only for London society and placed no value on his estate beyond the fact that being Hawthorne of Gardsley gave him position.

She could look for work. Wistfully she thought of Anna McCall, who had been her governess and friend for six years. Anna had been discharged on Ariel's eighteenth birthday because Sir Edwin had not wanted to continue paying her modest salary.

Anna had gone to a fine position with a family near London. Perhaps she could help Ariel find a situation, for the two women still corresponded. But Anna was older and much more clever, while Ariel was young and vague and had no skills except drawing. No one would want her for a governess or teacher.

If she wouldn't marry Bratchett, couldn't stay at Gardsley, and was incapable of supporting herself, she had only one other choice: accepting Falconer's proposal. Of the paths open to her, it was the hardest to evaluate. Yet even if the man was lying and he wanted to use her to slake his mysterious male needs, he couldn't be worse than Bratchett. If he genuinely wanted no more than to offer her a home, she might be happy at Belleterre.

Lifting her head, Ariel gazed at the dark stranger who waited patiently for her answer. She wished she could see his face. No matter how misshapen his visage was, it would be less alarming than the hood. Nonetheless, she said steadily, "If you truly wish it, Lord Falconer, I will marry you."

Humor again lurking in his voice, he said, "You've decided that I'm the best of a bad lot?"

"Exactly." Her lips curved up involuntarily. "Apparently I inherited some of my father's gambling blood."

"Very well then, Ariel," he said, his deep voice making music of her name. "We shall marry. I guarantee that your life at Belleterre will be no worse than your life here. If it is within my power, I shall see that it is better."

She could hardly ask fairer than that. Nonetheless, that night in her bed, she cried herself to sleep.


They were married three and a half weeks later after the calling of the banns. Ariel's father had insisted that she must have a fashionable wedding gown, so he took her to a London dressmaker.

She hated the noise and the crowds of people. Even more, she hated the white silk gown, with its bustle and train and elaborate flounces that made her feel like an over-decorated cake. Most of all, she had hated the corset and steel hoops she must wear to make the dress fit properly.

Just before they left the dressmaker's salon, she heard Sir Edwin tell the proprietor to send the bill to Lord Falconer of Belleterre. So her father would not spend his own money even for his daughter's wedding gown. Any sentimental regrets she had about leaving her home vanished then.

She slept badly during the weeks between her betrothal and her marriage, and she went to the church on her wedding day with dark circles under her eyes. She wouldn't have been surprised if the groom took one look at her and changed his mind, but he didn't. She suspected that he was as nervous as she, though she wasn't sure how she knew that when he was completely invisible under his cowled robe.

For a moment she had the hysterical thought that she might not be marrying Lord, Falconer, for anyone could hide under a robe. She reminded herself that his face might be hidden, but his height and smooth, powerful movements were proof of his identity.

The wedding was very small, with only Ariel and her father, the vicar and his wife, and an elderly man who stood up with Lord Falconer.

Based on a faint but unmistakable scent, Ariel surmised the elderly man worked with horses. She'd invited Anna McCall, but her friend had been unable to come, for the interesting reason that she herself was getting married the same day.

Though the ceremony went quickly, there were several surprises. The first came when the vicar referred to the bridegroom as "James Philip." Ariel knew that his family name was Markland, but with a small jolt she realized she hadn't known his given name.

He was a stranger, a complete stranger—and she had agreed to marry him without knowing either his name or what he looked like. She glanced up at his face, but the church was old and shadowy, and the cowl effectively prevented her from seeing anything even though she stood right next to him.

The service progressed. The next surprise came when Falconer lifted her icy hand so that he could slide the ring on her finger. He used both hands to hold hers, and she found his warm touch comforting.

She glanced down. She hadn't seen his hands closely before, for he tended to hold them so they were not readily visible. Now she saw that his left hand was so heavily scarred that the two smallest fingers must be almost useless. She could not help but stare.

He saw her reaction and dropped his hands as soon as the ring was on her finger. The sleeve of his robe fell over his wrist, and once more the damage was invisible.

She wanted to tell him that her reaction had
been simple surprise, not revulsion, but she
couldn't do that in the middle of the wedding
ceremony. She bit her lip as the vicar concluded
the ritual, declared them man and wife, and said
jovially that it was time to kiss the bride.

Ariel had wondered what would happen at this
point. Would her new husband abstain, or would
he actually kiss her and she might learn something of what he looked like?

Once again, he surprised her by lifting her
right hand and kissing it, very gently. His lips
were warm and smooth and firm, just the way
lips should be. She wanted to weep, and didn't
know why.

They turned and left the church, married. No
wedding breakfast had been planned, for Ariel
guessed that Lord Falconer would be uncomfortable at such an event. Nor would there be a
honeymoon; they would go directly to Belleterre
where her possessions should have already been
delivered.

Before stepping outside, she saw Falconer give
an envelope to her father, but she said nothing
until she and her new husband were alone in their
carriage. As she arranged her billowing skirts, she
asked, "How much did it cost you to buy me?"

He shifted uneasily on the leather seat, but
didn't avoid the question. "I canceled a loan of
ten thousand pounds and gave your father ten
thousand pounds beyond that. He's supposed to
use it to settle other debts, though I doubt that
he will."

She inhaled the spicy sweet scent of her bouquet of white rosebuds and pale pink carnations. "That's a high price to pay for a good deed. You could have endowed another hospital for twenty thousand pounds."

"I suppose so," he said uncomfortably, "but I consider it money well spent."

Ariel was looking straight ahead, her eyes on the velvet lining of the carriage. He took advantage of that to study her profile again, this time from much closer than on the occasion when he'd first seen her. But today she wasn't that carefree girl under the apple tree. Beneath the veil, her flaxen hair was drawn up in a complicated style of coils and ringlets and her gown made her look terrifyingly fashionable.

Her beauty and sophistication alarmed him. Where had he ever found the audacity to offer for such a paragon? It was tragic that because of her father's fecklessness, she was now tied to a man wholly unworthy of her. "A pity that you never had a London Season. There you could have found a husband to your taste instead of being forced to choose between two unpalatable alternatives."

To his surprise she smiled humorlessly. "I did have a London Season when I was eighteen."

He frowned. "Then why aren't you married? You must have been a stunning success."

She began plucking the ribbons that trailed from her bouquet. "Oh, yes, I was a success. Proclaimed a Beauty, in fact. There were several proposals of marriage. Fortunately they were improperly made to me rather than my father, so I was able to decline without him learning about them."

"Why did you refuse? Were they all men like Bratchett?"

She twined a ribbon around one slender finger. "None were so dreadful as he, but neither did they want to marry *me*. They just wanted to win the latest Beauty. And win is the right word. Courtship was a sport, and I was one of the Season's best trophies. None of the men who proposed marriage knew anything about, me, or cared about the things I cared about." She looked up at him, her blue eyes stark. "To be a Beauty is to be a thing, not a person. Perhaps you, more than most men, can understand that."

Her words struck him with the impact of a blow. For the first time he realized just how much more she was than the beautiful child he had seen on the hillside. "Yes, I understand what it is to be a thing, not a person. I don't blame you for resenting that. But even so, you would have been better off married to one of those men, someone who would have given you a real marriage and a position in society."

"I'm not sure I would have been better off. I spoke the truth when I told my father that I preferred a quiet life in the country. He can't bear quiet. I suppose that's one reason we've never understood each other very well." Visibly shaking off her mood, she said, "I don't believe I've properly thanked you for saving me from Bratchett. I really do appreciate what you've done." After a slight hesitation, she added, "James."

Startled, he said, "No one calls me that."

"Would you rather I didn't?"

"Do as you will," he said, his voice constricted. He was deeply moved to hear her use his name. No woman had done so since his mother had died.

Thinking of his mother's death, he dropped his left hand from sight behind his thigh. Ariel had viewed the scars with distaste when he had put the ring on her finger. That was to be expected since she was without flaw herself. But she had the good manners of natural refinement and had done her best not to show her distaste.

For the rest of the journey to Belleterre neither of them spoke, but the silence was less awkward than he had expected. When the carriage pulled up in front of his home, he helped her out, saying lightly, as if the matter was unimportant, "After this moment, you need never endure my touch again."

He started to remove his right hand from hers, but she clung to it. Softly, her great blue eyes staring up at him, she said, "James, you mustn't think that you repel me. We are almost strangers, but you have been kind to me, and now we are married. Surely we will have some kind of relationship with each other. I hope it will not be a strained one."

He pulled his hand from her clasp, knowing that if he felt the touch of her slim fingers any longer, he would want to do more than just hold her hand. "It won't be strained. You will scarcely see me, except by chance around the estate."

She frowned. "It sounds like a very lonely life. Can't we at least be friends, perhaps sometimes keep each other company?"

To be friends with her would be difficult, but obediently he said, "If that is your wish. How much company do you want?"

She bit her lower lip, looking enchantingly earnest. "Perhaps ... perhaps we might dine together every night? If you don't mind?"

"I won't mind." He reminded himself that her request stemmed from the basic need for human interaction rather than any special liking for him, but even so, joy swirled through him at the knowledge that she'd actually requested his company on a regular basis.

She took his arm as they began walking up the steps, surprising him again. She was a brave child, and an honorable one, willing to do her duty. Solemnly he promised himself that he would not take advantage of that willingness.

The servants were lined up inside the house to meet the new mistress. Ariel knew she would never remember all the names until she knew them better, but she was impressed by the general air of well-being. If orgies were held at Belleterre, they didn't seem to distress the servants.

Nonetheless, she sensed deep reserve among them, as if they were doubtful about her. She supposed it was only natural for them to be wary about a new mistress. Once they discovered that she didn't intend to make sweeping changes, they would relax,

Introductions over, Falconer turned her over to the housekeeper to be shown to her rooms. Mrs. Wilcox was remote but polite when she took her new mistress upstairs. As she passed through rooms and halls, Ariel observed that her new home was furnished in excellent, if rather austere, taste. If was also well kept, with floors and furniture gleaming with wax and not a speck of dust anywhere.

On reaching their destination, the housekeeper opened the door and said, "Your belongings were delivered and the maids have unpacked them, your ladyship. If there is anything that you want, or if you wish to make changes, you have only to ask."

Ariel's first impression was that she had stepped into a garden, for every available surface was covered with vases of welcoming flowers. She drifted through the scented rooms, awed by the size and luxury of her accommodations. Not only was there a well-furnished bedroom and sitting room, but another large chamber that was almost empty:

It took a moment for her to realize that the room was a studio, for there was a north light and an easel in the corner. Her eyes stung. Had he known what this would mean to her? He must have guessed. Though he was a stranger, he understood her better than her own father had.

Behind her a soft Kentish voice said, "I'm Fanny, your ladyship, and I'm to be your personal maid. Do you wish to take off your gown and rest before dinner?"

Gratefully Ariel accepted the girl's suggestion,

for the stress of the day had left her exhausted. She slept well and woke refreshed.

Fanny appeared again and helped her dress. There was an entire armoire full of new clothing. Apparently the dressmaker in London had been commissioned to make Ariel complete wardrobe as well as the wedding gown.

Her husband had judged her taste well, for most of the dresses were loosely cut tea gowns. They would be perfect for daytime in the country, particularly for painting and walking. The colors chosen were clear, delicate pastels that suited her fair hair and complexion. Ariel was beginning to suspect that the Black Beast had the eye of an artist.

When she went down to dinner, she found her husband waiting in the morning room. He greeted her gravely and inquired if everything was to her taste. She assured him that her rooms were lovely, especially the studio. Then they went together into the family dining room. He tensed when she took his arm and she wondered if he found her touch distasteful.

The family dining room was still very large, and one end of the room was quite dark even though the summer sun had not yet set. Ariel had thought that when her husband ate he might put his hood back, but he didn't. Since his chair was in the dark end of the room and she was a dozen feet away at the far end of the polished table, she saw nothing of his face.

The dinner was a quiet one until the end, when bowls of fruit had been served. After the footman had left the room, Ariel said, "Do you always sit or stand in the shadows?"

He paused in the act of peeling a peach. "Always."

"Is that necessary?"

"To me it is." He began to peel away a spiral of peach skin, his long fingers deft. In the shadows it was impossible to see the scars on his left hand. "I have said that you can do whatever you wish at Belleterre. In return, Ariel, I ask that you respect my wishes in this matter."

She bit her lip. "Of course, James."

The rest of the meal passed in silence. When they were done, they rose and went into the hall. Ariel had thought that perhaps they would sit together after dinner, but her husband only said, "Good night, my dear. If you wish to read, the library is through that door on the left. The selection of books is wide, and of course you are welcome to add anything you want to the collection."

She realized that he had been quite serious when he'd said they would see little of each other. She'd wanted a quiet life, and it appeared that her wish would be granted. She was just saying good night when a scrabble of claws sounded on the polished marble floor.

Ariel looked up to see a dog trotting eagerly down the hall. It was the ugliest dog she'd ever seen, rawboned and splotchy and of very dubious parentage. But its shaggy face glowed with canine bliss as it reached its master, then reared up and balanced on its haunches.

Falconer scratched the dog's head, and a pink tongue lolled out of its panting mouth. "Did you come to meet your new mistress, Cerberus?"

Amused by the name, Ariel said, "Cerberus has no interest in me. It's you whom he adores with his whole canine heart."

Falconer's robe quivered, as if in a slight breeze. "It doesn't take much to win a dog's heart."

Ariel realized she could read the movements of the fabric to determine her husband's moods. Very useful since his face was concealed. Though she was new to the art of robe reading, she guessed that he was uncomfortable with her comment about being adored. Did he feel unworthy of even a dog's devotion?

With sudden ferocity, she wanted to know more about the stranger she had married. She wanted to know what had made him what he was. In time, surely, she would. After all, they were living under the same roof.

From the corner of her eye, Ariel caught more motion, and she turned to see a black-and-white cat entering the hall. It moved very strangely because it was missing one foreleg. Still, the cat seemed to have no trouble getting around. Ariel knelt and rubbed her fingers together, hoping the creature would come to her.

"That's Tripod," Falconer said. "Her leg was accidentally cut off by a scythe."

After a disdainful look at Cerberus, the cat hopped over to Ariel and rubbed against her out-stretched fingers.

She smiled. "Thank you for condescending to

meet me, Tripod."

Jealously the dog trotted over to ask for some attention. As Ariel ruffled the droopy ears, she murmured, "What a funny-looking fellow you are. You remind me of a picture of a musk ox I once saw."

In a low voice her husband said, "Any ugly creature is assured of a home here."

Ariel froze for a moment, feeling that she had committed some dreadful faux pas. Then she rose to her feet and said calmly, "You are a very kind man, James, to take in waifs and strays. After all, I am one of them. Good night."

Then she went upstairs to the charming rooms where she would spend her wedding night alone.

Though he had seen her with his own eyes, conversed with her over dinner, Falconer had trouble believing that she was under his own roof. In his mind he never used the name Ariel. To him his wife was *she,* as if she were the only woman in the world.

What he had not expected was how torment-ing her presence would be. It had been years since he had lain with a woman, and he had become reasonably comfortable with his monk-ish life. But no more. Though he still wore the robes of a monk, he ached with yearning. He wanted to touch his wife's blossom smooth skin, bury his hands in her silky hair, inhale her sweet female scent. He wanted more than that, though he would not allow himself to put words to his base thoughts.

After she had gone to bed, he went outside and walked from one end of Belleterre to the other as dusk became night. Cerberus trotted obediently behind, ready to defend his master from the lethal attacks of rabbits and pheasants.

As soon as it was dark enough, Falconer pushed back his hood, welcoming the cool night air, for he burned. He despised himself for his body's weakness, for it was unthinkable that a monster such as he could lie with the angel he had married. Unlike Bratchett, he knew that he was a monster. But in his heart he was no better than the other man, for he could not stop himself from desiring her.

It was very late when he returned to the house. To his surprise, when he went upstairs a light showed under his wife's bedroom door. Was she also having trouble sleeping? Perhaps he should go and talk with her, reassure her about her new life.

Though he knew he was lying to himself about his motives, he literally could not prevent himself from going down the hall and tapping on her door. When there was no answer, he turned the knob and eased the door open, then crossed the room to the bed.

She had fallen asleep while reading and she lay with her head turned to one side, her pale blond hair spilling luxuriantly over the pillow. She wore a delicately tucked and laced nightgown, and she was the most beautiful being he had ever seen.

He picked up the book that she had laid on

the coverlet. It was one of his volumes of William Blake, the mystical poet and artist. A good choice for a girl who was also an artist. He set the volume on the table by a vase of roses, turned out the lamp, and ordered himself to leave the room.

But he allowed himself one last look. The bedroom curtains hadn't been drawn, and in the moonlight she was a figure spun of ivory and silver. He drank in the sight, knowing he could never permit himself to do this again, for he could not trust himself so close to her.

When he had memorized her image well enough to last a lifetime, he turned to go. He was halfway to the door when his resolve broke and he spun back again. Against his will his hand lifted, began reaching out to her.

With a violence that was all the more intense for being subdued, he turned to the vase of roses and gripped the stems with his left hand. Ignoring the thorns stabbing into his fingers, he stripped the blossoms away with his right hand. Then he slowly scattered the fragile scarlet petals over her like a pagan worshiping his goddess. They looked like black velvet as they drifted down the moonbeams.

One petal touched her cheek and slid over the soft curve, coming to rest on her throat, exactly the way he longed to touch her. As the intoxicating scent of roses filled the air around him, more petals spangled her gilt hair and delicate muslin gown, rising and falling with the slow rhythm of her breath.

When his hand was emptied, he took a shuddering breath. Then he turned and left her room forever.

# AUTUMN

ARIEL ADDED A bit more yellow paint to the mixture, stroked a brush full across her test paper, then critically examined the result. Yes, that should do for the base shade of the leaves, which were at the height of their autumn color.

In the next two hours, she made several watercolor sketches of the woods, more interested in creating an impression of the vibrant scene than rendering an exact copy. As James said, now that photographers were able to reproduce precise images, artists had more freedom to experiment, to be more abstract.

The work absorbed her entire attention, for watercolor was in many ways the most difficult and volatile medium. When she finally had a painting that satisfied her, she began packing her equipment into the special saddlebags that a Belleterre groom had made to carry her supplies around the estate. The glade was deeply peaceful. Above her head tall, tall elm trees rustled in the wind like a sky-borne river.

It had not taken long for her life to fall into an easy routine. As her husband had promised, she had quiet, freedom, and anything else that money could buy. The size of the allowance he gave her was staggering. She'd been thrilled to order the finest papers and canvases, the most expensive brushes and pigments, and never have to consider the cost.

It also proved educational to have such wealth at her disposal. She found that after she had bought her art supplies, there was little else to spend the money on. She scarcely even needed to buy books, for the Belleterre library was the finest she had ever seen. Nor did she have to buy clothing, for she had the wardrobe her husband had given her when they married.

He had also given her an exquisite, beautifully mannered gray mare. Foxglove was the prettiest horse on the estate, for the rest of the beasts were an odd-looking lot. Though quite capable of doing their jobs, they tended to have knobby knees, lop-ears, and coats that were rough even after the most thorough grooming. The pairs and teams didn't match at all. She suspected that like Cerberus and Tripod, the horses had been given a home because they hadn't been appreciated by a world that valued appearance over capability.

Ariel found the mismatched horses endearing and almost resented the fact that her husband had bought Foxglove for her. Did he think she was incapable of appreciating anything that wasn't perfect? Apparently. Yet because his intention had been to please her, she could hardly complain.

James had given her exactly the life of peace and freedom that he had promised. She could draw and paint to her heart's content for she no longer had to spend most of her time trying vainly to oversee her father's neglected estate. Her work was improving, and some of the credit for that must go to her husband, for they often discussed art over dinner. His knowledge of painting was remarkable and his insights very helpful, for her abilities were more intuitive than analytical.

Yet instead of mounting to ride back to the house, Ariel put her arms around Foxglove's neck and buried her face against the mare's glossy, horse-scented hide. She was a very lucky young woman. That being the case, why was she so miserable?

"Oh, Foxy," she said in a choked voice. "I'm so lonely. Lonelier than I've ever been in my life. Sometimes it seems as if you're my only friend." Though it sounded perilously like self-pity, the statement was true. If she hadn't asked that her husband dine with her, days on end would have passed without her seeing him.

She looked forward all day to those meals, for he was the pleasantest of companions, well-read and amusing, able to discuss any subject. Despite her youth and ignorance, he was never rude or disdainful of her opinion. In fact, the discussions were making her much more knowledgeable and she enjoyed them enormously.

Yet no matter how pleasant the meal, as soon as it was over James would bid her a polite good night and withdraw. She would not see him again until the next evening, except perhaps by chance in the distance as he rode about the estate.

The Belleterre servants were a surprisingly reserved group. Ariel had been on easy terms with everyone at Gardsley, but Falconer's people were as distant now as they had been the day she arrived, four months earlier.

The one exception was Patterson, the old, half-blind groom who had been her husband's best man at the wedding. He at least was always friendly, though not very forthcoming. Patterson, Foxglove, Cerberus, and Tripod were almost the whole of Ariel's social life. Even her friend Anna hadn't written in months, presumably because she was absorbed in her new family.

With a sigh Ariel mounted and turned Foxglove toward home. She had always been able to live quite happily in her own world. She had never been lonely until she came to Belleterre. Now she reckoned it a good night when Tripod deigned to sleep on her bed.

She had changed, and the blame could be laid at her husband's door. Solitude was no longer enough because she loved being with him. Loved hearing his deep, kind voice, loved laughing at his dry sense of humor. She would have been happy to trail around after him like Cerberus.

But she couldn't, for she knew James wouldn't like that. She was just a young and not very interesting female. Though he was willing to share one meal a day with her, more of her company would probably bore him to tears. She didn't dare jeopardize what she had by asking for more than he was willing to give.

As she reined in Foxglove at the stables, Patterson ambled out to help her dismount. When her feet were safely on the ground, Ariel impulsively asked a question inspired by her earlier thoughts. "Patterson, why are all of the servants so reserved with me? Is it something I've done?"

The old man continued unpacking her painting materials. "No, milady. Everyone considers you very proper."

"Then why do I feel as if I'm being judged and found wanting?" Ariel said, then immediately felt foolish.

The groom took her words in good part. "'Tisn't that, milady. You're much admired," he said. "'Tis just that folks are afraid you might hurt the master."

She stared. "Hurt him? Why would I do that?" A horrible thought occurred to her. "Surely no one thinks I would poison him so that I could be a wealthy widow!"

"Not that, my lady," he said quickly. "'Tisn't that sort of hurt that folks are worried about." He heaved the saddlebags from the mare. Without looking at Ariel, he said, "Don't need a knife or gun or poison to break a man's heart."

"His lordship scarcely knows I'm alive," she said, unable to believe the implication. "I'm just one more unfortunate creature that he brought to Belleterre because I needed a home."

"Nay, milady. You're not like any of the others." In spite of the cloudiness of his eyes, Patterson's gaze seemed to bore right through her. "I've known that boy most of his life, and he never brought home anyone like you."

Ariel's mind unaccountably snapped to the morning after her wedding. Blood red rose petals all been scattered over the bed when she woke. She had been surprised and a little uneasy, until she decided that some of the flowers had fallen apart and been blown by the wind. But they had fallen very strangely if it was the wind.

She had a mental image of James scattering her with rose petals, and an odd, deep shiver went through her. Was it possible that he cared for her as a man cared for a woman? She rejected the idea. He didn't want her for a wife. His nature seemed as monkish as his clothing.

As she hesitated, caught in her thoughts, Patterson said, "I think he's in the aviary, milady. If you like, I can take your pictures up to the house."

As a hint, there was nothing subtle about it. "Please do that, Patterson. And thank you."

Ariel's steps were slow as she walked through the gardens to the aviary. If she understood the old groom correctly, James did care about her, at least enough that she had the potential to hurt him. She would never do so, but the opposite side of that potential was that she might be able to make him happy. She often felt deep sadness radiating from her husband, and the possibility that she might be able to reduce that was tantalizing.

Her steps became even slower when she came within sight of the aviary. It was an enormous enclosure made of elaborately molded, white-painted cast iron. Not only was it large enough to include several small trees and a little pool, but there was a vast shed where the birds could shelter during bad weather.

The aviary was home to dozens of birds, most of them foreign species that Ariel didn't recognize. She often came by to watch them fly and chatter and play. In particular she enjoyed coaxing the large green parrot into conversation. Several times she had done sketches of the aviary's residents, trying to capture the quick, bright movements.

Today her gaze went immediately to her husband, who was inside the enclosure. Instead of his usual calf-length robe, he was garbed in a dark coat and trousers such as any gentleman might wear for a day's estate management. However, his head and shoulders were swathed in a cowled hood that concealed his face as effectively as the longer robe.

Ariel had occasionally seen him dressed this way, but always in the distance. Close up, he was a fine figure of a man, tall and strong and masculine. His black coat displayed the breadth of his shoulders. His movements fascinated her, the turn of his powerful wrist when he stretched out his hand so that a small brown bird could jump onto it, his gentleness as he stroked the small creature's head with one forefinger, his warm chuckle when the parrot swooped down and landed on his shoulder with a great thrashing of wings.

The birds loved him, not caring what his face was like. The same was true of all the creatures who lived at Belleterre, and all the humans, too, including Ariel.

Perhaps what she felt for her husband wasn't quite love, but it could be if given a chance. She yearned for his company, for his touch. In her limited life she had never known anyone like him, not only for the obvious reason of how he dressed, but for his kindness and knowledge. It no longer mattered that she didn't know what he looked like. She was so accustomed to his hood that it had in effect become his face.

But how could an ignorant young woman tell a mature, educated man that she yearned to be more to him?

Praying that inspiration would come, Ariel unlatched the door and entered the aviary. Cerberus, who had been lying outside, lurched to his feet and tried to enter with her, but she firmly held him back.

As the door clinked shut behind her, James turned. "I thought you were painting, Ariel."

"I was, but the light changed, so I decided to stop after I did a picture that I was somewhat satisfied with."

A smile in his voice, he said, "Is an artist ever wholly satisfied with her own work?"

She said ruefully, "1 doubt it. I know that I never am." While she tried to think what to say next, the parrot flew to a branch and crooned, "Ar-r-riel. Ar-r-riel."

Surprised, she said, "When did he learn that?"

James shrugged. "Just now, I Imagine. He's a contrary creature. Once I spent hours unsuccessfully trying to teach him to say 'God save the

Queen.' The only thing he learned that day was the phrase 'Deuce take it!' which I said just before I gave up in exasperation."

The bird obligingly squawked, "Devil take it! Devil take it!"

Ariel laughed. "Are you sure that 'deuce take it' is what he learned that day?"

Her husband joined her laughter. "It appears that my bad language bas been exposed. Sorry."

"James ... " Not sure how to say what she wanted, she took several steps toward her husband.

To her dismay, he moved away. "Have you ever seen one of these parakeets close up?" He laid a hand on a branch and a bird hopped on. "Lovely little creatures." It was neatly done, as if he was not retreating but had merely seen something that caught his attention.

Ariel felt tears stinging in her eyes. Patterson was wrong. If James cared for her in a special way, he would not flee whenever she approached. She was struggling to maintain her composure when the blue-breasted parakeet suddenly skipped up her husband's arm and disappeared into the folds of the hood that wrapped around his throat.

For Ariel it was the last straw. Even that silly little bird, which wouldn't make two bites for Tripod, was permitted to get closer to James than she was. Her loneliness and yearning welled up, and with them her tears. Humiliated, she turned to leave the aviary, wanting to get away before her husband noticed.

But he noticed everything. "Ariel, what's

wrong?"

She shook her head and fumbled with the
door, but the latch on this side was stiff. As she
struggled with it, her husband came up behind
her and hesitantly touched her elbow. "Has your
father tried to reach you, or upset you in some
way?"

It was the most natural thing in the world to
turn to him, and for him to put his arms around
her. She was crying harder than she ever had in
her life, even when her mother died. But dear
God, how wonderful it felt to be in his embrace!
He was so strong, so warm, so safe.

Tall as well. The top of her head didn't quite
reach his chin, which put his shoulder at a convenient height. Trying to stop her tears, she gulped
for breath, pressing her face into the smooth dark
wool of his coat.

"Ariel, my dear girl!" he said, rocking her a little. "Is there anything I can do? Or ... or are you
crying because you're married to me?"

"Oh, no, no, that's not the problem!" She slipped
her arms around his waist, wanting to be as close
as she could. "It's just ... I'm so lonely here. Would
it be possible for us to spend more time together?
Perhaps in the evenings, after dinner? I won't dis-
turb you if you want to work or read, but I'd
like to be with you." It was as close as she could
come to putting her heart in his hands.

He didn't answer for a long time, so long she
feared she might suffocate because she couldn't
seem to breathe normally. One hand stroked
down her back, slowly, as if he were gentling a

horse. Finally he said, "Of course we could, if that's what you want."

"But will you mind?" she asked, needing to know if he was willing or simply indulging.

She felt a faint brush against her hair, from his hand or perhaps his lips. "I won't mind,' he said softly. "It will be my pleasure."

She was so happy that her tears began to flow again. That was sufficient excuse to stay just where she was, in his arms.

She would never tire of his embrace, for she felt as if she had come home. Besides happiness, she felt deeper stirrings that she couldn't identify. They frightened her a little, but at the same time she knew that she wanted to explore them further, for they had much to do with James.

She became aware how much tension there was in her husband. Reluctantly she stepped away, for she didn't want to wear out her welcome. "It's getting late." Suddenly aware of the untidiness of her hair and the stains on her painting clothes, she said, "I must go and change for dinner."

"This evening, if you like, we can sit in the library," he said hesitantly. "I've some letters to write, but if you don't think you'll be bored ... "

"I won't be." She was almost embarrassed at the transparent happiness in her voice. "I'll see you at dinner." This evening would be the first step, and eventually there would be others. She wasn't sure exactly where the path would lead, but she knew that it was one she must follow.

The meal was the most lighthearted they had
yet shared. Falconer wondered if his wife was
looking forward to spending the evening together
as much as he was, then decided that was impossible. But she looked happier than he had ever
seen her.

Though he hadn't realized until now, when the
difference was obvious, she had been growing
increasingly quiet, her characteristic glow muted.
He reminded himself that even self-contained
young women who enjoyed solitude needed
some companionship. For Ariel, he was the available companion. He would not take her desire
to see more of him too personally, but that didn't
mean that he couldn't enjoy it.

They retreated to the library for coffee, still
talking, tangible warmth between them. Falconer
was careful not to strain that fragile web of feeling, for he wanted it to grow stronger.

She took a chair and gracefully poured coffee
from a silver pot. Garbed in a blue silk gown,
she looked especially lovely tonight, her delicate
coloring as fresh as spring flowers. As she handed
him his cup, she said, "Today I got a letter from
my former governess, Anna. Have I ever told you
about her?"

When he answered in the negative, Ariel
continued, "After leaving Gardsley, she found a
position teaching the two daughters of a widower
who lives in Hampstead, just north of London."

He stirred milk into his coffee. "Is the man
intellectual or artistic, like so many of those who
live in Hampstead?"

"Indeed he is. Mr. Talbott designs fabrics and furniture for industrial manufacture and is quite successful with it. He also has the good sense to appreciate Anna. In fact, they married on the same day we did. They went to Italy for a honeymoon and have only just returned. Anna apologized for not writing but said that she's been so busy and happy that she didn't quite realize how much time had gone by. She has invited us to visit her in Hampstead. She says the house is very large."

Ariel looked shyly over her coffee cup. "Would you be willing to do that sometime? You'll like Anna, and Mr. Talbott sounds like a wonderful man."

Falconer frowned, but he didn't want to spoil the mood of the evening. "Perhaps someday."

Ariel regarded him thoughtfully, then changed the subject. They talked of other things until the coffee was gone. Then she stood. Falconer feared that she had changed her mind and was going to go upstairs until she said, "I'll read while you do your letter writing." She gave him a bright, rather nervous smile. "I don't want to distract you from your work."

When she was this close, it was hard to think of letters, but obediently he went to his desk and started writing. He had a large and varied correspondence, for letters were a way to be involved with people without having to meet them face-to-face.

Cerberus was pleasantly befuddled by having them both in the room and wandered back and forth, flopping first by Falconer, then ambling to the chair where Ariel was reading. Tripod was lazier and simply curled up on the desk on top of a pile of notepaper.

Falconer could not remember when he had been happier. The library, with its deep, leather-upholstered furniture, had always been his favorite room, and having Ariel's presence made paradise itself seem inferior.

But the evening became even better. Hearing a sound beside him, he absently put his left hand down to ruffle the dog's ears. Instead, he touched silken hair. Glancing down, he saw his wife curled up against his chair. "Ariel?" he said, startled.

She glanced up, both teasing and apologetic. "Cerberus enjoys having his head scratched, so I thought I'd try it." Her smile faded. "I'm sorry, I shouldn't have disturbed you."

"No need to apologize." He turned his head away so that she couldn't see under the cowl. "I'm ready for a break." His fingers twined through her shining tresses as if they had a life of their own. He'd thought his scarred fingers had little sensation, but now he would swear that he could feel each gossamer strand separately.

With a soft, pleased sigh she relaxed against the side of his chair. For perhaps a quarter of an hour they stayed like that while he stroked her head, slender neck, and delicate ears. As he did, joy bubbled through him like a fountain of light and his mind rang with the words of Elizabeth Barrett Browning's famous sonnet. *How do I love thee? Let me count the ways ….*

For he did love this exquisite girl who was his wife. On their wedding day, when she had expressed her dislike of being courted solely for her beauty, he had felt ashamed, for he could not help but be bewitched by her loveliness. Yet even that first moment, when the sight of her had been like an arrow in his heart, he had sensed that her beauty was even more of the spirit than of the body.

The idyll ended when Tripod, deciding that she needed attention, jumped down into Ariel's lap. She laughed and straightened up. Falconer started to withdraw his hand, but before he could, she caught his fingers. Then she very deliberately laid her cheek against the back of his hand.

Her skin was porcelain smooth against the coarse scars that crippled his two smallest fingers and made the rest of his hand hideous. Yet she did not flinch.

He began to tremble as waves of sensation pulsed through him, beginning in his fingers and spreading until every cell of his body vibrated. For the first time he wondered if it might be possible for them to have a real marriage. She did not seem repulsed by the scars on his hand. Was there a chance that she might be able to tolerate the rest of him?

The thought was as frightening as it was exhilarating. His emotions too chaotic to control, he got to his feet, then raised her to hers. Hoarsely he said, "It's time for bed. But perhaps in the morning, you might join me for a ride?"

Her smile was breathtaking. "I'd like that."

He turned out the lights, then escorted her upstairs to her room, the animals trailing along behind. At her door she turned to him. "Good night, James. Sleep well."

In the faint light of the hall, she looked eager and accessible, her lips slightly parted, her hair delectably disheveled from his earlier petting. Instinct told him that she would welcome a kiss, and perhaps more. But she was so beautiful that he couldn't bring himself to touch her.

"Good night, Ariel." He turned and walked away, feeling so brittle that a touch might shatter him. The idea that they might build a real marriage was too new, too frightening, to act on. He might be misinterpreting her willingness. Or, unspeakable thought, she might believe herself willing but change her mind when she saw him. One thing he knew: if she rejected him after he had begun to hope, he would be unable to endure it.


Ariel went to bed in a state of jubilation. He had been happy to have her with him, she *knew* it. He hadn't even minded when she had foolishly succumbed to her desire to come closer. Best of all, he wanted her to ride with him. Perhaps they might spend all day together. And perhaps even the night ... ?

The idea filled her with blushing excitement. She was unclear what happened in a marriage bed, but knew that holding and kissing were involved. She definitely liked those things; she still tingled from the gentle fire of his touch.

If intimacy began with a kiss, in what exciting place might it end?

Her fevered emotions made it impossible for her to sleep. Finally her tossing and turning elicited a growl of protest from Tripod, who needed her twenty hours of sleep every day. Ariel surrendered and got out of bed.

As she lit the lamp on her desk, she decided that the best use of her high spirits was to answer Anna's letter, for she was now in the same elevated mood that her friend had been.

Her stationery drawer contained only two sheets of notepaper, which wouldn't be enough. She must get more from the library.

Humming softly, she donned her robe, then took the lamp and headed downstairs. The shifting shadows made her think of ghosts, but if there were any about, they would surely be benevolent ones. She must ask James about Belleterre's ghosts. Any building so old must have a few.

With ghosts on her mind, Ariel opened the library door, then blinked, with surprise. In the far corner of the room, framed by dark shelves of books, floated an object that looked horribly like a skull. She gave a sharp, shocked cry.

A flurry of sounds and movements occurred, too quick and confusing for Ariel to follow. The object whirled away, accompanied by a soft, anguished exclamation. Almost simultaneously there came a thump, a swish of fabric, then a resounding slam of the door at the far end of the library.

Shaken and alone, Ariel knew with a certainty beyond reason that something catastrophic had just occurred. She raggedly expelled the breath she had, been holding, then walked to the far corner of the room. A low lamp burned on a table; that was how she had seen ... whatever it was that she had seen.

A book lay open on the floor, and she knelt to pick it up. Elizabeth Barrett Browning's *Sonnets from the Portuguese.*

Dear God, the other occupant of the library must have been James with his hood down! She tried to recall the fleeting image that had met her eyes when she had entered the room, but try as she might, she could remember no details. The floating object had been the right height for his head. The skull-like whiteness must have been his hair, pale blond like hers, or perhaps prematurely white. Covered by his dark robe, the rest of his body had been invisible in the dark, which had made the sight of him so uncanny.

With sick horror, she realized that he'd dropped the book and fled because of her shocked exclamation. She leaned dizzily against the bookcase, the volume of poetry clutched to her chest. He must have thought she was reacting to his appearance with disgust.

But she hadn't even really seen him! She'd simply had ghosts on the mind, then been disconcerted when she saw something ghostly.

But to James, who was so profoundly ashamed of his appearance, it must have seemed as if she had found him repulsive. He would not have fled like that without a word if he hadn't been deeply wounded.

Anguished, she realized that this was what the servants had feared. She had the power to hurt her husband, and unintentionally she had done so. He must ache all the more because they had been starting to draw closer together. Certainly that fact magnified her own pain.

Determined to explain to him that it had all been a ghastly mistake, she turned out the light he had left, then lifted her own lamp and went upstairs to his rooms. She hesitated outside the door, for she had never been inside and to enter uninvited was an invasion of the privacy that he wrapped around himself as securely as his cowl.

But she couldn't allow the misunderstanding to go uncorrected. The pain in her heart was well-nigh unbearable, and he must hurt even more.

She turned the knob to his sitting room and the door swung smoothly inward, but there was no one inside. Swiftly she searched the sitting room and the bedroom next door. Nothing but solid, masculine furniture and richly colored fabrics. She opened the last door and found herself in his dressing room, but he was not there, either.

She was about to leave when her eye was caught by a small, framed picture. She was startled to see that it was one of her own drawings, but not one she had done since coming to Belleterre.

Frowning, she examined the sketch, which was of her favorite oak tree at Gardsley. She'd made it in springtime. The paper had been crumpled, then flattened, and some of the charcoal lines were blurred.

Realizing that it was a drawing that she had discarded, she cast her mind back to when she must have sketched this particular subject. Yes, it was the day she had first seen James, when he had visited her father. He must have found the drawing then.

She touched the elaborate gilded frame, which was far more costly than the sketch deserved. No one would frame such a drawing for its own sake, so it must have been for the sake of the artist. She felt incipient tears behind her eyes. He must care for her, little though she deserved such regard.

Swallowing hard, she withdrew and quietly searched the public areas of the house, stopping when she discovered that the French doors in the drawing room were unlatched. The housekeeper would never have permitted such laxity, so James must have gone outside this way.

He could be anywhere. She refused to believe that he would harm himself, so soon he would return home. Determined to wait up for him, she returned to his rooms and curled up on the sofa with a knee rug around her. But in spite of her intention to stay awake, eventually fatigue overcame her.

She was awakened by his return, though he made no sound. Her head jerked up from the sofa and she stared at her husband. His hood was firmly in place, and he was so still that she could tell nothing of his mood. Her lamp was guttering, but outside the sky was starting to lighten.

Quietly he said, "You should be in bed, Ariel."

She drew a shaky breath and went straight to the heart of the matter. "James, what happened in the library—*nothing* happened. I didn't see you, just unexpected movement. That's why I was startled."

She was still fumbling for words when he raised one hand, cutting her off with his gesture. "Of course nothing happened," he agreed in an utterly dispassionate voice. "It has occurred to me that since you've been lonely, perhaps you should visit your friend Anna for a few weeks."

Ariel rose from the sofa, the knee rug clutched around her. "Don't send me away, James," she begged. "You don't understand!"

Ignoring her words, he said, "You'll like Hampstead. It's close enough to London to be interesting, far enough away to be quiet. Send Mrs. Talbott a note today and see if it's convenient for you to come."

He stepped to one side, holding the door open in an unmistakable command to leave. "You might as well go. With winter coming there's much to be done around the estate and I won't have much time for you. Rather than being bored, you should visit your friend."

She repeated desperately, "James, you don't understand!"

"What is there to understand?" he asked, still in that soft, implacable voice.

Defeated, she walked to the door. She paused a moment when she was closest to him, wondering if she should take his hand, if touch might convince him where words couldn't.

Sharply he said, "Don't!"

A moment later she was in the hall outside and his door shut behind her. Numbly she pulled the knee rug around her shivering body and walked down the long passage to her own rooms.

Perhaps she should do what he suggested. Not only would she benefit from Anna's warm good sense, but if she was gone for a fortnight or so, it would give her husband time to recover from the unintentional hurt she had inflicted. When she returned, he would be more open to her explanation. Then they could begin again. Really, the incident had been so trivial.

She refused to believe that he might not recover from it.

*Talbott House, Hampstead*
*October 20th*

*Dear James,*

*Just a note to tell you that I've arrived safely. It's wonderful to see Anna again, she is positively blooming. Mr. Talbott is a broad, merry elf who is everything hospitable. He makes wonderful toys for the children. I had wondered if his daughters might resent the fact that Anna went from being their governess to their mother, but they adore her. Apparently their own mother died when they were very young.*

*I'll finish this now so that it can go out in the next post, but I'll write a longer letter tonight.*

*Your loving wife,*
*Ariel*

*Talbott House, Hampstead*
*November 10th*

*Dear James,*

*You were certainly right about Hampstead. It's a charming place, full of interesting people. Not at all like the ghastly society sorts that I met during my Season.*

*Remember the letter I wrote where I wondered who owned Hampstead Heath? I've since been told that the gentleman who held the manorial rights to the heath recently sold them to the Metropolitan Board of Works so that the area will be preserved for public use forever. I was glad to learn that, for people need places like the heath. Walking there reminds me a bit of Belleterre, though of course not so quiet and lovely.*

*Last night we dined with a young literary gentlemen, a Mr. Glades. He is something of a radical, for he teased me about being Lady Falconer. He's very clever—almost as much so as you—but his mind is less open, I think.*

*I know you must be terribly busy, but if you found time to scribble a note to tell me how you are, I would much appreciate it. Of course, soon I'll be home myself, so you needn't go to any special bother.*

*Your loving wife,*
*Ariel*

*Belleterre*
*November 20th*

*My dear Ariel,*
*No need to rush back. I'm very busy doing a survey of improvements needed on the tenant farms. My regards to your amiable host and hostess.*
*Falconer*

*Talbott House, Hampstead*
*December 1st*

*Dear James,*
*Last week, to amuse the girls I made some sketches illustrating the story of Dick Whittington's cat. Without my knowing, Mr. Talbott showed them to a publisher friend of his, a Mr. Howard, and now the fellow wants me to illustrate a children's book for him! He says my drawings are "magical," which sounds very nice, though I don't know quite what he means by it. While I'm flattered by his offer, I don't know whether I should accept. Would you object to having your wife involved in a commercial venture? If you don't like the idea, of course I shan't do it.*
*Almost time for tea. I'll add to this later tonight. I miss you very much.*
*Your loving wife,*
*Ariel*

Belleterre
December 3rd

My dear Ariel,
Of course I don't object to you selling your work.
Very proper of Mr. Howard to appreciate your talent.
In fact, perhaps you should purchase a house in Hampstead since you've made so many friends there. It will be convenient if you decide to illustrate more children's books. Find a house you really like. Cost is no object.
Falconer

Talbott House, Hampstead
December 4th

Dear James,
While I like Hampstead, I'm not sure we need a second house, and I certainly can't buy one unless you see it. We can discuss the matter when I come home.
Also, I want to ask your opinion of the financial arrangements Mr. Howard has suggested. I don't particularly care about the money, for your generosity gives me far more than I need, but I don't want to be silly about it, either. Later this evening I'll copy out the details of his proposal, then post this letter in the morning. I look forward to your reply.
Your loving wife,
Ariel

*Belleterre*
*December 6th*

*My dear Ariel,*

*Mr. Howard's contract seems fair. However, I can't recommend that you return to Kent just now, for the weather has been very gray and dismal. Far better to stay with your friends since Hampstead and London are more amusing than the country. Besides, from what you've said, I gather that all of the Talbotts grieve when you talk about leaving. And what of the literary Mr. Glades? You said he claims you are his muse. Surely you don't wish to leave the chap inspirationless.*

*Falconer*

*Talbott House, Hampstead*
*December 7th*

*Dear James,*

*When I mentioned your letter to Anna, she suggested that you might like to come to Hampstead and we could spend Christmas with the Talbotts. She says there is much jolliness and celebration. Perhaps too much. I'm not sure that it would be the sort of thing you'd like. Also, as much as I love Anna and her family, I would rather my first Christmas with you was a quiet one, just the two of us. And Cerberus and Tripod, of course. Has Tripod forgiven me for going away? Cats being what they are, she has probably expunged me from her memory for my desertion.*

*Eagerly awaiting your reply,*
*Your loving wife,*
*Ariel*
*P.S. The only inspiration Mr. Glades cares for or needs is the sound of his own voice.*

Falconer finished the letter, then closed his eyes in pain.

He could hear her voice in every line, see her vibrant image in his mind. It was torture to read her letters, and she wrote faithfully every day, with only rare, faint reproaches for his almost total lack of response.

Yet what could he write back? *I am dying for love of you, beloved, come home, come home!* Not the sort of letter one could write to a woman who had been horrified to see his face.

Drearily he got to his feet and stared out the library window. The fitful weather had produced a brief bit of sunshine, but it was winter in his heart. Loyal child that she was, Ariel would come home if he let her, but to what? Her life in Hampstead was full and happy. What would she have at Belleterre but disgust and loneliness? He could not allow her to return.

Mr. Glades, the literary gentleman, figured regularly in her letters. Clearly the man was besotted with her, though she never said as much. Perhaps, in her innocence, Ariel did not realize the fact.

Falconer had had the man investigated and discovered that the Honorable William Glades was handsome, wealthy, and talented, part of a glittering literary circle. He was also considered an honorable young man. A bit full of himself, like clever young chaps often were, but otherwise he was exactly the sort of man Ariel should have married.

Falconer leaned heavily against the window frame. He'd once read of savages who could will their own deaths. Though he'd been skeptical at the time, now he believed that it was possible to do such a thing. In fact, it would be easy to die ....

He wrapped his arms around himself, trying to numb his despairing grief. The heart of his spirit was dead, and it would only be a matter of time until his physical heart also stopped.

The sunshine was gone and the sky had darkened so quickly that he could see his own face faintly reflected in the window glass. He shuddered at the sight, then returned to his desk and lifted his pen.

*Belleterre*
*December 8th*

*My dear Ariel,*
*I never celebrate Christmas. It's a foolish combination of sentimentality, exaggerated piety, and paganism. But I don't wish to deprive you of the festivities, so I think you should stay with the Talbotts for the holidays.*
*Falconer*

After reading her husband's latest letter, Ariel lay down on her bed and curled up like a hurt child. She did not cry, for in the previous two months she had shed so many tears that now she had none left to mourn this ultimate rejection. Though James was too courteous to say so outright, it was obvious that he didn't want her to ever return to Belleterre. She still believed that he had once cared for her, at least a little, but plainly his feelings had died that night in the library.

She forced herself to face her future. Though she loved her husband, he would never love her. He couldn't even bear to have her under his roof. Therefore she might as well take his suggestion and buy a house in Hampstead.

There was a charming old cottage for sale only five minutes' walk from the Talbotts. It had a lovely view over Hampstead Heath and was just the right size for a woman and a servant. Though James would have to pay for it, she vowed to work hard at illustration so that eventually she would no longer need his money to survive.

Supporting herself now seemed possible. It would be far harder to make the rest of her life worth living.

# CHRISTMASTIME

"DID YOU HAVE a nice walk?" Anna called.

"Splendid." Ariel knelt and helped little Jane Talbott from her cocoon of coat, bonnet, scarf, and muff. "Even in winter the heath is full of wonderful, subtle colors. I never tire of it."

The older girl, Libby, said, "Hurry, Janie, for we can't help decorate the tree until we've had tea!"

Anna, a tall woman with nut brown hair, entered the front hall. "Thank you for taking the girls for a walk to wear down their high spirits." She smiled indulgently as the children scampered off to the nursery. "They're so excited that I'm afraid they'll vibrate to pieces between now and Christmas. And if they don't, I will!"

"Courage! Only two more days to go." Ariel removed her own coat and bonnet. "Did anything come in the post for me?"

"This package arrived from Mr. Howard." Anna lifted it from the hall table and handed it over.

"Nothing from Belleterre?"

"No, dear," Anna said quietly.

Ariel glanced up and made herself smile. "Don't look so sorry for me, Anna. I daresay this is all for the best."

Her friend's eyes were compassionate, but she was too wise to offer sympathy when Ariel's emotions were so fragile. Instead she said, "Everyone in Talbott House will be in raptures if you buy Dove Cottage. You'll never get Jane and Libby out from under your feet."

"I love having them around," Ariel said. "Libby has real drawing talent. It's a pleasure to teach her."

Glancing at the package from the publisher, she continued, "If you'll excuse me, I'll go up to my room. Mr. Howard said he was going to send another story for me to consider."

As Ariel climbed the stairs, she gave thanks for Anna's understanding. The Talbotts had been wonderful. Ariel didn't know how she would have survived the last two months without their warmth and liveliness.

As a Christmas present to the family, she'd painted an oil portrait of the four of them together. It was one of the best pieces of work she'd ever done; sorrow must be honing her artistic skills.

As she expected, the package contained the project that Mr. Howard wanted her to do next. He had been so pleased with *Puss in Boots* that he was now talking of doing an entire series of classic fairy tales, all to be illustrated by Ariel.

With a stir of interest she saw that he had sent her two different *Beauty and the Beast* books.

Though Ariel had a vague knowledge of the story, she had never read one of the many versions of the old folk tale. Lifting the larger of the volumes, she began to read and soon discovered that it was a much more powerful story than *Puss in Boots*. Moreover, the visual possibilities were enticing.

Ariel was halfway through when the back of her neck began to prickle. In an odd way the tale resembled her own life, though reality was sadder and more sordid.

At the end it was a relief to learn that Beauty and her Beast lived happily ever after. Ariel supposed that was why people read such fanciful tales: because real life couldn't be trusted to end as well. But as she set the story aside, she was haunted by the image of the Beast, who had almost died of sorrow when Beauty left him.

The rest of the day was taken up with festivities. She helped the Talbotts decorate the tree. After the girls were sent giggling to bed, the adults went to a nearby house where they shared hot mulled wine and conversation with a dozen other neighbors.

The small party helped distract Ariel from her misery. As she went to bed, she gave thanks that the next few days would be so busy. By the beginning of the New Year, she might be prepared to face her new life.

But the old life was not done with her, for she fell asleep and dreamed of *Beauty and the Beast*. She herself was Beauty, young and confused, first fearing the Beast who held her captive, then learning to love him. What turned the dream into nightmare was the fact that her captor was not a leonine monster but James. He was a haunted, noble creature who was dying for lack of love, and as life ebbed from him, he called out to her.

She awoke with an agonized cry. How could she have left him? How could she have let him send her away?

Even awake, she heard his voice in her mind, the deep, desolate tones echoing across the miles that separated them. She slid out of her bed, determined to leave instantly for Belleterre.

As soon as her feet hit the icy floor, she realized the foolishness of her impulse. It was three in the morning and she couldn't leave for hours yet. But she could pack her belongings so that she would be ready first thing. She threw herself into the task with frantic haste and was done in half an hour.

The thought of the hours still to wait made her want to shriek with frustration. Then inspiration struck. She settled down at her desk with drawing paper, pen, and ink.

Feeling as if another hand guided her own, she drew a series of pictures with feverish, slashing strokes. She had not bought a Christmas gift for her husband since he had been so firmly opposed to celebrating the holiday. Now she was creating a gift so vivid that it might as well have been drawn with her heart's blood rather than India ink.

As she wept over the last drawing, she prayed that he would accept it in the spirit offered.

The footman opened the front door of Belle-terre and blinked in surprise. "Lady Falconer?"

"None other," Ariel said crisply as she swept past him into the front hall. "Is my husband in the house?"

"No, my lady. I believe he intended to be out on the estate all day."

"Very well." She surveyed her surroundings, unsurprised to see that there wasn't a trace of holiday decoration. "Please ask Mrs. Wilcox to join me in the morning room immediately. Then have my things taken to my room. Be particularly careful of the drawing portfolio."

As the footman hastened to obey, Ariel went to the morning room, which was the smallest and friendliest of the public rooms. While she waited for the housekeeper, Tripod came skipping into the room.

The cat was halfway to Ariel before she remembered her grievance. With ostentatious disdain, Tripod sat down, her back turned to the mistress of the house who had dared to go away for so long. Only the twitching tip of her tail betrayed her mood.

"We'll have none of that, Tripod!" Ariel scooped the cat into her arms and began scratching around the feline ears. Within a minute, the cat started to purr and stretch her neck so that her chin could be scratched. Ariel hoped wryly that her husband would be as easy to bring around.

Soon Mrs. Wilcox joined her. Always dignified, today the housekeeper was positively arctic. In a voice that was only just within the bounds of politeness, she said, "Since your arrival was unexpected, your ladyship, it will take a few minutes to freshen your rooms."

Ignoring the comment, Ariel said, "How is my husband?" When the housekeeper hesitated, Ariel prompted, "Speak freely."

Mrs. Wilcox needed no more encouragement. "Very poorly, my lady, and it's all your fault! The master seems to have aged a hundred years since you left. How could you go away for so long, after all he's done for you?"

How bad was "very poorly"? Though she ached, Ariel kept her voice even. She was mistress of Belleterre, and she intended to fill the position properly. "I left because he sent me away," she said calmly. "It was very bad of me to obey him. It shan't happen again."

She set down the cat and stripped off her gloves. "I want every servant in the house put to work decorating Belleterre for the holidays. Greens, ribbons, wreaths, candles ... everything! Send a man to cut a tree for the morning room, and have the cook prepare a Christmas Eve feast. I realize that time is limited, but I'm sure Cook will do a fine job with what is available. Oh, whenever the table is set in the future, always put my place next to my husband's rather than at the far end."

Mrs. Wilcox's jaw dropped. Ariel added, "When doing the decorating and cooking, don't stint on the servants' quarters. I want this to be a holiday

Belleterre will never forget. Now off with you! There's much to be done."

"Yes, my lady," the housekeeper said, her eyes beginning to shine. She paused just before leaving the room. "You won't leave again, will you? He needs you something fierce."

"Wild horses won't get me away unless he comes, too," Ariel promised. She needed her husband something fierce herself.

# CHRISTMAS EVE

THE THOUGHT OF going back to the empty house was almost more than Falconer could bear. He was so weary in spirit that he didn't notice how brightly lit the house was, but when he entered the front hall he was struck by the scent of pine and holly.

He stopped, blinking at the sight that met his eyes. The hall was wreathed in garlands of greenery accented by scarlet berries and bows and a footman stood on a ladder, tucking shiny holly leaves behind a wall mirror for the final decorative touch.

Falconer demanded, "By whose order was this done?"

As the nervous footman fumbled for a reply, a clear, light voice said, "Mine, James."

He would recognize her voice anywhere, yet it was so unexpected that he couldn't believe she was really here. Even when he turned and saw his wife walking down the hall toward him, he was sure he must be hallucinating. Exquisite in a scarlet-trimmed gown, her flaxen tresses tied back simply with a black velvet bow, she had to be an illusion born of his despairing dreams.

But she certainly looked real. Stopping in front of him, Ariel said, "Come and see the tree before you go up to bathe and change for dinner."

Bemused, he followed her into the morning room, which was scented by tangy evergreens and sweet-burning apple wood logs. Ariel gestured at the tall fir that had been set up in one corner. "Patterson chose the tree. Lovely, isn't it?"

Hoarsely he said, "Ariel, why did you come back?"

"I am your wife and Belleterre is my home," she said mildly. "Where else would I be at Christmas?"

"I told you to spend the holiday with your friends!"

She linked her fingers together in front of her, the knuckles showing white. "When we married, you offered me a home. Are you withdrawing that offer?"

"You don't belong here!" Anguish lanced through him, as if a knife was being turned in his heart. He had thought that she understood and accepted that their lives should lie apart, but apparently not. Now he must go through the agony of saying the words out loud as he sent her away again. "You mustn't blight your life through misplaced loyalty, Ariel. Our marriage is one of convenience only. I'm almost twice your age. You're scarcely more than a child."

"I'm old enough to be your wife," she retorted.

He edged toward the shadowed end of the

room, trying desperately to keep his defenses from crumbling. "I never wanted a wife!"

"But you have one," she said softly. "Why do you run from me, James? I know I'm not clever, but I love you. Is it so unthinkable that we be truly married?"

"Love?" he said, unable to suppress his bitterness. "How could a beautiful girl like you possibly love a man like me?"

His words acted like a spark on tinder. "How dare you!" she said furiously, looking like a spun sugar angel on the verge of explosion. "Because men think me beautiful, do you think I have no heart? Do you think I am so superficial, so blinded by my own reflection in the mirror, that I cannot see your strength and kindness and wit? You insult me, my lord!"

Helplessly he said, "I meant no insult, Ariel, but how can you love a man whose face you have never seen?"

Her blue eyes narrowed. "If I were blind and could see nothing, would you think me incapable of love?"

"Of course not, but this is different."

"It's *not* different!" Her voice softened. "I fell in love with you because of your words and deeds, James. Compared to them, appearance is of no great importance."

When the black folds of his robe quivered she knew that he was deeply affected, but not yet convinced. She knelt by the tree and pulled out the portfolio of drawings she'd brought for him. "If you want to know how I see you, look at these."

Hesitantly he took the portfolio and laid it on a table.

Ariel stood next to him as he paged through the loose drawings. If any of her work had magic, it was this, for the drawings came straight from her heart and soul. The images made up a modern *Beauty and the Beast* and showed exactly how she had seen her husband, from her first glimpse of him at Gardsley to the present. Under each picture she had written a few spare words to carry the story.

James was the focus of every picture, forceful, mysterious, larger than life. Though his face was never shown, he was so compelling that the eye could not look elsewhere. He was the enigmatic Black Beast of Belleterre, his dark robes billowing about him like thunderclouds. He was the compassionate, patient Lord Falconer, caring for everyone and everything around him. And he was James, surrounded by adoring birds and beasts, for every creature who knew him could not help but love him.

Then he sent Ariel away. The last drawing showed him lying in the Belleterre woods on the point of death, his powerful body drained of strength and his great heart broken. Ariel wept beside him, her pale hair falling about them like a mourning veil. The legend below read, "*I heard your voice on the wind.*"

He turned to the last sheet and found a blank page. "How does the story end?" he asked, his voice shaking.

"I don't know," she whispered. "The ending hasn't been written yet. The only thing I know is that I love you."

He spun away, his swift steps taking him into the shadows at the far end of the room. There he stood motionless for an endless interval, his rigid back to Ariel, before he turned to face her. "I was ugly even as a child. My mother used to say what a pity it was that I took after my maternal grandfather. But that was normal ugliness and would not have mattered greatly. What you will see now is a result of what happened when I was eight."

She heard his ragged inhalation, saw the tremor in his hands as he raised them to his hood, then slowly pulled the folds of fabric down to his shoulders. Her eyes widened when she saw that he was entirely bald. That explained why she'd had the fleeting impression of a skull when she'd glimpsed him in the library.

Yet the effect, though startling, was not unattractive, for his head was well shaped and he had dark, well-defined brows and lashes. He might have modeled for an Asiatic warlord in a painting by one of the great Romantic artists.

Voice taut, he continued, "My mother was taking me to Eton for my first term, so we spent the night at Falconer House in London. That night there was a gas explosion in her bedroom. I woke and tried to help her, but she was already dead."

He raised his damaged left hand so Ariel could see it clearly. "This happened when I pulled her body from the burning room. The smaller scars on my scalp and neck were made by hot embers that fell on me." He touched his bare head. "Afterward I was struck with brain fever and was delirious for weeks. They thought I would die. Obviously I didn't, but my hair fell out and never grew back. I was never sent to school, either. It was considered 'unsuitable.' Instead my father installed me at a minor estate in the Midlands so he wouldn't have to see or think about me."

James closed his eyes for a moment, his expression stark. "Can you be as accepting in the particular as you were in the abstract?"

Ariel walked toward him, and for the first time their gazes met. His eyes were a deep, haunted gray-green, capable of seeing things most men never dreamed of. Coming to a stop directly in front of him, she said honestly, "You have the most beautiful eyes I've ever seen."

His mouth twisted. "And the rest of me? My father refused to look at me, my tutor often told me how lucky I was to have my hideousness visible rather than concealing it as most men do."

She smiled and shook her head. "You're a fraud, my love. I'm almost disappointed. I'd expected much worse."

His expression shuttered. "Surely you're not going to lie and call me handsome."

"No, you're not handsome." She raised her hands and skimmed her artist's fingers over the planes of his face, feeling the subtle irregularity of long-healed scars, the masculine prickle of end-of-the day whiskers. "You have strong, craggy bones. Too strong for the face of a child. Even without the effects of fire and fever, it would have taken years to grow into these features. Did you ever see a picture of Mr. Lincoln, the American president who was shot a few years ago? He had a similar sort of face. No one would ever call it handsome, but he was greatly loved and deeply mourned."

"As I recall, the gentleman did have a good head of hair," James said wryly.

Ariel shrugged. "A bald child would be startling, almost shocking. Yet now that you are a man, the effect is not unpleasant. Rather dramatic and interesting, actually."

She stood on her tiptoes and slid her arms around his neck, then pressed her cheek to his. As tension sizzled between them, she murmured, "Now that you have nothing to hide, will you promise not to send me away again? For I love you so much that I don't think I could survive another separation."

His arms came around her with crushing force. She was slim but strong, and so beautiful that he could scarcely bear it. "Unlike the Beast in your story, I can't turn into a handsome prince," he said intensely, "but I loved you from the first moment I saw you, wife of my heart, and I swear I will never stop loving you."

Her laughter rang like silver bells. "To be honest, in both the books Mr. Howard sent me, the handsome prince at the end was quite insipid. Your face has character. It has been molded by suffering and compassion and will never be boring." She tilted her head back, her shining gilt hair spilling over his wrists. Suddenly shy, she said,

"Did you notice what's above your head?"

He glanced up and saw mistletoe affixed to the chandelier, then looked back at her yearning face. Curbing his fierce hunger so that he wouldn't overwhelm her, he bent his head and touched his lips to hers. It was a kiss of sweetness and wonder, a promise of things to come. His heart beat with such force that he wondered if he could survive such happiness.

Instinct made him end the kiss, for they risked being consumed by the flames of their own emotions. Far better to go slowly, to savor every moment of the miracle they had been granted.

Understanding without words, Ariel said breathlessly, "It's time we changed for dinner, for it's going to take some time to decorate the tree. I brought some lovely ornaments from London. I hope you'll like them."

He kissed her hands, then released her. "I'll adore them."

Christmas Eve became a magical courtship. He discarded his robe. Then they dined close enough to touch knees and fingers rather than being separated by a dozen feet of polished mahogany. Laughing and talking, they turned the tree into a shining, candlelit fantasy.

The whole time, they were spinning a web of pure enchantment between them. Every brush of their fingertips, every shy glance, every shared laugh at the antics of Cerberus and Tripod, intensified their mutual desire.

When they went upstairs, he hesitated at her door, still not quite able to believe. Wordlessly she drew him into her room and went into his arms. As they kissed, he discovered an unexpected aptitude for freeing her from her complicated evening gown.

Her slim, curving body was perfect, as he had known it would be. With lips and tongue and hands, he worshiped her, as enraptured by her response as by the feel of her silken skin under his mouth. She was light and sweetness, the essence of woman that all men craved, yet at the same time uniquely Ariel.

She gave herself to him with absolute trust, and the gift healed the dark places inside of him. He could actually feel blackness crumbling until his heart was free of a lifetime of hurt and loneliness. Such vulnerability should have terrified him, but her trust called forth equal trust from him. Already he could scarcely remember the haunted man who had been unable to believe in love.

In return for her trust, he gave her passion, using all of his skill, all of his sensitivity, all of his tenderness. Their bodies came together as if they were two halves of the same whole that had finally been joined, and when she cried out in joyous wonder, it was the sweetest sound he'd ever heard.

After passion had been satisfied for the first time, they lay tranquil in each other's arms. He had never known such rapture, or such humility.

In the distance, church bells began to toll. "Midnight," he murmured. "The parish church rings the changes to celebrate the beginning of Christmas Day."

Ariel stretched luxuriously, then settled against him again. "Christmas. A time of miracles and new beginnings. What could be more appropriate?"

"Indeed." He brushed his fingers through her hair, marveling at the spun-silk texture. "I'm sorry, my love. I didn't get you a present."

She laughed softly. "You gave me yourself, James. What greater gift could I possibly want?"

THIS RECIPE IS my variation of a soup invented by a writer friend. Easy and hearty enough for a main meal.

## SAUSAGE SOUP

2 lb. bulk hot sausage (I use Jimmy Dean Hot, but not their Seriously Hot. Any well flavored sausage should do.)
2 – 3 large onions
4– 5 large, very firm, red potatoes cut into small cubes or rectangles or whatever. (Do not use potatoes that turn mushy easily!)
1 large (28 oz) can diced tomatoes, not drained.
1 regular can diced tomatoes, not drained
1 large can kidney beans, not drained

Brown sausage with onions, breaking up the sausage into smallish pieces. When brown, I usually drain to reduce the grease. Add tomatoes and kidney beans to meat and onions, bring to a simmer. Add cut up potatoes and cook gently until the potatoes are tender, about half an hour or so. You can correct the seasonings, but I find that the flavoring of the hot sausage is usually enough,.

Tasty and it matures and freezes well. Great on a cold winter day with crusty French or whole grain bread.

# ABOUT THE AUTHOR

A New York Times bestselling author, Mary Jo Putney was born in Upstate New York with a reading addiction, a condition with no known cure. Her entire writing career is an accidental byproduct of buying a computer for other purposes. She has won numerous awards, has had eleven RWA RITA nominations, two RITA wins, and RWA's 2013 Nora Roberts Lifetime Achievement Award. Though best known for her historical romances, she has also written contemporary women's fiction, paranormal historical, and YA historical time travel. Her stories invariably contain history, romance, and cats. She loves writing Christmas stories, and she's so distractible that she's amazed that she ever finishes a book.

FOR MORE INFORMATION, VISIT:
*https://maryjoputney.com/books/*
*https://books2read.com/u/38dQWd*
*https://books2read.com/u/mdD7Xd*

# The Kissing Bough

## PATRICIA RICE

# THE KISSING BOUGH

## PATRICIA RICE

THE KISSING BOUGH first appeared in A REGENCY CHRISTMAS in 1989. At the time, I was mostly writing American westerns with my characters making an occasional sailing stop in London. Due to my fascination with English literature and my need to know more about the historical events in the books I was reading, I'd been studying English history for years. The thought of having one of my  stories appear in an anthology with Mary Balogh and the late, great Edith Layton inspired my imagination.

I happily dug into obscure pamphlets on English Christmas traditions to research my story, but to my dismay, Christmas as we know it now was more Victorian than Regency. My soldier heroes wouldn't be coming home to huge fir trees adorned with hand-made ornaments. But kissing boughs are steeped deep in medieval English tradition, when a small tree top was hung at the entrance as a symbol of the holy trinity. The practice became more elaborate over time— and thus Diana could decorate the drawing room with greenery to her heart's content. And even with his one good arm, Jonathan could match her love and determination by hauling in the Yule log.

I hope my first Regency story inspires a lovely green Christmas of your own!

~*Patricia*

*A wounded warrior - a love lost long ago - can a kiss under the mistletoe change everything?*

DIANA CARRINGTON BALANCED a fragrant bundle of evergreen roping in one hand and precariously clung to the ladder with the other. Holding her breath, she lifted one kid slipper from the second rung to the third.

She had seen her father do this for years, and it had always seemed so simple. She just needed a little practice. Only it seemed such a long way down.

"Mama won't approve," her sister Elizabeth announced the instant she entered the drawing room.

Diana leaned toward the chandelier and swung the end of the greenery in what would have been a graceful arc had their father done it. The evergreen branches caught in the full sleeve of her black mourning gown and the whole loop tumbled. She shoved a disheveled brown curl out of her face and sighed in exasperation at the tangle.

Diana glanced down at Elizabeth's neat golden curls and sighed even louder.

Even in the black of deep mourning, Elizabeth's sunny coloring brightened the shadowed room. Diana felt like a crow despite the violet satin ribbons trimming her modishly cut black velvet. Black was simply not her color—or a Christmas color.

With another abrupt tug at the recalcitrant greenery, she almost succeeded in making the second loop match the first. "I am determined to make this a happy holiday. Papa would have wanted it," she said, as much for herself as Elizabeth.

"Papa would have wanted what?" The harried voice drifting in from the hall became a gasp of horror as Mrs. Carrington entered to see her eldest daughter swinging precariously near the crystal chandelier. "Diana, get down from there at once. I vow, I should think the twins nuisance enough without you adding to their deviltry. Elizabeth, fetch Goudge and have him bring down this nonsense at once!"

"No, Mama." Diana set her lips in a manner that she knew resembled her late father's stubborn expression. "Papa would have wanted to have the kissing bough just like every other Christmas. It's a tradition, and he wouldn't want us to break tradition."

"Diana, we're in mourning. Such decorations are inappropriate," Georgina Carrington remonstrated without conviction, reaching for her handkerchief to hide the tears.

Diana finished securing the garland without looking down at her mother's matronly figure. She wanted to cry herself, not just for the loss of her father but for all the heart-breaking losses of her twenty-two years. She had drowned her pillow with tears too many nights to count, and they had never made the pain go away. What she needed now was happiness and light, and she was determined to have it even if she must go against her mother's wishes.

"And what if Charles is allowed to come home? Do you want his first Christmas home in four years to be without candles and greenery? After all this time at war, should he be greeted with gloom?" Diana asked with the independence she'd learned these last months while her mother grieved.

At this mention of her eldest child, Mrs. Carrington surrendered the argument. "Don't raise your hopes, either of you," she warned. "And don't mention it to the boys. We don't know for certain that Charles can come home. It's been two months since he sent the letter, and he hasn't come yet. Maybe there is some difficulty in selling out his commission, and he hasn't wanted to worry us."

Or maybe he'd had the ill fortune to be wounded or killed after writing he was coming home, but Diane did not say the words they were all thinking. They had suffered one loss already these last months. To bear another would be too cruel a fate.

"He'll be here for Christmas if he can. Charles always loved Christmas. And who would carry in the yule log if he didn't come?" Elizabeth asked defiantly.

The ten-year-old twins burst into the room trailing the cold, fresh scent of the outdoors and carrying a basket of apples from the cold cellar. Oblivious to the solemn atmosphere in the dim drawing room, they bounced excitedly beneath the ladder, both talking at once.

"It's snowing, Di! Can we go sleigh riding?"

"Here's the apples, Di. Can I hang one, can I, Di, please?"

Mrs. Carrington closed her eyes and shuddered while Diana backed down the shaky ladder.

"We can't hang the apples until we tie on ribbons. Freddie, go ask Goudge what Father used to hang them. Frank, you need to fetch a box of candles. We can't go sleigh riding until there's enough snow for runners."

With a whoop, both boys ran off, content to be keeping busy.

"Perhaps we might have mincemeat pies and a pudding, after all," Mrs. Carrington said thoughtfully. "Charles might come home, and it would be dreadful to disappoint him." She trailed after the twins.

Sorting through the box of Christmas ribbon, Elizabeth cast a pensive glance at Diana. "Have the Drummonds heard from Jonathan? Do you think he and Charles are together?"

Diana pasted on a smile to hide her weepy fear and started back to the ladder with a green and red plaid streamer. "The Drummonds will be here tomorrow. You can ask, but I should think they would have written if they had had word."

"Fustian!" Sixteen-year-old Elizabeth expertly tied a bow in a red satin sash. "Mr. and Mrs. Drummond are so stiff-laced they read Marie's letters before she can post them. They won't allow Jonathan's name to be mentioned, but I know he writes. I just thought maybe Mrs. Drummond had said something to Mama."

Perched on the top of the ladder, Diana reached down for the bow Elizabeth handed to her. If she concentrated on her task, she could almost forget Jonathan existed. It had been four years, after all. She should be very good at pretending now. "Jonathan always was one to write. Remember when they went off to Oxford together, the only way we ever heard about Charles was when Marie brought Jonathan's letters to read to us? Maybe they have had a letter and Mr. Drummond won't let them speak of it. Mama will persuade it out of him tomorrow, if so."

The thought of Jonathan writing to his family cheered Elizabeth but only increased Diana's dismals. She had every reason to remember Jonathan's letters. Since they hadn't been formally betrothed when he went away to Oxford, he could not in all propriety write to her, but somehow he had managed to smuggle a missive or two to her whenever he could. Of course, it was only the continuation of a childish game, she told herself, but at the time those letters from her brother's handsome friend had been like diamonds and gold to her.

Even during the holidays Jonathan had still hidden letters in their secret cache, and she had left him flowers and favorite poems and whatever trinkets had pleased her that day. He had delighted in teasing her for her choices, but he had worn the flowers in his lapel and memorized the poems to surprise her.

She had loved him wildly then. Too wildly, she knew now. Looking into those passionate gray eyes and hearing his deep voice speak the poem she had said only to herself, she had fallen head over heels for Jonathan's charm despite the fact that he had never declared himself.

For the second time that evening tears threatened, and she jerked hastily on the streamer she was wrapping around the pine boughs. A loop started to come loose, and she grabbed for it just as the drawing room door bounced open again, admitting the twins.

"A coach and four! A smack-dab-up-to-the-rigs coach and four! Come see it, Diana! It's coming down the lane now!" Both young voices exclaimed this litany of excitement more or less in unison.

Diana steadied herself and threw an anxious look at the tall, mullioned windows covered now in heavy maroon drapery. Charles! It had to be Charles. He was the only one they knew mad enough to hire a coach and four to carry him to the back of nowhere. Her heart set up an erratic beat, but she dared not let her hopes rise too high.

"Well, it must be some poor person out in the

snow looking for shelter for the night. Or perhaps the Drummonds are here early. Go tell Goudge we're to have visitors while I try to finish this up. Hand me the apples, Freddie."

Diana's disinterest didn't douse the twins' excitement, and even Elizabeth deserted her to run to the windows and look out. Drawing back the draperies revealed a winding country lane filling with snow, the flakes white and dainty against the velvet backdrop of the night. Within minutes the carriage lamps grew brighter and the crack of a whip and a faint "Halloo!" echoed down the road. The twins dashed for the foyer, screaming with delight.

Determinedly, Diana continued hanging the ribbons amid the greenery. She dearly wished to see her brother again, safe and sound and at home at last, but she could not bear the thought of some stranger descending from that carriage.

"Two gentlemen, Diana! I see them climbing out!" Elizabeth reported from the window where she peeked discreetly from behind the draperies. "They've tall beaver hats and greatcoats and mufflers and Hessians, Di! Oh, they look very grand, just like they must in London. Oh, Diana, do you think I will ever be allowed to go to London with Marie?"

Since this complaint had been heard ever since Elizabeth had turned sixteen, Diana ignored it in favor of the description of the gentlemen. They knew few London gentlemen, so these must be strangers come to ask the way. They would probably drive on shortly. Or perhaps Mama would ask them in for tea before turning them out again to the cold. She really ought to climb down and make herself respectable, but her heart wasn't in it. She so much wanted it to be two other gentlemen out there that she wouldn't be able to hide her disappointment.

"Oh my, Diana! I think they're a trifle foxed! One just slipped on the road, and the other is laughing and holding him up. Oh, Diana, it has to be Charles. I know it does!"

Elizabeth flew from the room, leaving Diana perched on the ladder biting back tears and praying as rapidly as she knew how.

The draft from the opening of the double front doors spun the ribbons and threatened the candle flames. Diana kept to her self-appointed task despite the excited chatter outside the drawing room door.

Two gentlemen, Elizabeth had said. It couldn't be. She wouldn't believe it. Superstitiously, she remained where she was, doggedly reaching for the next apple and the next bough. If she climbed down, it wouldn't be them. If she stayed on the ladder, it had to be them.

"Diana! I've brought you a Christmas present! Where in blazes are you?"

The laughing, familiar voice filled her heart with joy, and Diana turned eagerly, nearly toppling the ladder in her haste to greet her older brother. He was, indeed, wearing a snow-dusted great coat and looking exceptionally proud of himself.

Behind him, another caped figure emitted

a curse, presumably at the sight of her swaying indelicately on the ladder.

Before she could hasten down, an elegantly clad arm with the strength of a vise clasped her waist, and she was lifted from her precarious throne. She scarcely had time to register astonishment before she was on her feet again, staring into once familiar eyes that had turned cold and forbidding since she had seen them last. He'd been injured!

She covered a cry of shock with her hand. He dropped his arm and turned away.

The chestnut hair she remembered falling over a high, intelligent brow now tumbled over an ugly raw gash. The arm that had so easily hauled her from the ladder sported a hand useless in its cover of white gauze. His undamaged hand gripped a walking stick to prevent placing weight on a leg he obviously favored.

Irrationally, when he turned away, fury swept through her.

The hand Diana had raised to cover her shock should have worn a ring he knew by heart, but it didn't. The knowledge hurt, but her shock at his appearance stabbed more bitterly than any wound he had suffered at the hands of Napoleon's army.

Stiffly, Jonathan Drummond glared at the traitorous friend who had forced him here. "I told you I shouldn't have come, Carrington. The coach can take me on to the manor. I'll be on my way, then."

"You great clodding sapskull, you terrify my sister and then expect to walk out without apology or explanation? Besides, there's no one at the manor; if you remember the letter I showed you. This is our year to do the celebrations. Take off the dratted coat, and I'll find us some brandy."

Jonathan glowered while his friend basked in the attention from his family. Charles's hair gleamed golden in the firelight as he threw off his hat, and the elderly butler happily gathered up his outer garments. While Mrs. Carrington tearfully hugged her prodigal son, the twins and his younger sister crowded around with excited chatter.

Charles deserved his homecoming. The two of them had seen too much war.

Jonathan withdrew into the shadows, doubting his welcome given the circumstances of his departure.

As the brandy materialized, Jonathan gripped the goblet and watched Diana deliberately turning her back on him while she hugged her brother. Jonathan studied the lovely young woman who had grown from the pretty girl he had once courted. Her soft brown curls hung in charming ringlets about a throat as graceful as any swan's. The laughter he had remembered curving mischievous lips had faded. He understood and wished only that the floor would open up and swallow him. He should never have come, not like this, perhaps not at all.

When she left her brother's side and turned in his direction, Jonathan bowed politely. "I apologize if I frightened you, but you had no business on a ladder. You could have tangled your feet in the hem of that flimsy little gown and broken your neck."

The dangerously tottering ladder had raised visions of all the deaths he'd seen during four years of war. He had reacted instinctively—and stupidly.

"It looks to me as if I have learned to take better care of myself than you have, Mr. Drummond," she said with a hint of irritation. "And it's my neck, if I choose to break it, as you have so recklessly chosen to risk yours."

"Diana! Upon my word, is that any way to greet a guest? Jonathan, give me that coat and go sit yourself by the fire. Your mother will never forgive me if I let you catch a chill. Here, Goudge." Mrs. Carrington took the greatcoat Jonathan grudgingly surrendered and handed it to the servant. "Frankie, Freddie, give Charles a hug and take yourselves upstairs to Nanny. He'll still be here in the morning when you come down."

When the twins protested, Charles grabbed their elbows and steered them toward the hall and stairs, whispering something excruciatingly funny in their ears. Bereft of her sons, Mrs. Carrington fluttered uncertainly about the room, then hurried off on other errands, leaving Elizabeth and Diana to entertain him.

Apparently unaware of any tension, Elizabeth practiced the formal etiquette of the tea table. Jonathan was surprised that she was old enough to do so, and that Diana allowed Elizabeth to take her place pouring tea.

Instead of sitting down for a cup so he might join her, Diana defiantly returned to the ladder.

"Did you stop to see your family in London before bringing Charles home, Mr. Drummond?" Elizabeth inquired politely.

Just out of the schoolroom, she was unaccustomed to dealing with elegant male strangers, particularly ones who favored brandy to tea and glared at her sister with such ... venom? Elizabeth didn't think that was the word, and she cast a quick look at Diana, now fastening the last batch of apples on the boughs.

Her sister looked particularly pretty tonight with her cheeks all flushed from working so hard on the kissing bough and her curls all disheveled just like in the ladies' books. The black velvet gown with the lovely violet ribbons contrasted nicely with the whiteness of her throat and shoulders, and Elizabeth wished she had thought of fastening a ribbon about her neck since jewelry was forbidden. It looked quite fashionably simple, and she had a glimmer of understanding of why Mr. Drummond kept staring at Diana.

This near-stranger tore his gaze away from Diana to reply. "My parents apparently left before us. Since they don't seem to be here yet, I suppose they chose to rest overnight while we rode on. That's their usual style. They should be here by morning, I venture to say."

Above them, Diana gritted her teeth at this stilted speech. The Jonathan she had known had been full of life and laughter and eagerness. He

had defied his father by saving his quarterly allowance until he had enough to buy his commission
into the cavalry. He had gone off to war determined to defeat Napoleon and return a hero.

Now here he was, wounded and ill and probably half-foxed, sounding as pompous and bored
as his curmudgeon father. She had half a mind
to throw an apple at him where he sat sulking
behind the barricade of a great wing chair.

As if in answer to her thoughts, Charles returned,
glanced from her to Jonathan, and scowled.

"Get down from there, puss. That's my job."
Charles grabbed her waist and hauled her down.
Then, throwing off his long-tailed frock coat, he
climbed the flimsy ladder, nearly reaching the
ceiling when he stood on the top rung. "Now
give me the rest of those apples. You would never
have got this top branch right."

"Charles!" Diana gasped as he swayed alarm-
ingly. "Do come down, Charles. You do not look
at all safe up there."

Jonathan observed his friend's assumption of
the role of man of the house with wry interest,
and he, too, raised a skeptical eyebrow. "I daresay
you enjoyed the innkeeper's punch a trifle too
much, Carrington. You'll make a proper botch
of a perfectly good garland if you don't climb
down."

"I can hold my liquor as well as you, Drummond, and you had twice as much of the grog.
You just rest there like a proper invalid and let me
take care of things. Diana, where's the mistletoe?"

"Mistletoe?" Diana stared dubiously upward at

her slightly wobbly brother. He looked remarkably handsome in his crisp white cravat and linen, and she was thrilled to have him home again, but he was just a wee bit too tipsy for his own well-being. "You do remember this is a house of mourning, Charles? I don't think Mama would approve of something quite as frivolous as mistletoe."

Her words had an instant effect. Charles stared down at his sisters in their stiff mourning and went silent. He climbed down a few steps, then suddenly slumping over the ladder, he propped his elbows on a rung and held his head in his hands. "Do you think I can forget, Diana? Do you think for one instant of these last months I have thought of anything else but you and Mama and the children and how selfish I have been? I should have been here. I shouldn't have to be notified by letter a month after the fact. Devil take it, I left him to die alone with only women and children at his side." His voice rose as he spoke, and he pounded the trembling ladder with his fist for emphasis.

Jonathan rose and grasped his arm to help him down. "He was proud of you, Carrington. You showed me his letters, remember? He was as proud of your accomplishments as if they had been his own. Be glad of a father like that. You could have had mine."

Shocked by the bitterness she had never before heard in Jonathan's voice, Diana glanced in his direction—as she had tried very hard not to do since he'd entered.

Even with the vicious scar across his brow, Jonathan was a handsome man. His deep-set eyes held wells of compassion. She had seen his heavy eyebrows frown like thunderclouds when he observed injustice. His aquiline nose and distinguished cheekbones revealed his pride, however. The years of war had worn away any forgiving softness, and the taut lines of his features revealed the man who had once been a pampered boy. She gulped back a heartbroken sob at what had once been and was now lost.

Mrs. Carrington entered as Charles climbed down, dispelling the silence that had fallen. "I have the servants airing your rooms and warming baths for the both of you. You must be weary. Elizabeth, it's time for you to retire. I will need your help with the twins in the morning. Diana, if you would come to the kitchen, I need to discuss tomorrow's menu."

Diana and Elizabeth exchanged glances of surprise over their mother's renewed energy, but hastened to comply. While Elizabeth trailed in their mother's wake and Charles carried out the box of ornaments, Diana gathered the nearly untouched tea tray and cups. Jonathan lingered in the doorway, watching. She studiously pretended he had left with the others.

"I liked your father. I have not offered my sympathy at your loss."

Diana started. His deep, masculine voice had had often caught her by surprise when he came home for the holidays and spoke from behind a door or wall or tree. The same thrill went through her now when she had no right to feel it.

She swung around to face him. He was not just a fantasy in her mind any longer but a man, a soldier returned from war, a person with dreams and a life of his own. Once, she had thought that life would include her. His cold silence since he had departed for the war had taught her differently.

"He was ill only a brief time. Perhaps it was better that way. It just seems very ... strange, without him." To her disgust, Diana felt her eyes filling with tears again. She so desperately wanted to be cosseted and told everything would be all right, but as the eldest, she had been the one to comfort the others. There had been no time for self-indulgence.

Jonathan heard the way her voice broke over the words, felt her anguish, and wished he had the power to give her the comfort that she needed. She had made her antipathy clear from the moment he had walked into the house, however, and he had too much pride to take a second rejection. He still did not understand the first.

"Things have changed all over, Janey." He used the secret name they had chosen when they were children. "It's a part of life and growing up. Sometimes it's for the good, sometimes it's not." He shrugged and glanced around him. "This room, even. I like the painting of the hunt. That's new. But I miss the old secretary. Whatever happened to it?"

At this casual mention of the old hiding place for their childish notes and secret love letters, Diana turned away. "The twins ... The twins decided to experiment with fire with the pair of candles we kept there. The blotter they were test-ing—" she hiccuped on what could have been a sob or laughter— "went up in a sheet of flame, scorching the desk, not to mention their little fingers. Mama always meant to have it refinished, but she never did. I suppose it's still up in the attic."

A sudden, extremely painful thump paralyzed Jonathan's heart. It could not be. It was not pos-sible, was it? All these years, all these confounded lonely years thinking she had rejected him ... Could she really not have known he would never have left her without a word?

Tentatively, he probed for more information. "That must have been some time ago. They look too old for such mischief now."

Diana gave a shaky laugh and finished gath-ering the last of the cups. "They are only just recovering from broken bones after falling from the apple tree, but at least they have learned their lesson about fire. It's been nearly four years since they've touched a candle, since a little after that Christmas when you left, as a matter of fact."

A little after Christmas. There had been time, then. She should have found it. He had no rea-son to hope. Jonathan sighed and offered a polite bow. "Then we can all go to our beds without fear of waking up in flames. I'll leave you to your tasks, Diana. Good night."

Once the door closed behind this cold stranger,

the tears flowed, accompanied by great wrenching sobs. Diana curled up on the window seat,
buried her face in a pillow, and cried like the
child she had once been. For years, she'd har-
bored just the tiniest sliver of hope… But that
hope was smashed now. Jonathan didn't love her,
had probably never loved her. Somehow, she had
to pretend it didn't matter.

Her mother had to plan the Christmas menu
without her help, after all.

By the next morning Diana had recovered
from her momentary lapse of self-pity, and no
trace of last night's tears remained. Since it was
the day before Christmas, she defiantly decided
the occasion warranted her first break from full
mourning, and she donned a lavender percale
gown that pleated gracefully in back. Although it
was a simple morning gown, the velvet-ribboned
sleeves and shoulder ruffles made her feel femi-
nine and sophisticated.

She crimped the hair about her face so it curled
attractively for a change. Let Jonathan see what
he had given up when he had chosen life as a
soldier over her.

She was late coming down, but Charles was
later. There was no sign of her brother as Diana
joined her mother and sister in the dining room.
Jonathan, however, had apparently overcome last
night's excesses and sat sipping coffee at one end
of the table. Diana noticed his untouched plate
in passing, but thought nothing of it until she sat
down with her own breakfast of muffins, ham,
and soft-boiled egg. The minute she held her egg

cup with one hand and lifted her knife to crack her egg shell with the other, she understood Jonathan's dilemma.

"Good morning, Diana," said her mother. "Will you be certain Cook doesn't double up the spices in the pudding this morning? I want to freshen the linens in the guest rooms before everyone arrives." Without stopping for her daughter's agreement, Mrs. Carrington smiled at their single guest. "I hope you slept well last night, Jonathan. Your appetite didn't used to be so poor."

"I've learned to live without, Mrs. Carrington. It will take some time to develop the habit of eating well again." Jonathan looked up at Diana's entrance, and in the spirit of Christmas, offered a tentative smile in greeting.

Diana buttered her muffin, then set half on his plate. "Then you should begin breaking bad habits now. That dreadful brew will ruin your digestion, else-wise."

Jonathan's smile grew as he accepted her muffin. "You always did have a way with words, Diana," he murmured before biting hungrily into the muffin he could not have managed to butter with one hand.

"I should rather like to be thought of as a person who acts instead of talks," she responded tartly, breaking open her egg and neatly scooping the contents onto his plate, mashing it so he could use a fork to eat it instead of chasing the egg cup about the table. "Words aren't very reliable."

"It is common knowledge that actions speak

louder than words," Jonathan agreed. The egg was delicious, but he couldn't show his gratitude while she poked at still festering wounds. Diana was never one to carry out conversations on a single level. She was baiting him, and he didn't like it. He didn't think he would like being treated as an invalid, either, but Diana was somehow making it very easy to accept his limitations.

Perhaps that was because she thought of him more as a brother than a lover, or even a rejected lover. In all these years of puzzling over her actions, he had never once considered that possibility, and it was a very likely one. They had grown up together. Just because he had felt their relationship had been a special one did not mean she thought of him as more than her brother's friend. The likelihood depressed him even further, and he couldn't bring himself to say thank you when she matter-of-factly placed the cut-up sections of ham on his plate.

A startling bellow interrupted from above stairs. "By the devil, I'll have you martyred and hung upon the cross if you're not out of here at once!"

"Charles!" Scandalized, Mrs. Carrington hastily pushed away from the table and hurried to chastise her eldest and to assess the twins' damage.

Charles didn't wait for help to arrive. He appeared in the upper hall still in shirt sleeves and stockings, one guilty twin caught by the collar in each hand. Seeing his audience streaming from the dining room below, he shook the rascals and held them up for all to see.

"They're too blood—" he cut his curse off

short and rephrased the oath— "too young for catechism class! They've made the Last Supper out of my last bottle of wine. Where the h—" Again, he stopped to rephrase. "Where is their d—" Giving up in disgust, he released his brothers. "The army is easier. Where's their nanny? I can't dress with this mess stinking up the room."

Jonathan smothered a grin, but Diana's muffled giggles made it difficult to keep a straight face. The twins looked decidedly green around the edges as they ran to their mother for comfort.

"Don't worry, Charles," Diana called out sweetly. "The maids haven't forgotten how to take care of drunken little boys. I'll send someone straight up."

Charles glared down at her. "See if I do you any more favors, Miss Jane."

"And when have you ever done me any?" she demanded, irked that he had used the private name only Jonathan should have known. She turned but Jonathan was leaning against the door jamb, eating his toast and watching the entertainment.

From his lofty perch, Charles glared down at his friend. "Drummond, we're going after the yule log just as soon as I break my fast. No excuses." He stalked back up the stairs.

Puzzled, Diana studied Jonathan's noncommittal expression, but he merely shrugged and asked, "He didn't have his cravat on yet, did he? It will be another hour before we see him again. I, for one, prefer to return to the table." And he did so, leaving Diana to stare after him with bewilderment and a new awareness of his physical presence that left her shaken.

The boy's shoulders she remembered so well had broadened into those of a man, a man accustomed to the rigors of a soldier's life. Muscular arms strained the seams of his civilian coat, and his athletic grace and masculine strength made a mockery of any injuries. Obviously, his wounds were such as not to limit a man of his stature to any great degree.

She could detect no bandages beneath the knit of his trousers, but she suspected Jonathan's pride would prevent him from wearing bandages if they were at all to be avoided. She almost felt his wince of pain as he entered the dining room and reached for a chair. Were his wounds so painful that he could not relax and be himself, or had the war changed him?

She had loved Jonathan Drummond for as long as she could remember, since she had been too little for him to notice. He had been just one of her older brother's many friends, but he had always been special. He was the only one who had spoken to her, treated her as an equal, and she had adored him. Later, when they were older, their families had shared their holidays, and there were picnics and romps and theatricals where they had just naturally paired off together, or against each other, depending on their ages or the game.

Diana remembered a particular snowball fight where she managed to catch him squarely in the head, and he had chased her until they both tumbled down a hill of snow, soaking themselves thoroughly. They had both caught a chill that day, but he had arranged to send her a bouquet from their greenhouse to cheer her sickroom. It was that next summer when his nonsensical notes began to take a more serious vein. The hiding place in the old secretary that had been their cache of secret jokes became a place to exchange private thoughts.

Diana watched as Jonathan adjusted his injured leg beneath the cloth and propped his bandaged hand upon the table. Four years couldn't have made him a total stranger. Charles had not changed that much. Why should Jonathan hate her now when he had at least considered her to be a friend before?

She could no longer bear the suspense of wondering. He was alive and here and she would find out. That was the smallest price he would have to pay for leaving her with a heart that would not open to anyone else.

He nodded without smiling when she returned to her breakfast. Mrs. Carrington and Elizabeth had run off to direct the settling of the twins' latest disaster, so there was no one to monitor their conversation. Not that Jonathan invited conversation, Diana thought wryly as he lifted his cup of coffee with his undamaged hand.

"Where did you take your injuries?" Trying her best to be as cool and sophisticated as this stranger across from her, Diana added more hot water to her tea.

"No grand battle but the retreat from Burgos," Jonathan said with distaste. "Your brother has been seeing to my welfare. That is why he was so late in returning. I don't suppose it occurred to him to write and tell you that, and unfortunately, I was not in a position to do so. I am exceedingly grateful for his care. The army surgeons would no doubt have insisted on amputation, and I would still be in some fly-infested tent if he had not come to my rescue."

Diana's eyes widened in horror as she gazed on the gauze-enshrouded hand resting amid the china and silver. That was his writing hand, his right hand. He could have lost it forever. The fear of loss must have been as great as the physical pain.

Determined not to let Jonathan see how he had upset her, Diana rested her gaze on the raw scar of his forehead and quizzically raised an eyebrow. "Amputation of the head would have been a tri-fle drastic, but I daresay it would have relieved any concern about the flies."

His table companion said this with such a straight face that Jonathan nearly choked on a swallow of coffee. He had forgotten Diana's dry sense of humor, or rather, he had forgotten its effect on him. She was much too beautiful in the mornings for his senses to resist. The physical urge to gather her into his arms and kiss that sassy mouth into submission had to be prevented in some way.

"Your sympathy is gratifying. I shall always remember it with fondness." Collecting himself, he returned to his coffee.

"Then let me give you something else to

remember with fondness." Diana rose precipitously from her chair and overturned his plate and carefully cut breakfast into his lap.

Without further word, she sailed from the room trailing lavender ribbons.

Jonathan almost smiled as he contemplated the remains of his breakfast running down his once immaculate trousers. In some ways, Diana hadn't changed at all, and he felt oddly relieved that the little hoyden still remained behind all her stylish beauty. And there certainly couldn't be any pity lingering there if she felt free to take advantage of his temporary handicaps. In another time and place he would have chased after her and made her pay for her temerity, but he was no longer that heedless boy, just as she was no longer the pigtailed girl who would wrestle him to the ground. Just the thought of such a combat roused definitely unchildish desires.

With a grimace at his response to a woman who had made it quite clear that she held him in disfavor, Jonathan struggled from his lonely seat and set out to find clean trousers.

Charles found him sometime later—staring up the narrow back stairs to the attics. He slapped a hand to Jonathan's back and steered him toward the main staircase. "The maids don't sleep up there, old fellow, if you've taken a sudden penchant for slap and tickle. It's too damn hard to heat those rooms."

Jonathan scowled. "I bloody well don't give a damn where they sleep. I owe you a great deal, Charles, and don't think I'm ungrateful, but this won't work. You should have left me in London."

"To do what, may I ask? Hide from your father? Or Diana? Or both? Devil take it, Drummond, but you're a bloody great hero on the field, and a complete horse's ass on home ground. You have the courage to stand up against the worst Boney could send you, but you haven't the backbone to stand up to one sharp-tongued female. You're the one who has thrown his cap over a wind-mill for that frippery sister of mine. I could have warned you it was a foolish piece of business. Diana's a right one, but she can be mighty high in the instep when she wants to be. She's not so easy-natured as your Marie."

"Marie is a senseless chit, even if she is my sis-ter. And I'm damned sorry you ever got near me while I was fevered. Remind me never to become ill again."

The two men clattered down the last of the stairs and into the hall where the butler waited with their greatcoats and mufflers. Unoffended by Jonathan's irascibility, Charles grinned and shrugged into the caped coat.

"On the contrary, you should be ill more often. It's quite an enlightening experience. You're a damned close-mouthed devil, Drummond. I had no idea your passion for my sister had gone so out of hand as to stoop to pet names! Come on, nodcock, let us find a log that will last into eter-nity. That will show them what kind of stuff we're made of."

They disappeared into the blowing cold of a white-laced winter wonderland.

The yule log arrived while Diana was completing the greenery in the drawing room later on Christmas Eve. Besides the kissing bough in the center of the ceiling, she had decorated the mantel candelabra with ivy and holly and made a centerpiece of evergreen branches intertwined with ivy for the spinet. Already several small gifts dangled tantalizingly from the boughs on the ceiling, and Diana smiled as a gust of wind from the open front door sent them dancing. Her father had initiated the tradition of hanging gifts when they were very young and the kissing bough's mistletoe meant nothing to them. This year, only the gifts would be there. The mistletoe was not only perilous to cut down from the thorny hawthorn, but inappropriate for a house of mourning. But she could not resist the gift tradition.

Jonathan and Charles carried in the enormous log meant to burn for the next twelve days. Not many houses had fireplaces large enough for the old custom, but the drawing room in the old part of Carrington House was ideal for the purpose. The enormous room had a fireplace that engulfed one wall. Dwarfed by the towering stone and timber fireplace, Diana balanced precariously on the edge of a wing chair as she added another piece of ivy to her bouquet.

She climbed down from her perch, nearly dancing with delight as she inspected the beribboned log. "It is lovely. I do believe it is the best log ever. It will make a splendid sight when you light it tonight. Do we have any of last year's chips left to light it with?"

"How am I supposed to know? You were here, not me, but I shouldn't think Father would have forgotten to set a few pieces aside," Charles admonished, brushing off his gloves.

At this mention of their father, Diana's delight faded. Last year, that had been her father lowering the log to the grate. As much as she admired Jonathan's strength in maneuvering it with one hand, he was not the father who had loved her. Nor the man she had hoped would love her. Half-heartedly, she pressed a kiss to her brother's cheek in gratitude.

Charles pulled off his gloves and circled her shoulders. "I'm sorry, Di. I have been tormenting myself for weeks for not being here when you needed me. It's hard to come home and act cheerful when there's this big gaping hole that he used to fill."

Diana nodded in understanding. "I keep waiting for him to come through the door and yell for the twins and spin Mama around the room as he did when he had a good day. I miss talking to him in the evenings. I even miss his scolding. I catch myself sounding just like him sometimes when the twins are in the briars."

Jonathan slipped unobtrusively to the door to escape this family scene, but Charles caught him before he could escape.

"Don't bolt yet, Drummond. The greenery ain't up yet in the hall and unless you want Diana climbing up there to do it by herself, you'd better stay here to help. The twins are in their best clothes, and I promised Mama to keep them entertained until their keeper returns from the village, so I'm taking them out." He ignored Diana's dubious look. "Goudge ain't much help, but he may lend a hand if you need him."

Releasing Diana, Charles reached up to spin one of the dangling packages. "Or, Jonathan, you can take the twins and I'll help Diana."

"Heaven forbid." Jonathan raised expressive eyes to the ceiling. "I'd rather face Boney himself than those two. Were we ever like that?"

Diana nibbled a fingernail as she contemplated her older brother and his friend. "Don't I remember a time when the two of you put me in an empty barrel and sent me down Scott's Hill? And then, of course, there was the time—"

"Don't let her start!" Charles dodged a Chippendale sofa in his effort to reach the door before she could continue. "She'll make the heathens look like saints before she's through."

He was gone, leaving her with a pensive Jonathan. "I am nearly done decorating," she lied. "You don't need to help me unless you wish. Mama's right. This is a house of mourning—I should not be so frivolous."

"I should think a little frivolity is what we all need right now. I speak for myself, of course." He grimaced as he gestured with his bandaged hand. "But the twins and Elizabeth are young yet. They need things to be the way they used to be, just for a little while. It's hard on them."

"You've changed, Johnny." She saw him stiffen

at this boyhood name and regretted her famil-
iarity. He was no longer a lanky adolescent but
a man full grown, a gentleman she had trouble
recognizing. His windswept chestnut hair tumbled across the sun-darkened brow of a seasoned
soldier who had spent years on foreign shores.
What had made her think he would have any
interest in a country miss such as herself? She had
not even a London bronze to catch his eye or
hold his attention.

"You've changed, too," he reminded her.
"You're not a skinny little girl in pigtails or a
bluestocking with her nose in a book or even
a hoyden who can climb trees with the best of
them. We all grow up."

Diana cut viciously with her pruning shears at
the evergreen branch she was trimming. "I still
read books and can climb trees as well as the twins.
In happier times, I even know how to laugh. But
not you. You look just like your father when you
glare at me like that with your nose up in the air
and that disapproving frown between your eyes."

"Do I?" To put the lie to her words, a twinkle began to gleam in those maligned features.
He removed the branch she was butchering and
gave a quick twist to the wire tying it to a second branch. "Then perhaps my father will find
me so changed he will forgive me for my tres-
passes. One can always hope. And what about
you, Diana? Have you found a suitor who will
read poems to you and admire your collection of
antiquities?"

"Oh, they always read poems to me when

they find out I like them," she answered crossly, twisting a ribbon around the roping taking shape beneath his capable fingers. Even with one hand Jonathan managed the unwieldy branches better than she. "And they mutter suitable exclamations when I show them my pieces of Roman pottery. And then they go on to talk as if I hadn't half a brain in my head or the wit to know the difference. I really don't think men are all that necessary. I can keep the accounts as well as my father could. He had managers to oversee his various interests. I could do that if they'd let me. But no, they must pat me on the head and tell me what a good little girl I am, and why don't I fetch them a cup of tea? Men! They are a thoroughly useless lot."

"You go too far, Janey. Would you march to war without us?"

"There wouldn't be any war without men," she answered blithely.

"You have a point there. But look at the women you know. How many of them are capable of keeping the government running?"

"About as many as there are men." Diana looked up from her ribbon-tying to find Jonathan watching her, a grin pulling at the corners of his mouth. He was leading her down the garden path, but she didn't care. She'd never played coy with Jonathan and would not start now. She twitched his self-importance again. "Why should a woman marry when all it ensures is a lifetime of cooking and cleaning while the man carouses? Any sensible female must see that marriage isn't made in heaven but in a much more earthly place."

"Oh, I'll agree with that. If it weren't for earthly pleasures, no self-respecting male would find himself leg-shackled to a shrewish female who complains night and day and gives him no peace until he is in his grave. I am certain it is only the desire to breed heirs that keeps the custom of marriage alive. I can't remember your feeling that way before. You certainly have changed more than I imagined. It is a relief to learn that now."

"You are not what I once thought you to be either," Diana responded tartly. "I can remember once when you enjoyed my company instead of calling me a shrewish female. But of course, that was when you were inclined to wager on whether the first leaf would fall from the oak or birch, and you enjoyed wrestling on the lawns with children and teasing shrewish females. That was back before you lost your sense of humor and became your father, when you knew how to laugh."

"Ah yes, I remember that time. And didn't I used to pull hair ribbons and run away and hide them where shrewish females couldn't find them? Like this?" And to Diana's dismay, Jonathan leaned over the table and slipped one of the ribbons from her hair, causing a tumble of thick tresses to cascade over her shoulder. Before she could grab it away, his long legs carried him toward the door, his limp not hampering his swiftness to any great degree.

"Jonathan Drummond, you give that back! I

haven't another to match and your family will be here any minute!" Brushing a shower of evergreen branches from her lap, she jumped up and raced after him.

"You'll never find it!" he cried out from the top of the stairs as Diana dashed into the hall.

"Jonathan, upon my word, I will pull every hair from your head if I catch you!" Lifting her skirts, Diana raced up the stairway after him.

Diana located Jonathan perched on the attic stairs with no sign of the ribbon in sight. She grinned in satisfaction and sat comfortably on the step below him. The high stickler from the drawing room now appeared more like the Jonathan she remembered, with his hair down over his forehead and a smile dancing about his lips.

"You can't hide up there anymore. Mama keeps the attic locked ever since Freddie fell asleep in one of the trunks and disappeared for hours. So now give me my ribbon."

Jonathan ignored her outstretched hand and looked contemplatively at the door that kept him from discovering the secrets of the old desk. Perhaps it was better he not know if the ring remained concealed in the hidden drawer. What could he do if it still were? Diana was a grown woman now, not the impressionable little girl he had hoped to persuade to wait for him.

Besides, he had even less to offer her now than he had had then. His father most likely had disowned him, and if there were any chance his hand would not mend properly, he had few means of making a living. With neither home nor means of support, he could not renew his suit. It would be better to let old wounds heal, but in four years the one in his heart showed no sign of closing.

"I guess that eliminates a fast game of hide and seek. Shall we bob for apples next?" Jonathan pulled the crumpled ribbon from his pocket and dangled it tauntingly just out of her reach.

"You may join the twins at the apples, if you wish. Besides, hide and seek isn't any fun. You always knew my favorite hiding place, even if you pretended you didn't."

In the narrow, walled stairwell, Diana seemed dangerously close to him. They must have been much smaller when they used to hide up here and talk while the others searched for them. Jonathan's leg now rested daringly close to her knees. Yet, boldly, she didn't flinch from the proximity.

"I wanted to make certain I was the one to find you. I was an amazingly selfish young man, wasn't I?"

"You most certainly were," Diana said. "I'll not ever forgive you for slipping off to war without thinking to tell me first. That was the height of your selfish career,"

"You don't know the half of it, my lovely Janey." Wistfully, Jonathan swung the ribbon within her reach and watched as she grabbed it to twist and bind in her straying locks. In an effort to determine just how and where she had found out about his leaving—had it been from his letter or some other source first?—he asked, "Where were you when you heard the news?"

"Sick in bed." Diana made a face of disgust.

"I caught the twins' chicken pox. I was so mad at them, and then I was mad at you and Charles when I heard the news. I couldn't believe it. I must have been delirious. I was going to ride out after you and ring a proper peal over your heads. I suspect my mother gave me laudanum to keep me quiet. When I woke, Elizabeth brought me a rose on my breakfast tray, and I knew you weren't coming back. I never have been able to pry out of her where she found a rose at Christmas, but it was like receiving a funeral wreath, I guess. I just knew you weren't coming to hold my hand and make me laugh anymore."

"A rose?" The word emerged more as groan than question. A rose. She had thought it a farewell.

He had assumed Diana would find the signal indicating a message waited for her when he placed it on the old desk. A rose in winter. He had been very proud of that romantic gesture.

But she had never seen it on the desk and had never known he had sneaked through the window that night to place it there. How could she have known? What a stupid, childish fool he had been. The chances were very good she had never found his letter, and now it lay resting somewhere above, moldering away with his dreams. "It was warm that winter. Sometimes the potted roses continue blooming in the greenhouse."

Diana glanced sharply at him. "Your greenhouse, you mean. We don't have one."

He was saved from responding by a loud rap from the front door knocker. They sat in silence as they listened to the doors being thrown open and cries of greeting filling the air.

"Your family," Diana whispered, throwing him a hesitant glance. Did he know his father had not mentioned his name since he left? From the bleak look on Jonathan's face she surmised he had some inkling of the situation. "I will go down and tell them you are resting. After a few cups of Mama's lambs-wool, your father will be much more amiable."

Jonathan offered her a crooked grin. "Maybe you haven't changed so much, after all. You always were a wicked liar."

"It will at least give you time to straighten your cravat and wash the dust smeared across your cheek," she replied tartly. "Do as you wish."

"You know what I wish, don't you?" He leaned forward and caught her shoulder.

His warm breath caressed her cheek and his lips lingered tantalizingly near her own. She had a very good suspicion of what he wanted, but she wouldn't let him do that again, not like this, not in secrecy anymore. She stood up hastily and brushed out her lavender skirt.

"Don't mistake me for someone else, Jonathan. I haven't changed that much." She marched off without another word.

Damn! Jonathan hit his thigh with his fist as Diana disappeared down the hall. She hadn't guessed. After all these years, she hadn't guessed where that rose came from. Or perhaps she didn't want to know.

Sadly, he glanced over his shoulder at the door

behind which the answer lay. If Diana had spent four years thinking he had run away from her, she would not be very likely to welcome his suit now, but he was too miserable not to know.

Jonathan rose and, brushing the dust from his trousers, started down the back stairs.

He knew the keys were kept in the kitchen. As a child, he had been allowed full run of the house, and he didn't think the routines had changed greatly. If he could just somehow slip down unnoticed and figure out which was the attic key, it wouldn't be a moment's work to run up the stairs and find the old desk. He had to know whether she had found his letter.

He chased away all the doubting thoughts about what difference the knowledge could make. He certainly couldn't repeat his offer. In that case, it would be better if the letter were safely in his pocket where it could cause no misunderstanding. If it was there.

That's what he had to know. At the risk of repeating the same blow he had suffered when she had not replied the first time, he had to know. If she had found it and chosen not to reply, he would at least know where he stood. He could leave now and not submit himself to the torture of sharing this holiday with people who no longer wished to include him in their lives.

But Diana had not behaved as if she had cast him aside as she had her childhood. True, she was not as outgoing and lavish with her affections as she had once been, but people change. He, of all people, should know that. Once, all he had wanted was the adventure and thrill of seeing the world and fighting to save his home and country. Now, he had seen his fill of war and wanted only the security of home and family. Unfortunately, neither war nor family would have him.

One of the twins sat munching an apple on a stool near the pantry where the keys were kept, his hair mussed and his best clothes slightly awry from whatever entertainment Charles had provided. Jonathan could hear the uproar in the kitchen beyond, but none of the servants were in the back hall to observe him. Just Frankie. Or Freddie.

The boy grinned at the sight of company, revealing a gap between his front teeth. Freddie, then. "You come to snitch an apple, too? All them smells make me hungry."

Jonathan hesitated. He hadn't counted on anybody seeing him purloin the key. But he needed it now, before confronting his father. If he could just enter the damned attic ...

"Me, too," Jonathan answered casually, easing around the stool for a glimpse into the pantry. The keys weren't there! "Why aren't you with Charles?" he asked desperately, looking for some way to rid himself of any witness.

"Mama said we had to come in and clean up but I was hungry. I hate coats." He shrugged at the confining shoulders of his best new suit, and he eyed Jonathan with caution. "Cook said she'd cut off my hand with an ax if I touched anything in there," he informed him helpfully. "Better just take an apple."

The obstacles only made Jonathan more determined. Giving the boy a level look, he said, "Actually, your mother sent me down for a key. They used to be in there. Do you know where they are kept?"

The boy brightened. "Mama hung them way up on the back of the door so we couldn't climb the shelves to reach them, but I can still get at them. Which one do you want?"

"Perhaps I'd better find it myself." With a wry lift of his eyebrows at the boy, he entered the pantry and found the key board. Row after row of polished brass keys hung in neat array, if he could only decipher their order. First row, first floor? Top row, top floor? No, there were too many. Frowning, he tried to think like Mrs. Carrington. How would she arrange the keys?

He panicked at the sound of voices. A child might believe his story of a guest being sent to the kitchen for a key, but no one else would. He was tempted to grab a handful and run with them.

The boy solved his dilemma. Slipping around the door, he pointed helpfully to a key dangling in the shadows at the very top of the door. "We can't reach that one. It's the attic key. We wanted to see if there were any ghosts up there, but the stool isn't tall enough."

Jonathan glanced down to his nemesis and savior. "There weren't any ghosts there last time I looked, but you know that back bedroom with all the boxes and dustcovers? I thought I saw one in there once. Where's Frankie? Fetch him and maybe you can see if it's still there."

The boy's whole face lit up and he stared at Jonathan with excitement. "Do you really think so? Let's go see. How did you know I was Freddie? Even Elizabeth sometimes mixes us up."

The voices came closer and Jonathan's desperation increased. "Because you're the one who does the talking. Frankie just waits for you to come up with ideas. Go on now. I hear Goudge, and he'll probably frown about that apple."

Freddie was off and gone without further argument. Reaching with his one good arm, Jonathan just barely pried the key off its hook. Pocketing it, he picked up Freddie's half-eaten apple and wandered out into the hall. Nodding at a suspicious Goudge, he ambled toward the back stairs, apple in hand, key in pocket. His heart thundered in his ears. Never in all those years of war had he reached such a pitch of nervous excitement.

The attic stairs were around the landing from the back stairs. All he had to do was keep climbing and no one would be the wiser. Just up one more flight of stairs ...

The twins sat perched expectantly where he and Diana had just been, blocking access to the attic door. Jonathan groaned inwardly.

Charles shouted his name from the hall. A servant would hunt him down shortly.

He'd never really had a chance. It had been foolish to think he could sneak around a friend's house like some damned thief. He would have to place his future in the hands of fate.

Downstairs, Diana surveyed the joyful arrival of the Drummonds. Excited greetings, winter wraps, and the brisk scent of cold air permeated the front hall. Jonathan's family had arrived from London with fashionable hats, fur-lined cloaks and muffs, a carriage full of trunks, and an air of sophistication that the country-bound Carrington household could never hope to attain.

Marie, the little girl who had once romped the fields on ponies with Elizabeth, was now a young lady with rosy cheeks framed by stylish auburn curls. Mrs. Drummond hadn't changed from her plump, shy self, but she seemed a trifle nervous as she shed her velvet pelisse. Glancing at the formidable frown on Mr. Drummond's brow, Diana had some idea of the tense scene ahead.

"Diana! Don't you look lovely! Come here and let me see you." Mrs. Drummond held out her arms in greeting as Diana came down the stairs. "We saw Charles out on the drive a few minutes ago. Doesn't he look dashing? Isn't it grand to have him home at last?"

All the lady's nervousness poured out in this voluble greeting, and Diana understood at once. Charles must already have told them Jonathan was here. She glanced anxiously toward the elder Drummond as she embraced his wife.

"It is such a relief. I could not have asked for a better Christmas gift," Diana murmured. "Jonathan is upstairs resting," she added with a hint of defiance. "It seems he was wounded and Charles would not come home without him." This she said loudly enough for Jonathan's father to hear.

He ignored the mention of his son as he allowed the butler to help him with his cloak. Mrs. Carrington sent her daughter an anxious glance at this breach of a forbidden subject, but she helped old Goudge with the gathering of outer garments.

Mrs. Drummond clutched Diana's elbow eagerly at this mention of her son and led her toward the drawing room. "How is he? He has not been seriously injured, has he? Oh, tell me, Diana, for I am in a frightful state. I did not think ever to see him again."

"His injuries are not grave, but a serious blow to his pride, I suspect. He will be down shortly, I am certain, and you will see for yourself. Come, let me pour you a cup of hot tea, and you can tell us how marvelously Marie fared in her first Season."

The two younger girls followed them in to rearrange chairs for a quiet coze.

"We should have come out together." Elizabeth pouted at hearing Diana's topic. "We had it all planned. I was to be the Snow Queen and Marie was to be the Rose. Now it is all spoiled."

"Oh, no, it is not!" Marie protested. "I shall be able to tell you which gentlemen are the best catches, and we can start out by favoring only the most eligible young men. It will be great fun, you will see."

Pouring the tea, Diana watched her mother offering Mr. Drummond his brandy, and she hid a smile of relief. Perhaps the brandy would warm his frozen features. If she were a miracle worker, her Christmas gift to Jonathan would be his father's forgiveness.

Charles and the twins had apparently repaired their best attire. They joined the company now all polished and immaculate. The twins had slicked back their brown cowlicks and wore their short coats. Charles had donned a formal hammer-tailed coat of chocolate brown over a gold waistcoat and fawn trousers. With his cravat starched and neatly tied and his blond hair gleaming in the candlelight, he made a striking picture.

"I should like to welcome you more politely than with snowballs," he said genially, holding out his hand to Jonathan's father.

For the first time, Diana thought with a pang of grief, Charles must act as man of the house. It seemed very odd to think of her older brother as a man and not the young scoundrel who came in foxed at night and crawled through windows when his father locked him out. But he acted the host with a maturity that had not been there when he left home.

"You'll have your hands full stepping into your father's place, I'll warrant," Mr. Drummond said gruffly, accepting the offered hand. "I'll lend a hand wherever you need it."

"I appreciate that, sir. Would you like Frankie or Freddie?"

Charles said it with such a straight face that the older man looked momentarily nonplused, but when the girls giggled and Mrs. Carrington rapped her son's arm with her fan, Drummond caught the joke and nodded. "Those young scamps will have you thinking twice about starting your own nursery. I can remember when you and ..." His voice trailed off as he realized his error in almost mentioning his son, and he returned morosely to his glass of brandy.

An awkward silence fell, into which Jonathan had the misfortune to step. He had attempted to brush back his unruly dark hair, but that only emphasized the healing gash along his brow. His navy tail coat fit his broad shoulders to perfection, but his cravat had a rakish angle created by his inability to use his right hand. The civilized cut of his silver-gray waistcoat and pantaloons did nothing to disguise the striking darkness of his visage or the bleakness of that whitely bandaged hand.

"Do I interrupt?" he inquired with brave frivolity.

"No, do come in, Jonathan, and have a seat," said Mrs. Carrington. "I was about to send Charles for the lambs-wool to take the chill out of everyone's bones. Charles?" She quirked an eyebrow at her eldest son, who, responding with alacrity, left the room.

"Yes, have a seat," Diana urged him. "Cook has prepared a light supper before we go off to church, and it will be ready shortly. Mama, the twins might stay up until then, may they not? The carolers will be here soon, and I think they're old enough to behave." Diana shot her younger brothers a meaningful look, and they returned it with bright grins.

The normal, everyday activities of the Carrington family removed Jonathan from the center of attention, and he settled into a large chair away from the fire where he was hidden in shadows. His attempt at disappearing from the company did not go unnoticed. Diana rose to perch like some malicious angel upon the arm of his chair when no one else seemed prepared to chastise him for his rudeness.

"How good of you to join us, darling. Wouldn't you care to step over here by the fire and warm yourself? I should think you would have learned to appreciate a good fire by now."

Since the word darling had once been an epithet they had thrown at each other when warned against calling each other impolite names, Jonathan didn't misunderstand Diana's message now. And since the yule log had not yet been lighted, she was veritably hitting him over the head with his misconduct. Instead of resenting her interference, he threw his avenging angel a grateful look for easing the awkwardness of his situation.

"You are quite right, my darling," he answered suavely, smiling and catching her off guard. "I am behaving like a graceless savage. I shall have to practice returning to civilized ways. Did Charles find the tinder from last year's fire?"

"He did," she assured him. "It's in the basket."

Jonathan rose and appropriated Diana's arm to lead her across the room to his mother. Mrs. Carrington nervously embarked upon a monologue about the supper she had prepared. The twins, of course, left to themselves, began to eye the kissing bough. They were on their own. He needed to speak with his mother.

"Mother, you are looking fine, as usual. Shall I light the fire for you? I'm sure Charles won't mind if I relieve him of one of his many duties this evening."

His mother ignored his father's furious expression and gazed up at him with adoration he didn't deserve. "It is good to have you back, Jonathan. Your letters have been the delight of my life since you've been gone."

Hiding his relief that she'd received his missives and wasn't entirely furious with him, Jonathan glanced down at Diana, who still clung to his arm. "Do you hear that? I haven't lost my touch. I think I shall take up writing letters for a living."

"All you have to do is find someone who will buy them," Diana replied solemnly. Then releasing his arm, she lifted the basket containing the remaining pieces of last year's log. "Shall you do the honors, sir?"

"Sir" was much more promising than "darling," and Jonathan graciously accepted. He was well aware he was goading his father into a greater fury, but he couldn't help himself. He resented having to win the affection of his own parent.

Charles entered carrying the steaming bowl of punch while Goudge managed the difficult job of drawing open the dining room doors. The twins shouted in joy at the heaping platters of the buffet revealed.

Their mother hovered at Charles's shoulder. "You are certain you added the proper amount of sugar? Your father always said if it was not done just the proper way ..."

"We shall let Mr. Drummond taste it to declare whether it is proper done or not, Mama." Charles lowered the silver punch bowl to the table and graciously ladled out the first cup for their guest. "I trust I haven't forgotten all of my father's teachings."

Mr. Drummond sipped experimentally at the mixture of hot ale, spices, sugar, and apples, and nodded his head in approval. "Your father taught you well, young man. He would be proud of you this day."

Jonathan winced at this chance remark, and Diana clenched his arm.

"You have spent four years risking your life so that they could celebrate this Christmas in safety," she whispered.

"It is not your place to interfere," Jonathan warned, but he might as well speak to the hounds in the hunting painting over the mantel.

"My father was proud of both Jonathan and Charles," Diana remarked on the comment that had not been made to her. "Papa always said if it weren't for such men as them, Napoleon would have walked across England as he has Europe."

She said it quietly, without defiance, but polite conversation all across the room died. Mr. Drummond turned as if noticing her and his son for the first time.

In the candlelight Diana's mahogany tresses

shimmered in a rich halo about features as fair as fine porcelain. Even his father couldn't fail to recognize that she had grown into a striking woman instead of the young chit who once got caught in the top of his best apple tree. He couldn't scold her as he would a child. Not only would it mar the memory of his late friend's words, but she was right.

Jonathan watched his father struggle with the dilemma of acknowledging her truths. He in turn, tried to put himself into his father's shoes. The old man had suffered humiliation when his only son had rejected his lands and position for the life of an adventure-seeking soldier. He would believe Jonathan had to be punished.

"Your father was quite likely right, Miss Carrington, as he was in many things." That was as far as his father could unbend.

Unprepared for his father's grudging admission, Jonathan crouched to set the fire licking at the brittle kindling beneath the log. He had no defense ready when Diana launched her attack.

"My father also said it was wrong for a son to act against his father's wishes without trying to understand his father's reasons. It is not always possible to adhere to the wishes of one you love, but if you truly love him, you would at least listen and consider his feelings."

Jonathan heard more in her words than he dared admit. Reluctantly, he lifted his gaze to the passion blazing in Diana's eyes, then turned to face his silent father. He had never been very good at apologizing, and he still felt himself the wronged party, but it was Christmas, and he could not abide this distance that separated him from his family. In her outspoken manner, Diana had offered him the opening he could never have made for himself. He took the cup of punch Charles shoved between his fingers, and raising it, nodded to his father.

"Your father was a wiser man than I, Diana. Perhaps it is still possible to learn from him. Charles," Jonathan caught his host's eyes and raised his cup in salute, "To fathers, past, present, and future, who must bear the ingratitude as well as the affection of their unthinking sons. May we bear the task as well when our turn comes."

Charles grinned and winked roguishly at the young ladies watching from the corner. "I'll drink to that. To fatherhood."

A loud "harrumph" of disapproval at the blatant flirtation removed the grin from Charles's face. Mr. Drummond lifted his glass to join in the toast. "Past, present, and future—that was very well said. I'll drink to that."

It wasn't a healing of the breach, but it was a rough acknowledgment that a rift existed.

The village musicians, who earned extra shillings at Christmas by roaming from house to house singing the ancient carols, arrived to fill the huge old drawing room with song and share the punch. Neighbors stopped by to enjoy the chorus and to exchange greetings, and the strained atmosphere dissipated in the general merriment.

Jonathan and Charlie became the center of festivities, but above the heads of his well-wishers,

Jonathan observed Diana as she entertained the guests. He could not decide whether she had defended him out of affection or her usual determination to see things right. It mattered little enough. His father obviously wasn't prepared to admit his own pigheadedness and welcome his erring son home. Jonathan couldn't blame him, he supposed, but he couldn't forgive him easily, either.

They had all chosen their paths; there was nothing for it but to go their separate ways, it seemed. The package he'd hastily wrapped earlier and stuffed in his pocket had no purpose anymore. He must have been crazed even to consider it.

Catching a glimpse of Freddie eyeing the highly polished apples adorning the branches of the kissing bough, Jonathan managed a wry smile in remembrance of Christmas past. He and Charles had often connived some means of reaching those tempting apples, even though their stomachs were filled to overflowing with delicacies from the table. Judging by the spills adorning the front of Freddie's coat, the lad had already sampled everything else, but the forbidden apples always looked more delicious than what was at hand.

Successfully evading several older couples saying their farewells, Jonathan slipped up behind Freddie and whispered, "What will you give me if I help you reach one?"

Freddie beamed up at him. Without hesitation, he offered, "Me and Frankie got the mistletoe like Elizabeth said. We gave it to Charles, but we'll fetch you some, too, if you like."

Jonathan chuckled. "Is that what you scamps were up to? I'll not send you back out in the cold. The information is sufficient payment, thank you. Climb up on my shoulders. We should be able to reach that low one there."

Since the branches were hung so that the lowest loop just barely missed his head, Jonathan could have plucked the apple for himself, but that wouldn't have been nearly as much fun for the boy. Without thought to the crease of his coat, he hoisted Freddie into the air where the lad triumphantly captured his prize.

From her corner of the room, Diana watched this display with a peculiar wrenching feeling in her midsection. A man like Jonathan should have children of his own. He had always been patient with Marie, more so than Charles had been with his younger siblings. She could tell by the smile on Jonathan's face that he was enjoying the mischief as much as Freddie.

Perhaps he hadn't changed as much as she had feared. Perhaps it was only his feelings toward her that had changed. Or perhaps she had only imagined those feelings in the first place, mistakenly thinking his attentions more than those of an older brother, when all he did was play the part he played with Freddie tonight.

"Look, that package has my name on it!" Freddie cried excitedly from his lofty perch. "And there's one for Frankie!"

"And it will still have your name on it in the morning when you come down." Charles strode to stand beside them and lifted the imp from Jonathan's back before Jonathan could discover the difficulty of lowering that hefty weight with a bad knee and one hand. "Where's Frankie? It's time you're both off to bed. The guests are starting to leave."

Both hands filled with apples, Freddie came down reluctantly. "Aren't you going to hang the mistletoe, Charles? Can we help you?"

Charles exchanged a laughing glance with Jonathan as his secret was revealed. "It can't be a kissing bough without mistletoe, can it?" To his brother, he added, "Go upstairs now and we'll see about the mistletoe later. It's a surprise, so not a word, mind you!"

They watched as Freddie located his twin and the two ran off whispering together. Jonathan followed Charles's gaze toward the three young women conferring in the corner by the fire. He doubted that Charles was watching his own sisters.

Thoughtfully, Jonathan studied Marie. She had turned into a beauty in the four years since they had left. She was almost a woman at seventeen. Had Charles truly fixed his interest there? She seemed terribly young.

Diana, now, was a different story. She had been a pretty child, like Marie, when they left. She was a stunning, self-assured woman now.

"Have you discovered yet if another has captured Diana's fancy?" Charles asked. "I can't believe you were fool enough to go off to war without securing her pledge. If I'd known Marie would become such a diamond, I would have sought hers. Now I suppose I'll have to fight her suitors away."

Jonathan quirked an eyebrow but did not look away from the focus of his attention. "Diana was young and had only been out one Season. I couldn't ask her to wait for a man who might never come back, not any more than you can ask Marie before she's had time to test the waters. So don't lecture me, Carrington."

"Then make haste while you can, sapskull, instead of idling time like some moonling. I'd see her wed to you before any other I know."

Jonathan shot him a wry look. "You'll not ever make a proper head of the household with that attitude. You haven't inquired into my prospects. They don't look particularly bright, you realize. I haven't a feather to fly on. My father still isn't speaking to me, and with a crippled hand, I have very little use in any position."

Charles gave him a look of disgust that spoke his opinion of these objections. "You're quite correct. You forgot to mention you haven't a wit in the old brain pan, either." With that frosty remark, he left to see off the remainder of their guests.

Diana was caught by surprise when she entered the dining hall some minutes later to discover the only other occupant was Jonathan. Almost everyone had left or retired upstairs to rest and freshen up before midnight services. She had intended to help in packing the boxes of left-over food for the needy.

The cold punch had been returned to the

kitchen, but Jonathan sipped tea kept hot over the
chafing dish while he sampled the moist remains
of a fruit cake. At Diana's appearance, he gestured
a greeting with his cup.

"I was hoping to speak with you, but you seem
to be avoiding me. Have I given you cause for
offense?"

Nervously, Diana glanced away. His eyes still
had the ability to send her heart into a rapid
flutter, although she had considered herself well
past the stage of girlish palpitations. His presence
made her more nervous than that of any man she
knew, which was senseless. Four years could not
have made that much difference in the person
she had known all her life.

"I've been trying to help Mama. It's been difficult for her. Forgive me if I have neglected you."

Jonathan winced. "It is I who have neglected
you, Diana. I wanted to thank you for what you
did earlier. My father and I are much alike in
some ways, as you have already thrown in my
face several times. The silence between us would
never have been broken without your aid."

"I only did what I've been scolded for time
enough again. It always surprises me when I'm
no longer ordered up to my room directly after
one of my outbursts." Diana managed a wry smile.
Despite the fact that Jonathan seemed almost a
stranger—an exciting stranger, she was forced to
admit—this was Johnny, and she had never kept
anything from her best friend.

"My father and I tend to keep our grievances
to ourselves," he continued. "You are like a burst

of fresh air between us. Perhaps that is why I have always admired you."

The tone of his voice and the warmth in his gaze heated her cheeks. She had not remembered his proximity disturbing her quite like this. She feared the moment he tried to touch her—he would know her heart then.

Perhaps they could still remain friends if she did not let him see how he affected her. "I daresay that is why you and Charles rub along so well. He is as light-headed as I am. Feel free to invite us over whenever you and your father are at loggerheads. We'll bring the twins and turn the house wrong side out. Elizabeth is the only sensible one among us."

"It is not likely that my father and I will be sharing the same household any time soon," Jonathan said in resignation. Changing the subject, he added, "I had supposed you would be married by now and helping your mother bring out Elizabeth. Is there a special suitor waiting for you when your mourning ends?"

Diana contemplated screaming at him and beating her fists against the starched linen of his broad chest until he awakened, but she resisted and smiled coolly, instead.

"I've had suitors enough, thank you. As I've told you before, marriage never seemed worth the effort."

She turned to walk away, but Jonathan halted her with his words. "None of them to your taste is that it, Janey? All too tame, perhaps?"

Diana swung back around. "You think I've had

no offers? There was old man Thompson, I suppose. He was quite wealthy and stuck his spoon in the wall only a year after he married the sixteen-year-old who finally consented to be his bride. I could be a wealthy widow today. Or if you think it is tameness I dislike, I'll have you know Lord Ashley asked for my hand just last spring. I suppose he thought my irreverent tongue covered a multitude of sins and we would suit."

"Ashley?" Jonathan's eyebrows shot up to his hairline. "The man's a rogue through and through. Whatever was your father thinking to entertain him?"

"Perhaps he was thinking I had enough sense to know a rake when I see one. Anyway, Ashley's married now, too. I hear his new wife is already expecting an heir and is currently enjoying her freedom while he dallies with his latest courtesan. But forgive me, I should not mention such subjects." Diana's tone grew more acerbic as she spoke. "I should entertain you with my other prospects. One is quite the gentleman and my mother is holding out fond hopes we will make a match of it. He is unfailingly polite, unlike some men I know. He has a considerable fortune, I am told. He is well-favored and quite persistent in his attentions. I am sure any woman would be delighted to be the object of his affections."

"So what is the delay in announcing your nuptials? Surely you'll not allow such a catch to escape?" Jonathan asked with a hint of unusual temper.

Diana couldn't continue to take out her bitterness on him. He had come home from a long, painful war, weary at heart and soul, to be faced by a cold father and little future. It was Christmas, and she could afford to be generous with her love for just a little while, just not enough to let him suspect. She gave him a wry smile offering a truce.

"We have no interests in common. The only topic we can discuss together is the weather. Can you imagine saying 'It is raining out today, dear,' and having exhausted all conversation for the remainder of the day?"

Jonathan choked back a laugh. Wickedly, he inquired, "Surely it cannot be so bad as that? After you were married, he would have to bring up a new subject or two, I daresay. What would he say ..." he hesitated and modified his original thought somewhat, "if he wanted to kiss you?"

Diana understood that tell-tale hesitation. She had not followed at her brother's heels and eavesdropped on his conversations without learning a few things, but Jonathan persisted in being a gentleman. She gave him the reply his question deserved.

"I should imagine he would say, 'It's Saturday night, dear. Shall we?" Then, not stopping to watch Jonathan's reaction to that conceit, Diana marched off to prepare herself for church. If he remained here much longer, she would have need of a prayer or two.

His laughter followed her up.

Diana absorbed the pleasure of both families returning to the house from the quiet, dark snow after church. The joyous choir still rang in her ears, greetings of "Merry Christmas" tingled her tongue, and the smile on her face reflected that of the others around her. If she couldn't have the exact perfect Christmas she had wanted, she at least had the quiet comfort of the familiar—and the presence of all her loved ones.

Despite his bandaged hand, Jonathan helped removed her pelisse as the others removed their outer wraps. While the rest of the company tried to shake the chill from their bones with a flurry of coats and scarves and stamping feet, Diana was conscious of the heat of Jonathan's proximity.

The yule log had been left to burn merrily, and Elizabeth and Marie naturally gravitated toward the drawing room. Their outburst of giggles gave fair warning of mischief ahead. With a worried frown, Mrs. Carrington hastened after them.

Diana raised her eyebrows in suspicion at Charles's grin, but he shrugged and gestured for her to precede him. Then he made a point of seeing that Jonathan followed her through the doorway.

She gasped at the sight of the silver-and-gold-be-ribboned mistletoe dangling from the center of the kissing bough. It was more elaborate than any attempt her father had ever made. The greenery glistened in the firelight, swaying teasingly with the draft from the hall. Marie placed herself beneath it, contemplating the brilliance of the ribbons with an innocent air.

To everyone's surprise, Charles took advantage of the poised beauty beneath the berried leaves. Skirting around Diana and Jonathan, he caught Marie's hand and lifted it to his lips.

The loud cough behind her reminded Diana of why her usually reckless brother had limited himself to such circumspect behavior. Taking Jonathan's arm so as to include him in the conversation, she turned to Mr. and Mrs. Drummond.

"It appears Father Christmas or some mischievous elves arrived while we were out. I do not remember half so many gifts hanging among the garlands when we left."

The frown on Mr. Drummond's face faded. "Well, let us investigate, shall we?" He nodded to where Charles was already reaching up among the branches to bring down a package addressed to his mother.

"I concur." With some formality but a trace of a smile, Jonathan steered Diana toward the garlands where Charles had already begun to reach for a package addressed to Marie.

Diana knew her brother had only followed the custom set by their father of tying tiny surprise packages to the greenery, but she could not help a slight flutter of anticipation as Jonathan purposely guided her toward the low-hanging branch where he and Freddie had snitched the apples. The Drummond family had been with them enough Christmases to join in the game also, but it could scarcely be expected that Jonathan would have had time to purchase any gifts.

Still, while everyone else was merrily tearing

into their surprises, Jonathan reached among the evergreens and pulled out a poorly wrapped and oddly shaped parcel addressed to Diana. His expression as he handed it to her was guarded.

"I have no roses as a reminder, and I'm not at all certain that my gift is appropriate any longer, but if it still reposes where I left it four years ago, I would like you to have it anyway. If it has already been found and discarded then I understand that, too. I only want all your Christmases to be happy ones."

Jonathan's words were spoken so low none could hear except Diana. The blush rising to her cheeks would give her away, so she turned aside to tear open her package.

Acting as host, Charles distracted the others by discovering more surprises hidden in the evergreens. She would have to be grateful that no one would notice the contents of her package besides the giver.

Inside the paper rested a key. Diana held it in the palm of her hand and studied Jonathan's dark face, desperately striving to keep hope from welling up inside her. "The attic key? However did you ..." Then noting the tension behind his stiff stance, she continued, "Shall we try it? Do you think anyone will come look for us if we do?"

"We shall be home free before they find us." Using the words of the child's game they had once played, Jonathan caught her elbow and escorted her from the room.

Jonathan was relieved that Diana needed no explanations of the paltry gift he had hidden in

the evergreens for her. He had not come prepared for the welcome he had found here. He
had taken his chances when he clumsily wrapped
that key with one hand. Now his heart rested in
his throat as Diana turned up the attic stairway.

He carried only the lamp from the bottom
of the stairs, and it threw odd shadows over the
walls as Diana bent to insert the key in the door.
With the silly anticipation of two children about
to engage in mischief, they kept their voices to
whispers while they rattled the lock.

"I feel like the twins must whenever they're
about something they shouldn't be." The latch
clicked and Diana gingerly pushed against the
door.

"That's because you were always forbidden
to hide up here and you always did, anyway,"
Jonathan reminded her. "I'm surprised the two
of them aren't on our heels, or down amid the
greenery. Their nanny must have given them laudanum."

Diana giggled. "At the very least. Ugh. I've
just walked into a spider web. Shouldn't we have
saved this expedition for All Hallow's Eve?"

"No." Jonathan's reply was surprisingly curt. He
lifted the lamp and led the way to keep her from
encountering any more unpleasant surprises. "It
has waited too long as it is."

Diana sent him a searching glance, but in the
shadows from the lamp she could barely discern
his face and certainly not his thoughts.

He had changed his coat and cravat to attend
services, and she smiled at the elegant figure he

cut in the dusty shadows of the attic. Had she been permitted, she would have blurted out the words "I love you" just because of that anxious frown between his eyes right now. She had never stopped loving him, of course. She couldn't imagine why she had thought she ever would. He was as much a part of her heart and soul as the air she breathed. She didn't know what nonsense had brought him up here in the middle of the night while all else drank punch in the warmth below, but she would have followed him into darkest Africa had he asked.

"There it is." Jonathan pushed an old trunk out of the way so she could maneuver her skirts around it with a minimum of damage to the hem on the dust-coated floor. He set the lamp upon the scarred old secretary and turned to take Diana's hand.

"Did you ever once think to open the desk after I left?" He watched her as she stared at the battered remains of their childish hiding place.

She glanced up at him quizzically. "You hadn't been home in months. You ran off to join the cavalry instead of coming home at Christmas. I thought you were gone forever. I put our hiding place aside as I did my childish toys." She could have said she had put the desk aside with her childish dreams, that she couldn't bear the heartbreak of knowing there would never be another message waiting for her again. But she was not so outspoken as to reveal thoughts she had never said to herself. She turned from the intensity of his stare to trace her fingers through the thick dust upon the burnt surface.

"Open it now, Janey, one last time. Please, for me?"

Startled by the urgency of his tone, she sent him a glance, then did as told. The charred drawer moved with difficulty, and Jonathan had to help her. But he stood aside as she reached behind the drawer to spring open the secret panel. They had thought themselves so clever when they found that hiding place when she was less than the twins' age. Now it squeaked open with less vigor, but she studied the cavity with the same excitement as then.

Diana searched the small chamber with her fingers, discovering the package hidden from sight.

Her exclamation of surprise brought a smile of mixed relief and joy to Jonathan's lips. "You really did not know it was there!" His smile faltered, but he only said, "Come, let us take it below where it is warmer. We can open it there without sneezing."

Diana closed her fingers fervently around the gay ribbons of the package. She said nothing, only nodding in agreement at his suggestion. She didn't dare hope too much, but her hand trembled on Jonathan's arm. She didn't want to leave the darkness. She wanted to stay here with his hand at her back, his long frame close to hers, pretending this was their world and no problems existed.

Still, she followed him, closing the attic door and locking it while Jonathan waited. They descended the narrow dark stairs in the light from the wall sconces below. She could see the brownness of long fingers closing around hers as he helped her to take their childhood seats on the stairs.

"I have no right to ask you to open that package any longer. I gave up that right when I left my home against my father's wishes. But for what we once had, I would like you to have it. Open it here, Diana. I would not wish to embarrass you by declaring my feelings in public."

Those words gave her the courage she needed. She opened her lips to speak but could find nothing to say. Jonathan touched a gentle finger to her chin to close them.

"Open it, Diana. I cannot say more until you do."

With shaking fingers she ripped the bright wrappings off the oblong box. The package was too thick to be a simple missive.

A thick vellum letter fell into Diana's lap, and from between the pages, a fragile golden ring dropped. Diana exclaimed in surprise and lifted the ring, but before she could look to Jonathan for explanations, a scream rang out below, shattering the fragile bonds of anticipation.

"Fire!"

That panic-stricken cry destroyed any further thought. Even so, Diana clutched her treasures when Jonathan helped her to her feet.

They both ran down the corridor toward the front stairs to the accompaniment of frantic cries and shouts. Diana's heart beat frantically at the smell of smoke. Fire in the old wood and heavy draperies of the drawing room would spread with terrifying swiftness. If not stopped at once, it could not be stopped at all.

They ran into the large room on a scene of chaos.

"We only meant to hide in the window seat until everyone left the room!" Frankie cried, dumping the contents of the teapot on a fiery bit of ribbon that had fallen from the boughs over-head.

"We wanted to see the presents!" Freddie was weeping, while dangling from the chandelier. Charles righted a chair beneath it to stand on.

The remaining toppled chair and stool beneath the dangling twin showed how the boys had attempted to reach the presents. Diana ran to stomp out the candles that had tumbled from the evergreens to ignite the litter from unwrapped gifts.

Flames danced across the carpet, fed by the drafts along the floor. Mr. Drummond stamped ineffectively at the tiny fires trailing dangerously closer to the older draperies and giving off clouds of smoke. The women milled frantically beneath Frankie, ignoring the fire perilously close to their long skirts.

Jonathan jumped across the burning debris to grab the teapot from Freddie.

"Go fill the punch bowl with snow!" he yelled at the terrified child. "Diana, the coal scuttle! Anything else you can think of! Charles, you have two hands, help with the buckets. I'll get the boy."

Goudge tottered into the room with a bucket

of water from the kitchen and nearly tripped and spilled it before Diana grabbed it from his hands to throw on the largest fire.

Understanding Jonathan's commands, Charles and Mr. Drummond scooped up the largest containers they could find and dashed outside for snow. Not only was it closer at hand and more abundant than the water from the old plumbing in the distant kitchen, but it would smother the flames more effectively.

Standing in the puddle Diana had created with Goudge's bucket of water, Jonathan grasped Freddie by his trouser waistband. "Steady on, old fellow. We've got you. Now let go."

With only one hand to grasp the boy, Jonathan had to put all his strength into his one good arm. The terrified little boy released his grip on the fragile chandelier, and Jonathan swung Freddie in an arc and down into the arms of his mother. The room erupted in sobs and cheers.

By this time, sleepy maids had joined them with all the pots and pans from the kitchen. Mounds of snow melted across the drawing room. The stench of burned carpet reeked in the air, and half of the kissing bough hung bedraggled and scorched to the floor, trailing smoking ribbons and bruised apples. With the flames doused, the company rested to survey the damage.

Jonathan searched for Diana and smiled with tired relief when he found her. She still clutched the crumpled letter and presumably the ring, although the paper was now wrapped around the bucket handle. Sensing his gaze, she blushed and glanced at the mess she had made of his careful missive.

"Good show, Drummond. Now I know how your troops survived all those battles." Charles wrapped a weary arm around his friend's shoulder and gazed about him. "Now admit it. We never caused this much trouble. The twins have us whipped."

"At least this is the kind of war you can fight in relative comfort." Jonathan shrugged off the praise, his gaze never leaving Diana. She seemed bewildered and alone and he wanted to go to her again, but she had not yet given him the right to do so. His heart ached as she set down the bucket and carefully smoothed his letter between her fingers. The ring sparked in the firelight. She held it pressed against her palm.

"You are too modest, son." Mr. Drummond stepped into the breach.

The twins' voices could be heard protesting as Mrs. Carrington led them back to the nursery.

Jonathan's mother was on the point of ushering Elizabeth and Marie off to their rooms to remove their wet clothing—but she hesitated at the tone of his father's voice. She turned with a question in her eyes that Jonathan couldn't answer.

He allowed hope to rise when his father approached him with his hand held out. "You thought more quickly than any of us," he said with some embarrassment. "You would be a valuable asset on the battlefield, or anywhere else you chose to apply your efforts."

Recognizing this as the only apology he would

ever receive for all those long years of agonizing silence, Jonathan accepted his father's hand in his undamaged left one. "I learned that trick in service, sir. You would have thought of it soon enough. I thank you for the kind words, though."

Smiling with delighted relief, Mrs. Drummond hastened the younger girls away. Charles returned to the punch bowl to fill cups for a toast.

It was Diana's future Jonathan decided in accepting his father's hesitant overtures. For her sake, if he thought he had a chance at all, he would swallow his pride and beg forgiveness. He watched in agony as she toyed with the ring while he and his father battled silently and stubbornly.

Almost absently, Diana slipped the ring on her finger.

At her gesture, Jonathan could breathe again. Instead of the cold, formal man he'd meant to be while accepting his father's stilted apology, he felt light as a boy, a boy filled with life, laughter, and love.

He hugged his father. "You will have to forgive me, Father. There is the matter of an unopened Christmas gift that the excitement interrupted."

Jonathan stepped away to stand before Diana. He lifted the hand wearing the ring and met her smiling eyes with hope. "You have not read the letter yet," he reminded her.

"I trust it includes some explanation of your abrupt departure," she answered solemnly, a teasing twinkle in her eye belying her tone.

"That, among other things. I asked your father's permission before I wrote it, of course."

"Papa? You spoke to Papa?" That knowledge brought tears to her eyes.

"His reply is in the letter, Janey. I wrote him from Oxford. He did not know I intended to leave, but his letter gave us his blessings. It was one of the happiest days of my life. I did not know it was to be my last for a long time."

"I didn't know, Johnny." She lifted her eyes to his, and he read the love and steadiness there. "He said nothing to me."

Charles handed Jonathan a punch cup and grabbed the letter from Diana's hand. "You mean to say there is a letter from my father in here? A kind of posthumous blessing, as it were?"

Instead of being annoyed at the interruption, Jonathan grinned. "Relieving you of the responsibility, old fellow. All I need is the lady's word. Now give it back and go away, if you would be so kind."

Mr. Drummond harrumphed from where he had been left standing across the room. "It seems to me, if you're entertaining ideas of taking a bride, that you will need some prospect of financial security to offer the lady. I know of a promising position, if you are willing to take direction from an obstinate old man."

Jonathan tore his gaze away from the glowing promise in brown eyes long enough to meet his father's look. "I am willing to learn from a man with more experience, sir, if he will have me."

"He'll have you all right, and with open arms." Embarrassing himself with this display of emotion, Mr. Drummond gestured curtly at Charles.

"Come, Carrington. If we harbor any hopes of getting these two off our hands, we'd better turn in. I don't think the carpet will suffer more if it waits until morning."

Grinning, Charles returned the letter to his sister, bussed her on the cheek, shook Jonathan's hand, and gesturing at the maid and butler hovering in the doorway, dismissed everyone but the lovers from the room. Obviously quite pleased with himself, he grabbed up the bottle of brandy and guided his distinguished guest out of the room for one last drink of celebration.

Smiling, Jonathan lifted Diana's fingers to his lips and admired the lovely color in her cheeks. He could not mistake the love he found in those clear, bright eyes, but he would have no mistake this time. Not daring to let himself hope more, he pressed the letter upon her.

"Read it, Diana. I do not think I can stand the suspense any longer."

Nodding, she unfolded the pages. For four years her happiness had been stored away in a secret hiding place. Four years were long enough. She read swiftly, starting with her father's letter to his best friend's son. She wept over the words of praise and caution, and by the time she read his approval at the end of the letter, she was blotting her eyes with her handkerchief.

Jonathan had not needed her father's letter to speak his case, but she had not realized how much her father's approval meant to her. Her tears blotted the pages she carefully tucked away for later perusal.

Jonathan's youthful letter, on the other hand, brimmed with life and hope and dreams. He explained his father's opposition to his only son's desires to serve his country, and his own need to do his patriotic duty. He spoke of the difficulty of his decision to buy a commission rather than return to his father's comfortable house. Then he spoke of the life and the love he wished them to share if she would wait. The ring was to be her signal that she was prepared to set all others aside in favor of him. He did not expect her to make the decision soon or even quickly, but only to mention her decision to wear the ring when she wrote to Charles.

It was a young man's letter, full of nonsense and dreams, but the man standing before her now waited with the same eagerness and anxiety as the youth who had written it. The healing gash upon his forehead whitened with tension.

Eyes streaming with tears, Diana lifted the letter and kissed it as she would have done had she discovered it four years ago. Then twisting the ring upon her finger, she gazed longingly into his handsome face.

"Four years I waited for this letter. Four years I could have been wearing this ring. Do you think we can make up the lost time somehow?"

"It won't be easy, but I'll try. I love you, Diana. If I promise to find other topics besides the weather, will you marry me?"

"You have four years of letter writing to catch up on," she said with a teary smile. "Do you think you can do it by the time my year of mourning is ended if I tell you how much I love you and how much I have missed you?"

"I can move mountains and learn to deal with Frankie and Freddie if you'll just show me how much you mean those words." Jonathan stepped daringly closer, sliding his arm around her waist as he reached to set the bulky letter aside.

"Jonathan!" Startled by his sudden brash behavior, Diana brought her hands to his chest to hold him off.

He smiled, glanced knowingly at the sparkling ribbons of the mistletoe still dangling among the remaining greenery overhead, and returned the heat of his gaze to her pink cheeks. "I caught you under the kissing bough, my love. You can't refuse."

"So I can't." Acknowledging defeat gladly, Diana slid her arms about his neck and felt the warm pressure of his lips against hers and melted into the strong embrace she had only been allowed to dream of for so many years.

In the hallway, peering through the crack between the doors, two young girls giggled with delight at the sight of their brother and sister embracing beneath the mistletoe.

Caught up in the romance of the moment, they failed to note the shadow sneaking up from behind, dangling a piece of greenery, until the branch hung over their heads. A whispered "Surprise!" caused them to glance in tandem at the mistletoe, and squealing, they bolted wildly for the stairs.

Elizabeth's protesting cry of "Charles!" as she

ran up the stairs made no impact on the pair in the drawing room. While the others raced madly through the upper halls, the happy couple laid more sedate plans for the future, all of them spoken through the magic of kisses, with the permission of the kissing bough above.

THIS TRADITIONAL CHRISTMAS punch has been served since the Middle Ages. The name probably refers to the fluffy white flesh revealed by the broken skin of the roasted apples which float on top of the bowl of ale.

## LAMBS WOOL PUNCH

4 eating apples
4 pints of ale or cider
6 cloves and 1 tablespoon of grated nutmeg.
Half a teaspoon of ground ginger. Pinch of allspice. I cinnamon stick, 1 – 2 tablespoons dark soft brown sugar

Heat oven to 400. Place the apples in a baking dish with a little ale, cider or water and cook for 30 minutes until the apple flesh is "woolly" in texture.

Meanwhile, heat the ale or cider, spices and sugar to taste in a large pan over a low heat until very hot, but do not allow to boil. Strain into a large serving bowl. Scoop out the apple pulp with a spoon, discarding the core and the pips and pile on the hot ale. Serve hot with a scoop of apple flesh.

# About the Author

With several million books in print and New York Times and USA Today's bestseller lists under her belt, former CPA Patricia Rice is one of romance's hottest authors. Her emotionally-charged contemporary and historical romances have won numerous awards, including the RT Book Reviews Reviewers Choice and Career Achievement Awards. Her books have been honored as Romance Writers of America RITA finalists in the historical, regency and contemporary categories.

A firm believer in happily-ever-after, Patricia Rice is married to her high school sweetheart and has two children. A native of Kentucky and New York, a past resident of North Carolina, she currently resides in Southern California, and now does accounting only for herself.

FOR FURTHER INFORMATION,
VISIT PATRICIA'S NETWORK:

*http://patriciarice.com*
*http://facebook.com/OfficialPatriciaRice*
*https://twitter.com/Patricia_Rice*
*http://wordwenches.com*

For more Christmas stories:

It's a magical time of year, and Patricia Rice delivers magical holiday stories to celebrate the season! This unique special collection brings together three of Patricia's favorite holiday romance stories in one joyful book: Christmas Angel, Christmas Goose, and Tin Angel. *https:// patriciarice.com/books/christmas-enchantment/*

Love mystery and romance?
Have a few free books on me!

Sign up for content and news of upcoming releases. Be the first to know about special sales, freebies, stories from my writer life, and other fun information. Join me on my writing adventures! Join here: *https://www.subscribepage.com/ricewebsite*

# From the Authors

WE HOPE YOU have enjoyed three of our favorite holiday stories! Visit our websites to discover more romances from Susan King, Mary Jo Putney, and Patricia Rice. And be sure to check out the Word Wenches blog that we share with some wonderful author friends. Visit us on Facebook and social media too!

*www.wordwenches.com*

*www.susankingbooks.com*

*www.patriciarice.com*

*www.maryjoputney.com/books*

Made in the USA
Columbia, SC
06 November 2021

48430446R00181